THE BLACK
MULDOON

THE BLACK MULDOON

A Western Trio

MAX BRAND

Skyhorse Publishing

"When Iron Turns to Gold" by George Owen Baxter first appeared in Street & Smith's *Western Story Magazine* (7/30/21). Copyright © 1921 by Street & Smith Publications, Inc. Copyright © renewed 1949 by Dorothy Faust. Copyright © 2010 by Golden West Literary Agency for restored material. Acknowledgment is made to Condé Nast Publications, Inc., for its cooperation.

"The Two-Handed Man" by George Owen Baxter first appeared in Street & Smith's *Western Story Magazine* (12/3/32). Copyright © 1932 by Street & Smith Publications, Inc. Copyright © renewed 1959 by Dorothy Faust. Copyright © 2010 by Golden West Literary Agency for restored material. Acknowledgment is made to Condé Nast Publications, Inc., for its cooperation.

"The Black Muldoon" by Peter Dawson first appeared in Street & Smith's *Western Story Magazine* (9/30/22). Copyright © 1922 by Street & Smith Publications, Inc. Copyright © renewed 1950 by Dorothy Faust. Copyright © 2010 by Golden West Literary Agency for restored material. Acknowledgment is made to Condé Nast Publications, Inc., for its cooperation.

The name Max Brand® is a registered trademark with the United States Patent and Trademark Office and cannot be used for any purpose without express written permission.

Skyhorse Publishing books may be purchased in bulk at special discounts for sales promotion, corporate gifts, fund-raising, or educational purposes. Special editions can also be created to specifications. For details, contact the Special Sales Department, Skyhorse Publishing, 307 West 36th Street, 11th Floor, New York, NY 10018 or info@skyhorsepublishing.com.

Skyhorse® and Skyhorse Publishing® are registered trademarks of Skyhorse Publishing, Inc.®, a Delaware corporation.

Visit our website at www.skyhorsepublishing.com.

10 9 8 7 6 5 4 3 2 1

Library of Congress Cataloging-in-Publication Data is available on file.

Cover design by Brian Peterson

Print ISBN: 978-1-63450-741-7
Ebook ISBN: 978-1-63450-742-4

Printed in the United States of America

TABLE OF CONTENTS

When Iron Turns to Gold

"Iron Dust," an eight-part serial, was Frederick Faust's fourth contribution to Street & Smith's *Western Story Magazine*. It appeared under his George Owen Baxter byline, beginning in the issue for January 15, 1921, and is in book form as *Iron Dust* (Skyhorse Publishing, 2016). It is the story of a young blacksmith, Andrew Lanning, who is goaded into a fight with the town bully. Believing he has killed the man, Lanning takes flight and is pursued by a posse led by trigger-happy Bill Dozier. By the end of the serial, Andy has befriended Bill Dozier's brother, Hal, who urges Andy to pursue Anne Withero, the girl he loves. The serial proved so popular that Faust wrote a sequel, "When Iron Turns to Gold," which appeared in the July 30, 1921 issue of *Western Story Magazine*.

I

Even though the slope was steep and broken and cut with boulders, Andrew Lanning let the reins hang slack and gave the mare her head. But, in spite of the difficulty of the course before her, Sally gave only half of her attention to it. She was mountain bred and mountain trained, and accordingly, she had that seventh sense in her dainty feet to which only mountain horses ever attain.

She knew a thousand little tricks. She knew that, when gravel began to slip beneath her, the thing to do was not to stop merely or to whirl and go back, but to spring like a cat to one side. For that small beginning might mean a landslide of no mean proportions. By that seventh sense on those small, black hoofs she understood the rocks; she sensed which of them were too slippery for acrobatics and which, for all their apparent smoothness, were so friable that she could get a toehold. She knew to a fraction of a degree what angle of a slope was practicable for a descent, and as for climbing, if she did not quite have the prowess of a mountain sheep, she had the same heart and the same calm scorn for heights. With this equipment it was no wonder that Sally went carelessly down the slope according to her own free will, sometimes walking, sometimes sitting back on her haunches and sliding, sometimes breaking into a beautiful, free gallop when she came onto a comparatively level shoulder of the hill.

But, no matter how busy she was, from time to time Sally tossed up a head that had made the heart of many a horse lover leap, and regarded the valley below her. It was a new country to Sally, and about strange things she was as curious, as pryingly inquisitive, as a woman. Everything about Sally, indeed, was daintily feminine, from the nice accuracy with which she put down her feet to the big, gentle, intelligent eyes, and there was even something feminine in the way her pricking ears quivered back to listen when her master spoke.

When he said, at length—"Ah, Sally, there's where I fight my big fight and my last fight"—she came to an abrupt halt and raised her head to look down into the shadowy heart of the valley. From here one could plainly see the little village of Martindale and every winding of its streets. For the mountain air was as clear as glass. Having surveyed it to her own content, she turned her head and regarded the master from a corner of her eye, as one who would say: "I've seen a hundred towns, better or worse than that one. What the deuce is there about it to interest you?" But Andrew Lanning nodded to her, and she tossed her head again and started on down the slope with the same nervous, cat-like placing of her feet. Plainly these two were closely in tune. He was among men very much what she was among horses, with the same clean-cut, sinewy, tapering limbs and the same proud lift of the head and the same clear, dark eyes.

But as they drew closer to the bottom of the valley, his face clouded more and more with thought. He even went the length of drawing his rifle from its case to examine its action, and then he tried his revolvers. Having looked to them, he was more at ease, as could be told by the way he settled back in the saddle, but still it was plain that he approached Martindale very much in doubt as to the reception that waited for him there.

As if to hasten the conclusion, the moment the hoofs of Sally touched the smooth trail that slid down the valley floor, he gathered her to a fast gallop. She came up on the bit in a flash, eager to stretch out at full speed, and under the iron restraint of his wrist, her neck bowed. There was no suggestion of daintiness about her now. She was all power, all flying speed, all mighty lungs and generous heart, and she rushed down the trail with that deceptively easy, long stride that only a blooded horse can have. But, even in the midst of her joyous gallop, the mind of the master guided and controlled her, not with the tug of the reins but with a word, and at his voice she canted her head just a trifle to one side, in the beautiful way that horses have, and seemed to listen and read his mind and his heart.

"Not so fast, Sally," he was saying. "Not so fast, old girl. We're going into Martindale at full gallop, and we may go out again with twenty men and horses on our heels. Well, that won't be anything new to us, eh?"

The wind had picked up a little whirl of dust before her; she cleared it from her nostrils with a snort and then came back to an easier gait, smooth as flowing water; her rider sat like a rock. And so they came to the outskirts of Martindale. It was one of those typical mountain towns, weather-stained, wind-racked, with the huddling houses that gave a comfortable promise of warmth in the winter snows and of cool shade in the summer. Andrew Lanning called Sally to a walk and went slowly along the main street.

If Martindale were awake, it only opened one eye at Andrew Lanning. There were no people at windows or on porches, so far as he could see, and very few sounds of life from the interiors of the shacks. The predominate sound was the dismal bellowing of a cow on a hillside pasture above the town, a disconsolate mother mourning for a son who had gone to make veal for the hungry. Not a particularly cheery welcome for Andrew Lanning, and his heart grew heavier with every step Sally took.

His manner had changed the moment he came between the two lines of houses that fenced him in. He sat bolt erect in the saddle, looking straight ahead of him, but his eyes had that curious, alert blankness of the pugilist who looks into your eyes and is nevertheless watching your hands. Andrew Lanning was watching, while he stared straight down the street, every window, every door, every yard that he passed, and when a little girl of nine or ten years came out on the porch of a shack, a quiver ran through the body of the rider before he saw that the newcomer was harmless. He turned squarely toward the child, whose great eyes were staring at the beauty of the horse. Andrew brought Sally to a halt.

"Hello, Judy!" he called. "Have you forgotten me?"

"Oh, my! Oh, my land!" exclaimed Judy, clasping her hands after a grown-up fashion. "Oh, Andy, you did come back."

He chuckled, but his glance slipped up and down the street before he answered. "Don't they expect me?"

"Of course they don't."

"Didn't Hal Dozier tell 'em I was coming?"

"He did, but nobody believed it. My dad said . . ." She stopped and choked back the next words.

He leaned a little from the saddle. "Judy, you ain't afraid of me?"

Her hands were clasped again. She came toward him with slow, dragging steps, as though her curiosity were gradually conquering her timidity, and all the while she peered into his face. Something approaching a smile began to grow on her lips. "Why, Andy, you ain't so much changed. You're most awful brown and you're thinner and you're older, but you ain't changed. I think you're even a lot nicer. Is this the hoss that everybody talks about all the time? Is this Sally?"

"This is Sally. Do you know where I got her?"

"Did you . . . did you . . . shoot somebody for her?"

His lips twitched. "A little boy gave her to me, Judy. What do you think of that?"

"I don't see how he could. I don't really, Andy."

She stretched out her hand with the palm up—man's age-old way of approaching a horse—and tried to touch Sally's face. Under the smooth-flowing voice of Andy the mare tremblingly submitted, and discovering that the soft, little, brown hand of the girl did no harm, Sally began to sniff at it.

"I know what she wants!" said Judy delightedly. "She wants apples or something. Ain't that it? Oh, you beauty! Might I ride her sometime?"

"Maybe. But what was it your father said?"

A shade of trouble came in her face. "I don't believe a single thing they say about you, Andy."

"Of course you don't. You and me are old friends, Judy. But what does your dad say?"

"He says that . . . that . . . inside a couple of days you'll shoot somebody or get shot. That ain't true, is it, Andy?"

"Who knows, Judy?" he asked slowly. "But I hope not."

He sent Sally down the street again with a touch of his heel, and then, remembering, he turned with a sudden smile and waved to the child. She brightened at once and waved after him. It comforted Andrew immensely to know that he had this one small ally in the town. Everything, it seemed, had changed , except Judy. Little Judy had grown lanky—even her freckles were bigger—but, inside, Judy was the same.

However, the town was different; it was more drab and shrunken, more hopeless. His discontent grew as he approached his destination, Hal Dozier's office. Rounding the bend of the street, he came in sight of it, and he also came in sight of the commercial district of the town, namely the hotel and store and the blacksmith shop. The hotel veranda, that social gathering place of the mountain towns, was filled with idlers. They stared at Andrew with casual interest, but when they saw the full beauty of Sally, their interest quickened. A buzz went up and down the length of the veranda, and every man came to his feet. Andrew knew then that they had recognized him.

Every nerve in his right arm began to tingle, as though it possessed a life of its own, and that life was endangered, and every nerve in his body called on him to whip out his gun. But he checked the impulse and fought it down with a great effort. Not a gun had shown on the veranda. One man or two had stepped back through the door, to be sure, but otherwise each man remained rooted to his place.

Andrew rode on, deliberately turned his back on them, and dismounted in front of Dozier's little town office. The big Dozier Ranch was far out of town among the hills, but Hal, who acted as a federal marshal, had written that he would be in town in his office. He rose with a brief, deep-throated shout at the sight of Andrew Lanning. Sally had been attempting to follow her master into the office, but the shout of the marshal drove her back. She slipped over to the window and cautiously put her head through the opening to overlook this interview and see that no harm came to her rider.

"I gave you up yesterday," said Hal Dozier as he wrung the hand of Andrew Lanning. "Gave you up complete. Did you get my letters . . . both of 'em?"

"I'll tell you why I waited for the second letter," said Andrew frankly. "I wanted to give you time to find out from the men around town how they would take my return. When you wrote in the second letter that you thought they'd give me a square deal and a chance to make good, I decided to come in. It wasn't that I distrusted you . . . not for a minute. I knew that you'd be better than your word. You've got the governor's pardon for me. That was the first big thing that gives me a chance to live like an honest man and hold up my head. But my job is to win back the trust of these people around here."

The marshal shook his head. "I know what you want to do. And when I wrote to you and told you that they were willing to give you a fighting chance, I meant what I said. Just that and no more. You see, Andy, these blockheads have it fixed in their brains that if a man is a killer once, he's a killer forever. I've tried to point out to them that you never were a killer, that you killed just one man, and that you killed him under excusable conditions. It makes no difference. They think the fever is in you, and that it will break out in gun talk, sooner or later."

"They're probably right," said Lanning sadly.

"Eh?" asked the marshal.

"I mean it. Look here."

He took the sheriff to the back window and pointed to the upstepping ranges of the mountains, ridge after ridge pouring into the pale-blue sky.

"That's been my country for these past few years," said Andrew softly. "I've been king of it. The law has fought me, and I've fought the law. A hard fight, and a hard life, but a wonderful one. Do you know the kind of an appetite it gives you to eat in a house surrounded by people who know there's a price of ten thousand dollars on your head? Do you know what it is to sleep with one ear open? Do you know what it is to go hungry for days, with towns full of people and food in plain sight and easy reach, but fenced away from you with guns? It's hard, but there's a tang to a life like that. I say I've lived like a king. My gun was my passport. It was my coin. It paid my debts and my grudges. And now I've stepped out of my kingdom, Hal, and I've come down to this."

He gestured despairingly toward the front of the little room at the street beyond. "Martindale! A rotten place for a grown-up man. No, Hal, it's hard to make the change. I'm going to fight hard to make it. I'm going to fight like a demon to be an honest man and work for my living, but every night I'll dream about the mountains and the freedom. And that's why I say that maybe they're right. Maybe I'll break loose before long. I've gone without roping for a long time. Maybe I'll jump the first fence I find in my way and land on another gent's property, or his toes."

Hal Dozier listened to this speech with a frown. "Then go away from Martindale. You know there's one place where you'd be welcome, a place where nobody has heard of you."

Andrew Lanning changed color. "Have you heard from her?" he asked huskily.

"I have." He handed Andy a letter, and the latter unfolded it slowly, breathing hard. He found written in a swift freehand:

I know he is up for a hard battle, but he'll win. He has too much true steel in him to lose any fight he really wants to win. Will you tell him that for me? And will you ask him to write?

"Well?" said Dozier as Andrew handed back the letter. "Will you do it? Will you write to her?"

"When I've earned the right to." He wandered slowly toward the door.

"What are you going to do now?"

"I'm going to find out for myself. I'm going to learn if those gents yonder on the veranda want me to stay or want me to go back to the mountains. They can have their way about it."

Hal Dozier attempted to stop him, but he brushed the restraint aside and walked slowly across the wide street toward the hotel. Dozier, thoughtfully rubbing his chin, looked after him, and Sally trotted after her master until she had reached his heels and then followed like a dog, reaching out and trying to catch the brim of the wide sombrero in her teeth, for Sally still kept a good deal of the colt in her makeup.

II

That evening Hal Dozier sat long at his desk, writing. Now and then he stopped to think, or even rose and paced the room until new ideas came to him, and it was late when he had finished a letter that ran as follows:

Dear Miss Withero:

I'm keeping the promise I made you to give you the news, as soon as there was news to give. To start with there's the biggest and best kind of news. Andrew has come into town!

He came as big as life, and very much as you must remember him; a little thinner, I think, and a little sterner, compared to the old Andy we used to know about Martindale. He came on Sally, of course, and Sally, at least, hasn't changed. I used to hate that horse. It was Sally, you know, who ran my Gray Peter to death. But she's such a beauty that I've forgiven her. She follows Andy about like a dog. If it weren't for her, he'd die of loneliness, I know.

But to get back to important facts. When Andy came in I ran over things as clearly as I could, told him that the governor had pardoned him for the past and hoped well for his future. I advised him to accept your invitation to go East, and I promised to help him in any way that I could.

But he was stubborn as steel. Under his gentle manner there's no end of metal. As for you, he refuses even to mention your name, far less write to you, because, he says, he hasn't earned the right to speak to you. As for going East and working out his life in a new country, he says that he loves these mountains, that he belongs here, that in the East he'd be a fish out of water, and that, if he isn't strong enough to work out his destiny in his own land and among his own people, he doesn't want to live at all. He said these things in such a way that I couldn't find answers. I told him that the people of Martindale were neutral and pretty suspicious. But they'd give him a chance.

Do you know what he did then?

He walked straight out of my office and went to the veranda of the hotel. Here a dozen or more men were sitting around, and Andy made them a speech. I wish you could have heard it, it was so straight from the shoulder. And I won't forget him standing up as straight as a soldier and looking them all in the eye. He has a hard look to meet, has Andrew, as you may know someday if you ever make him angry.

He told them in words of one syllable that he knew he'd led a bad life for the past two years. He didn't make any bones of it, and he didn't make any excuses. That isn't his way. After he got started, he acknowledged that he'd lived as an outlaw. He said that he wanted to come back to Martindale, where he was born, and show the people of it that he could live as a sober, hard-working citizen. He said it was a bargain. As long as he roved around the mountains, he was simply a burden, for he lived off the work of other people. If he was allowed to settle down peaceably in the town, he would cease being a burden for anyone to carry. It was up to them. If they wanted to get rid of him and didn't want him around, they had only to say the word, and he would jump on the horse that was standing behind him and ride away and never come back—peacefully. But if they allowed him to stay he would do his best to be as law-abiding as the next one.

Then he waited for his answer, but there was no answer made! They sat like owls on stumps and stared at him. They were afraid to give him a cheer and tell him to stay, and they were afraid to tell him to get out of town. Andrew waited a minute or two, and then he turned on his heel and walked away with his head down.

I tried to cheer him up and told him that the people of the town were simply waiting to see if he meant what he said, and that as soon as he showed them, they would be with him heart and soul. But he was too shrewd to believe me.

He went to his old blacksmith shop and opened it. Things were a little rusty, but pretty much as they had always been. He polished it up a bit and then sat down at the door to wait for work. But there's a new blacksmith shop in Martindale now, and all the work that came in to town today drifted right past Andy's old shop. They turned and stared at him, but they didn't ask him to shoe their horses.

Tonight he went back to his uncle's old house. I went to see him there. The old shack has run down since Jasper Lanning's death, and I found Andrew pacing up and down in the dust, with the old, warped boards of the floor creaking under him. Not a very cheery place for him, you see. And he was as restless as a wolf in a cage, and every once in a while he would stop his pacing at a window and look out at the mountains and then begin to walk up and down again, leaving his trail in the dust of the floor.

He was in an ugly mood, but he tried to keep it concealed. He swore that he would stay on as long as he could, and then I came back to my office to write to you.

I'm afraid for Andy, Miss Withero, I'm mortally afraid. He's closer to me than anything on earth. I went to kill him for the sake of the price on his head. He shot me down and then fought with four men to save my life. Men of Andy's stamp aren't turned out every day, and it's a pity to see him fail.

But fail he inevitably will. The men of this town are watching and waiting for an explosion, and the more they watch and the more suspicious they grow, the more nervous Andrew is. He knows that a lot of them hate him and would shoot him in the back if they could. Sooner or later someone is sure to get drunk and cross him, or some crowd will get together and try to bully him. If either of these things happens, someone is going to die. It won't be Andrew. After the explosion he'll be on Sally on his way back to the mountains and the free life he loves. So you can very well see that I live over dry powder, with sparks flying all the time. When will Andy blow up?

There's one thing that can dampen the powder. There's one thing stronger than Andrew's nervousness. You know what that one thing is—his love for you. It's more than a love; it's worship. You're more than a woman to him. He's dressed you up as a saint, aureole and all. When he speaks of you, his voice changes, and he lowers his eyes.

Well, Miss Withero, I think you would do a good deal to help Andrew. I want to find out how much. Will you come West to Martindale and see Andrew and give him patience for the fight? Five minutes of you mean more to him than five years of adventure and freedom.

He doesn't know that I've written to you. I don't dare tell him. He thinks he must make himself go through the trial and try to see you after he has proven himself. But I say that the trial is greater than his strength. What will you do?

Hal Dozier

The marshal wrote that letter in the best of good faith, never dreaming that out of that letter would come the hardest test young Andrew Lanning was ever to receive. Moreover, it was destined to enter many hands and put strange thoughts in many minds and bring great results, some of which the marshal hoped for and some of which were the opposite of his desires.

It began by interrupting an important conversation. The conversation in itself was the result of long planning on the part of Charles Merchant. For a month he had been laboring to bring about a meeting between himself and Anne Withero, and eventually he had been able to maneuver until he was invited to this weekend party at the house where Anne was a guest for the summer. It was a typical Long Island estate, with oceans of lawn washing away from a Tudor house, so cunningly overgrown with vines and artificially weathered that, although it was hardly ten years old, it looked 500. Beyond the lawns were bits of an ancient forest, although it was not quite so ancient as it looked. In one of these groves Charles Merchant would have greatly preferred to have the walk and talk. But the best he could do was to keep Anne strolling up and down in the formal garden, in full sight of the house, almost in hearing of the guests. It was one of those foolish, little handmade gardens, with hedges clipped and sculptured into true curves and rigid square edges, and flower beds planned like a problem in geometry. Stiff benches that no one in the world would ever dream of sitting on added to the artificiality, and imported French sculptures of the seventeenth century, dotted here and there—ladies with fat legs and silly, little grinning faces and simpering, corpulent cupids—completed the picture. It was one of those formal French gardens that call from every nook and cranny: "Man made me, and God had absolutely nothing to do with it!"

But from this garden one could look through graceful oaks on the edge of the hill, down to the blue of the sea. Through those trees the glances of Anne Withero went, but the glances of Charles Merchant never strayed from the face of the girl. He could not tell exactly where he stood with her, but he felt that he was making very fair progress. In the first place, she was listening to him, and that was really more than he had reason to hope. His argument was based on a very old doctrine.

"If I have done things that were wrong, and heaven knows I have, it was because I was fighting to keep you, Anne. And you know everything is fair in such a case, isn't that true?"

And she had answered: "To tell you the truth, Charlie, I'm trying to forget all about the mountains and what happened there. I'm trying to forget anything very bad that you may have done. Is that what you want to know?"

It was not all, and he was frank to tell her so. "If you succeed too well," he said, "you may forget me altogether. I'd rather be remembered a little, even if it has to be viciously."

He was convinced that he was very far on the outskirts of her attention, and it cut him to the quick. Had she not once been his prospective wife? But he clung to the task, and before long she was listening with more attention, although she persisted in confining their walk to the ridiculous little paths of that garden. He grew bolder as the moments passed. When she asked him when he was going West, he said: "When I have to give up hope."

"Just what do you mean by that?" she asked him, and she asked it so unemotionally, so far from either scorn or invitation, that he was abashed, but he said gravely: "I mean that I'm struggling to win back your friendly respect first, Anne. And when that comes . . . well, then I'll go on hoping for something else. Do you think I'm wrong to do so?"

He had always been a proud and downright fellow, and he knew that his humility was what was breaking down her dislike for him and opening her mind, but he was delighted beyond all bounds when she did not at once return a negative answer to his last question. Indeed, she did not answer at all, and when she straightened and looked wistfully at the rich blue of the sea beyond the yellow-green oaks, he knew that she was remembering pleasant things out of their mutual past. He had his share of intuition and cunning, and he discreetly kept silent.

It was at this very moment that the letter was brought to her. She glanced down at it carelessly and continued her walk, but, presently looking down again, she seemed to read the address and understand it for the first time. He saw her hand hastily cover the writing on the envelope, and at the same time her eyes became alert. She wanted to get rid of him at once, and he knew it. More than that, when she looked at him now there was a certain hardness in her eyes. Something about that handwriting had made her suddenly call up her old anger, her old distaste for him.

But still, although the test was a stern one, Charles Merchant was not a fool. He brought her back to the house at the first pretext and left her alone with the infernal letter, then he went to find Anne's maid.

When he had decided that life was not worthwhile without Anne Withero and that he must make a deliberate and determined campaign to regain his old position with her, he had, like a good general, cast about to find a friend in the enemy's camp. By means of a small subsidy, he had secured a friend in the person of Mary, Anne's maid. She had already proven invaluable to him in many ways. She could not only keep him informed of her mistress's movements, but she was also intelligent enough to catch the general drift of Anne's interests of the moment. When Anne was reading books of the West and talking about the mountains, Charles Merchant knew perfectly well that her mind was turning to Andrew Lanning, that strange adventurer who had literally dropped out of the sky to ruin his own romance with Anne Withero. And, when Anne read and talked of other things, Charles knew in turn that she was letting the memory of her outlaw lover grow dim. In time, and with three thousand miles between them, he was sure that the girl would forget the fellow entirely. Any other solution was socially impossible. But he remained uneasy.

He met Mary at their appointed rendezvous beyond the tennis courts, and he told her at once what he wanted.

"Your lady got a letter a few minutes ago," he said, "a fat letter on blue-white paper. You know, the cheap stuff and the big, sprawling handwriting. You can't mistake it. Now, I want that letter to be in my hands before the night comes, you understand?"

When Mary stood with her hands folded and her eyes cast down, there was a good deal of the angel in her pale face. When she glanced up quickly, however, one found a pronounced seasoning of mischief in her eyes. And now she looked up very quickly, indeed. In her heart Mary despised big, handsome Charles Merchant; she had her own opinion of men who could not take the queen of their hearts by storm, but had to resort to such tactics as bribing maids. Nevertheless, she had decided to serve Charles Merchant. It was really for her mistress's sake more than her own. For Charles Merchant was rich, and he was also weak. An ideal man for a master and, also, from Mary's point of view, for a husband. If Anne married him she, Mary, would retain a mighty hold on the purse and the respect of the master of the house. She might even stand at the balance between master and mistress of a great establishment. She would be the power behind the throne. All of these things were in her mind as she now looked into the face of Charles Merchant, but she could not keep back the small grimace of mockery.

"Mister Merchant," she said, "may I ask you just one thing?"

"Fire away, Mary."

"After you marry Miss Withero, will you keep on handling her the same way?"

He laughed, and there was a sigh of relief behind the laughter. "After we're married!" he exclaimed. "After we're married, I'll find a way of handling her, never doubt that. Plenty of ways."

There was something in his manner of saying this that made Mary's eyes grow very big, and a sudden doubt of Charles Merchant came to her. His short command for her to hurry sent her away before she had time to speak again, but she went away thoughtfully.

III

That night the letter was in the hands of Charles Merchant. He read it hastily, for Mary was waiting anxiously to take it back to its proper place. He detained her for a moment.

"Has she been talking about anything unusual?" he asked, almost fiercely.

"No, nothing."

"Thank goodness!" said Merchant. "You're sure? No mention of a journey?"

Mary grew thoughtful. "She asked me, when she was dressing for dinner, if I had ever been West, and if I'd like to go there."

Merchant groaned. "She said that?"

"What's in that? She was just talking about the mountains."

"Only the mountains?"

"And she said there was a different breed of men there, too."

"That's all!"

He slammed the door after her and, going back to the window, slumped into a chair with his face between his hands. For all that he shut out the light from his eyes, he was seeing too clearly the picture of the lithe fellow, straight, graceful, dark-eyed, and light and nervous of hand—that was Andrew Lanning. He cursed the picture and the name and the thought of the name, as his mind went back to the night, so long ago, when the figure had leaned over his bed and asked through the darkness: "Where is the girl's room?" And then, lest he make an outcry and alarm the house, Lanning had tied and gagged him.

In truth, the coming of Lanning had tied and gagged him forever, so far as Anne Withero's interest was concerned. Afterward the name of Lanning had grown in importance, had become a legend, one of those soul-stirring legends that grow up, now and then, around the figure of a stirring man of action.

An outlaw certainly was beyond the pale of Anne's interest, but Charles could see now that, perhaps, the very strangeness of the wanderer's position and character had made him fascinating in the romantic eyes of the girl. And then, striking back through a thousand dangers and risking his life for the sake of one interview, Andy Lanning, the outlaw, had come to the Merchant house again and seen Anne Withero once more. Only twice they had seen one another, but out of those two meetings had come the wreck of his own affair with her. He gritted his teeth when he recalled it.

Moreover, he was quite certain that Hal Dozier was right. Hal was a shrewd judge of men and events. If he said that the girl could tame wild Lanning and keep him a law-abiding man, then he was right. But he must also be right when he said that Lanning was balancing on a precarious edge, ready to fall into violent action and outrage society again.

Was it not possible, then, to knock the ground from beneath the tottering figure? Could not the necessary impetus be supplied that would throw Lanning off his balance and plunge him once more into a career of crime? There must surely be a way. And he, Charles Merchant, had money, could buy who he willed to buy. The cause was worth it! It was a crusade, this saving of such a girl as Anne Withero from the low entanglements of an ex-criminal.

He packed his things that night. In the morning he said good-bye to her.

"I'm going West, Anne," he told her. "I see that the past is still too close to you, and that you haven't been able to forgive me entirely. I'm going West and wait, for I haven't given up. I'm going to come back and try again. In the meantime, if it should happen that you need a helper, let me know. Will you do that?"

Even then he hoped that she might confide enough in him to admit that she was soon going West herself, but he was disappointed. She gave him a chilly farewell and no hint of her plans. In the morning he returned to New York and purchased a ticket for the West. Then he bought an early edition of an evening paper and went into the smoking room of the station to wait for his train. His eyes took in the headlines dimly. How could print catch his attention when a story of far more vital interest was running through his mind?

He turned the page, and a bulldog face caught his eye. He liked it for the ugliness that fitted in with his own mood of the moment. There was a consummate viciousness and cunning about the little eyes, protected under massive, beetling brows; there was power and endurance in the blocky chin, and the habitual scowl fascinated Merchant, for it was his own expression of the moment. He raised his hand and smoothed his forehead with grinding knuckles, and still the face held his eyes.

Lefty Gruger, he read beneath the picture, Pardoned!

It was placed in large letters—an event of importance, it seemed, was the pardoning of this Gruger. With awakened interest he followed the rather long article.

It developed that Lefty Gruger had been serving a life term on many counts. If he had lived to the age of two hundred, his term of punishment would still be unspent. But Lefty Gruger had been for eight years an ideal prisoner. Never once did the prison authorities have the slightest trouble with this formidable murderer, for such it seemed Lefty Gruger had been. The man had apparently reformed. The reporter quoted one of Lefty's quaint sayings: "I dunno what's in this heaven stuff, but maybe it ain't too late for me to take a fling at it."

In reality, during the eight years his life had been exemplary, he had never become a trusty on account of the appalling nature of the crimes attributed to him, but he was on the verge of this elevation when the outbreak came. It was one of those mad, unreasoning outbreaks that will come now and then in prisons. An unpopular guard was suddenly hemmed against the wall, and his weapons were torn from him by a dozen furious prisoners. He was already down and nearly dead when a small, but well-directed, tornado struck the murderers in the person of Lefty Gruger. He had come out of the blacksmith shop with the iron part of a pick in his hand, and he went through the little host of assailants, smashing skulls like eggs as he went.

In the sequel the guard's life was saved, and seven prisoners died from the terrible effects of Lefty Gruger's blows. But this heroism could not go unnoticed or unrewarded. The governor examined the case, determined to give Lefty a chance, and forthwith signed a pardon that was pressed upon him. The result was that the governor's benign face appeared in a photograph beside the contorted scowl of Lefty Gruger. That was worth at least fifty thousand votes in certain parts of the state, although it was pointed out, with grim smiles in the police department, that Gruger was freed from a life sentence because he had killed more men at one sitting than he had been condemned for in the first instance.

The major portion of the article had to do with the desperate heroism of Lefty Gruger to save the guard, then with a detail of his exemplary conduct while in prison, and finally there was a very brief résumé of Lefty's criminal career, now happily buried under the record of his more-recent virtues. It seemed that

Lefty had been a celebrated gunman for many years, that he had escaped detection so long because he always did his jobs without confederates, and that, although it had been long suspected that he was guilty of killings, it was not until he had spent ten years in criminal life that he was finally taken and convicted.

Once he was in the hands of the law, it turned out that there were various people willing to inform against the professional murderer, men who had been held back by fear of him until he was safely lodged in the hands of the law. Now they were ready and eager to talk. Into the hands of the police came more or less convincing proof that Lefty Gruger had certainly been responsible for five murders, and perhaps many more. But even this testimony was not of the first order. The result was that, instead of hanging, Lefty received a life sentence.

Now he was returning to his old haunts off the Bowery. The street address drifted into Charles Merchant's mind hazily. He was thinking with dreamy eyes, building a fairy story in the future. That dream lasted so long that the train departed with no Charles Merchant on it. Then he rose and sauntered into the street and took a taxi to the Bowery. At the stand where he had his shoes polished, in the hope of hearing chance news, the word was dropped: "Lefty's back. He's at Connor's."

Merchant, leaving his chair as the shine was completed, sauntered into a lunch counter across the street. Sitting at the end of the counter nearest the window, he kept a steady eye on the pavement and houses opposite. Still retaining that survey, he covertly counted out $100 in crisp bills and shoved them into a blank envelope.

Lefty Gruger was not long out of sight. Having become a hero overnight, he had to harvest the admiration of his fellows, and presently he was observed to stroll down the steps of his rooming house, preceded and surrounded by half a dozen as hard-faced fellows as Merchant had ever seen. But, among them all, the broad, scowling face of Lefty stood forth. Every brutal passion found adequate expression in some line or corner of his face. Suddenly it seemed to Merchant that he had known the recesses of that dark mind for years and years, and he felt himself contaminated by the very thought. He scribbled a few words on the envelope and left the lunch counter hurriedly. Crossing the street, he managed to intercept the course of Lefty's crew at the far corner. He sidled apologetically through the midst of them, and, passing Lefty, he shoved the envelope containing the money into the latter's coat pocket and went on.

Although he did not pause, it seemed to him that the stubby hand of Lefty had closed over that envelope, and the square-tipped fingers had sunk into the missive, and that he sensed the contents by their softness. But Merchant hurried on, took a taxi at the nearest corner, and went straight to a hotel. He had written on the envelope:

Inside two hours, at the corner of Forty-Seventh and Broadway, east side of the street.

In the hotel he flung himself on the bed, but he could not rest.

IV

He knew very little about such matters, but he imagined that once a notorious criminal was at large, the police must keep an eagle eye upon him. If Lefty came to that meeting place, there might very well be a whole corps of observers on the watch from hidden places, and they might follow Lefty and note the interview with Merchant. But then again it was very doubtful if Lefty would make his appearance at all. He had $100 in his pocket for which he need not make an accounting. There was only one thing to which Charles Merchant trusted, and that was, having made such a little stake of easy money, the killer might continue on the trail.

He wasted the two hours that remained before him with difficulty and then went out and took his place at the head of Times Square, in the full rush of the late-afternoon crowd. Eagerly he swept the heads of the crowd, but there was no Lefty. Presently he felt a light jerk at his coat, and then a stocky, little man hurried past him and shouldered skillfully through the mob. It was Gruger beyond a doubt. The rear view of those formidable, square shoulders was almost as easily recognizable as the face of the criminal. Merchant followed unhesitatingly.

Gruger opened the door of a taxi waiting at the curb and stepped in, leaving the door open. Merchant accepted the silent invitation and climbed into the interior. The abrupt starting of the engine flung him back to the seat, and the driver reached out an arm of prodigious length and slammed the door. It seemed to Merchant that he was trapped and a prisoner. An edge of paper in his own pocket caught his eye as he looked down. He drew out his own envelope and saw, as it bulged open, the money. He shoved it into an inside coat pocket and then for the first time turned to Lefty. The latter wore a faint, ugly smile.

"But I intended this . . ." began Merchant, oddly embarrassed.

"I know," said Lefty, "but I don't take coin till after I've done a job, and then I want spot cash."

There was something so formidable about the way he jerked out these words that it made Merchant feel as though the gunman had already done a killing and now demanded payment. He moistened his lips and watched the stocky, little man.

"But I thought you might be in need of a little stake," he ventured again.

"I ain't never broke," declared Lefty in his positive manner. "I got friends, mister. Now what you want?"

"I want in the first place to go where we can talk."

"You do, eh? What's the matter with right here?"

"But the driver?"

"Say, he's all right. He's a friend of mine."

"But suppose we were seen to have entered this cab and were followed?"

"Pal, nobody ain't going to follow him, not through this jam."

The driver was weaving through the press of traffic with the easiest dexterity, seeming to make the car small to slip through tight holes, and keeping in touch with his motor as though it were a horse under curb and spur.

"In the first place," began Merchant heavily, "I don't know how to let you know that you can trust any promises I make in regard to . . ."

"Money? Sure you can. You're Charles Merchant. You come out of the West, you got a big ranch from your old man, and your bank account would gag a mule. All right, I know you."

Charles Merchant swallowed. "How in the world . . . ?"

"Did I tumble to that gag? I'll tell you. You didn't think I let you do a fadeaway after you passed me the bunk, do you? Nope. I ditched the gang, done a sidestep, and slid after you to your hotel, grabbed your name off the book, and the rest was easy."

"How?"

"How? Why I got friends. They looked you up inside half an hour, and there you are. Now what's what?"

There was something startling in this abrupt way of brushing through preliminaries and getting down to the heart of things.

Merchant had expected long and delicate diplomatic fencing before he even broached the aim he had in mind. He found that he was brought to the heart of his subject inside the first minute.

"In a word," he said, breathing hard, "it is a task of the first magnitude."

Lefty studied him, not without contempt and just a touch of bewilderment.

"Guess I get you. Somebody to be bumped off? When and where, and what's the stake?"

Merchant gasped. Then he answered tersely: "As fast as you can get to the place. That place is Martindale, and it's a good two thousand miles from New York. The price is what you think it's worth."

"I don't like out-of-town jobs," said Lefty calmly. "They get me off my feed a little, and two thousand miles is pretty bad. Seeing it's you, ten thousand ain't too much to ask."

He said it in such a businesslike manner that, although Merchant was staggered by the price, he did not seriously object. A moment's thought assured him that $10,000 was cheap, infinitely cheap, if it brought him to his goal.

"And when do you want me to start, governor?"

"At once. About the money, what part will you want?"

"Ain't I told you that I'm never broke? I don't need any."

"The whole thing after . . . after . . . ?"

"After I deliver the goods? That's it."

"But how do you know . . . ?"

"That you'll pay? Easy! You think it over a minute, and you'll see why you'll pay."

And Merchant knew with a shudder that this was the last debt in the world that he would try to dodge.

"Now that we've settled things," he said, "I want to tell you about the man in the case."

"He don't matter," said Lefty largely. "He don't matter at all. All I want is his name."

Charles Merchant rubbed his chin in thought. It was strange that sectional pride should crop out in him in this matter of all matters. He looked coldly upon Lefty Gruger.

"Ever have a run-in with a Western gunfighter?" he asked.

"Me? Sure. Went as far West as Kansas City once and got mixed up with a tough mug out of the hills. They told me he was quick as a flash at getting out his cannon. Bunk! A revolver is pretty fair, but an automatic is the medicine for these Western gunfighters! They shoot one slug, standing straight up. I spray 'em by just holding down my finger. Fast draw? I don't draw. I drop a fist in my pocket and let her go!"

"Was that how it went with the gunman you met in Kansas City?"

"Sure it was. The boob didn't have a chance. He stood up straight like a guy getting ready to make a speech and grabs for his gat. I jumps behind a table and begins zigzagging. He didn't have a chance of hitting me. While I was jumping back and forth, I turn on the spray. Seven slugs, and they all landed. He wouldn't've held a pint of water, he was so full of holes when I finished with him."

Charles Merchant wiped his forehead. What he had looked upon as a forlorn hope changed to a feeling of far greater certainty.

"Now," he said, "listen to reason. You may be very good with a gun. Of course you are. But this fellow, Lanning . . ."

"First name?"

"Andrew. This Andrew Lanning is good with a gun, too. He's beaten the best men of the mountains. With rifle or revolver it doesn't seem that he can miss. You may be almost as good, but, if you stand up to him, you stand a fine chance of being killed, Lefty. Don't take the chance. Make a sure thing of it."

"Shoot him in the back?" said Lefty coldly. "That what you mean?"

"Why not? You'll get ten thousand just the same."

The voice of Lefty changed to a snarl. "Maybe you think," he said furiously, "that you're talking to a butcher? Maybe you think that?"

"I . . . I . . ." Merchant choked in his distress. "The fact is, in a business like this, I like to feel that my money is invested as safely as possible, and I think . . ."

"I want you to think this," said Lefty, and he shook a swiftly vibrating forefinger under the nose of his companion. "You're talking to a white man. I never shot a gent while he had his back turned. I never shot him when he was took by surprise. I never shot him when he was drunk. I never shot him when he was sick. I've fought every man face to face. They flopped, because they didn't have the nerve or the dope on gunfighting. That's my way. If a bird is good enough to flop me, then he collects, and I don't. That's all. If I didn't work for my coin, d'you think I could enjoy making it? No! I ain't a man killer, I'm a sportsman, mister, and you want to write it down in red. Gimme a good, sporting chance, and I take it. Give me a sure thing, and I tell you to go hang. I've never took up a sure thing, and I never will. But I'm after game, big game! Some gents like to go out into the jungle and hunt for tigers. I have more fun than that, because I hunt things a thousand times worse'n tigers. I hunt men. It ain't the money alone that I work for. I got enough salted away to do for me. But I like the fun, bo. It's in my nature."

He sat back again, contented, flushed after having expounded his creed, defying Merchant to argue further in the matter. It bewildered Charles, this singular profession of faith.

"This Lanning guy . . . ?" went on Lefty more gently. "You stop worrying. I'll plant him. I'll salt him away with lead so's you never have to worry about him none no more. That what you want?"

When Charles Merchant nodded, the gunman continued easily. "You just jot down the directions to the place. That's all I want."

V

From the roof to the bellows, there had been hardly a thing about the old blacksmith shop that did not need repairing. The anvil alone was intact. Even the sledgehammers were sadly rusted. He spent the first few days putting things in order and making repairs. But this was about the only work that came his way. To be sure, now and then, someone of the more curious dropped into his shop and had a horse shod in order to see the celebrated desperado at work. It would be something to ride home and point to the iron on the feet of a horse and say: "Andrew Lanning put those shoes on. I seen him do it."

But this made up a mere dribble of work, although Hal Dozier had sent in a few small commissions from his ranch. He had even offered to set up a shop for Andy on his ranch and said that he had ample ironwork to remunerate both himself and Andrew, but the ex-outlaw had other plans. He was determined to fight out the battle in Martindale itself.

There was something dreamlike about the whole thing. It had not been so many years ago since the men of Martindale looked down on the Lanning kid as being "yaller clear through." In those days they had greeted any mention of his name with a smile and a shrug. Then came the unlucky day when he knocked down a man and fled in fear of his life, leaving an unconscious victim who appeared to be dead. Feeling that he was outlawed by his crime, Andy had become an outlaw in fact. That was the small, the accidental, beginning that, it seemed, was to determine the whole course of his life. He had plenty of chances to think about himself, past and future, as he sat idly in the little shop, day after day, waiting for work.

His funds were dwindling meanwhile. An angle of the affair, at which he had not looked before, now presented itself. He might be actually starved out of the town. He might be starved into submission.

All day, every day, he could hear the cheery clangor of hammer on anvil in the new and rival blacksmith shop down the street. There was plenty of business there, plenty of it. His competitor had tried to placate this terrible rival soon after his arrival. He came to visit the latter in his shop at the beginning of the working day.

"I'm Sloan," he said, "Bill Sloan. Maybe you don't know me?"

"Sure," said Andy. "I know you."

"You and me being sort of business rivals, as you might say," said Sloan, "I got this to say for a start. I ain't going to use no crooked ways of getting customers away from you, Lanning."

"I guess you won't," said Andrew gently.

"Matter of fact, now and then, I get an overflow of trade. I might send some of it down to your shop, Lanning."

It touched Andrew, the embarrassment of this huge, sturdy-hearted fellow. He went to him and touched his shoulder.

"Sloan," he said, "I know what's on your mind. You think I'm getting mad at you, because you get the work. I'm not. Get everything you can, and don't send me any overflow. You're married, and you have kids. Get all the work you can. As for me, I'm not going to try to rustle trade with a gun."

* * * * *

On the afternoon of the next day Hal Dozier stopped before the shop with a suggestion.

"Andy," he said, "Si Hulan is in town. Staying up at the hotel right now. He's looking for hands. Why don't you trot up to see him? He'd be glad to take you on if he has any sense. Got a big ranch. Soon as he learns that he can trust you, he'd be apt to make you foreman. You're the man to handle that rough gang of his."

Andy Lanning was not at all enthusiastic.

"You see," he replied, "I'd be glad to do that, but Sally isn't much good at working cows. She's never had much experience."

"You could teach her."

"I could teach her, but that dodging and hustling around in a bunch isn't very good for a horse's legs."

"I know. Then ride another horse, Andy. Keep Sally for Sundays and holidays, eh?"

"Ride another horse?" asked Andrew. "Man alive, Hal, you don't mean that!"

"Why not?" asked the marshal.

Andrew was breathless. "Sally and me," he attempted to explain. "Why . . . Sally and me are pals, you might say, Dozier." He whistled softly, and at once the lovely head of Sally came around the corner of the shop. There she stood with her head raised, then canted to one side, her ears pricked, while she examined her master curiously.

"She plays out there all day," said Andrew, smiling at the mare. "I turn her loose in the morning when I come down to work, and she follows down here and plays around in the lot. Sometimes old Missus Calkin's dog, old Fanny, you know, comes over and plays a game with Sally. Game seems to be for Fanny to set her teeth in Sally's nose, and for Sally to let her come as close to it as she can without doing it. Hear Sally snorting and Fanny snarling, and you'd think they was a real battle on. Well, you see how it is. I couldn't very well get on with Sally if I rode another horse. Besides, the minute I got off another horse, Sally would kick the daylights out of the nag. That's Sally's way . . . jealous as a cat and ready to fight for attention. She'll come over here and nose in between us pretty soon if I talk to you and don't pay no attention to her." He rose as he spoke and winked at the marshal. "Watch her now."

He turned his back on Sally, and the marshal looked from one to the other of them. He thought them very much alike, these two. There was the same touch of wildness in both, the same high-headed pride, the same finely tempered muscles, the same stout spirit. Only one man had ever succeeded in riding Sally with a saddle, and that man was her present master. For the rest she was as wild as ever. And it came to the marshal that the same was true of the boy. One person in the world could tame him, and that was Anne Withero.

Sally had stood her exclusion from the conversation as long as possible. She now snorted and stamped with a dainty forehoof. It caused Andy to wink at the marshal, but he gave her no direct attention, and presently she came hesitantly forward and, in reach of Andy, she laid her short ears back on her neck and bared her teeth. The marshal stifled an exclamation, so wicked was the look of Sally at that moment, so snake like she was with her long, graceful neck and glittering eyes. The teeth closed on a fold of Andy's shirt at the shoulder, and she tugged him rudely around.

He faced her with pretended anger. "What kind of manners is this?" demanded the master. "You need teaching, and by hell, you'll get it. Now get out!" He threw up his arm, and the horse sprang sideways and back, lithe and neat footed as an enormous cat. There she stood alert, with ears pricking again.

"Look at that," said Andy. "Ready for a game, you see? What can you do with a horse like that?"

"Ain't you ever had to discipline her? Never used a whip on her?" asked the marshal.

"I should say not," replied Andy. "If I seen a gent raise a whip on Sally, I'd . . ."

"Wait a minute!"

Andy shuddered and allowed the interruption to silence him. "I dunno," he muttered. "I could stand almost anything but that. If they was to shy a stone at Sally, like they done the other day . . ."

"Did they do that?" asked the marshal softly.

"It was the Perkins kid," said Andy. "Sally dodged the stone a mile, but it was sharp edged enough to have hurt her bad. I went in to see Jim Perkins."

"You did? But you talked soft, Andy?"

"I done as well as I could. He said that boys will be boys, and then, all at once, I wanted to take him by the throat. It came to me like a fit. I fought it off, and I was weak afterward."

"Did you say anything?"

"Not a word, but Jim Perkins went to the door with me, looking scared, and he said that he'd see that they was no more stones thrown at Sally." The very memory of his anger made Andy change, and his mouth grew straight and hard.

"Then Sally doesn't get on very well with the folks in town?" asked Hal Dozier. He himself had been too much on his big ranch of late to follow things in Martindale closely.

"She gets on with the kids pretty fine, but if a man comes near her, she tries to take a chunk out of him with her teeth, or brain him with her heels. There was young Canning the other day . . . he just jumped the fence in time." He broke into riotous laughter.

"Wait a minute," cut in the marshal. "There seems to be two sides to this story. Is that a laughing matter? Canning might have been killed!"

"Served him right for teasing her."

The marshal shook his head. "You'd better see Hulan," he suggested.

After a little more talk, Andrew accepted the advice. The Hulan Ranch was neighbor to the town. He would be practically in Martindale, and all that he wanted was to convince Martindale of his honest determination to reform. Saying good-bye to the marshal, he went straight to the hotel.

VI

Business was slack; men were plentiful on the range at this season, so Andrew was not the only one who went to the hotel to call on old Si Hulan. He found that the rancher was in his room interviewing the applicants one by one. He had three vacancies, and he intended to fill them all, but only after he had seen every man who was asking for a place. There were a dozen men on the veranda, all waiting to be seen or, having been seen, they waited for the selection of the rancher. They were playing together like a lot of great, senseless puppies, working off practical jests that caused more pain than laughter, and every man was sharp-eyed for a chance to take advantage of his fellow. Even as Andy approached, someone happened to turn his head as he walked down the veranda. Instantly he was tripped and sent pitching across the porch. He stopped his fall by thrusting both arms into the back of another who was driven, catapulting, down the steps. This man in turn attempted to stop his momentum by breaking the shock at the expense of Andy Lanning.

The latter had his back turned, but a running shadow warned him, and he leaped aside. The other rushed past with arms stretched out, grinning.

There was a sudden cessation of laughter on the porch as Andrew turned. The man who had attempted to knock him down from behind came to a stumbling halt and faced about, deadly pale, his lips twitching, and the expectancy of the men on the veranda was a thing to be felt like electricity in the air. It was very clear to Andy that they expected him to take offense and, being a gunman, to show his offense by drawing his revolver. The white, working face of the big fellow before him told the same story. The man was terribly afraid, facing death, and certain of his destruction. But his great brown hand was knotted about the butt of his gun, and he would not give way. Rather die, to be sure, than be shamed before so many. Pity came to Andy, and he smiled into the eyes of the other.

"There's no harm done, partner," he said gently, and went up on the veranda.

He left the big man behind him, stunned. Presently the latter went to the hitching rack, got his horse, and rode down the street.

He would tell his children and his grandchildren in later years how he faced terrible Andy Lanning and came away with his life.

The crowd on the veranda began to break out of their silence again, but the former mirth was not restored. A shadow of dread had passed over them, and their spirits were still dampened. Covertly every eye watched Andrew. He went gloomily up the steps and laid his hand on the back of the first chair he saw, just as another man came hurriedly from the interior of the hotel.

"Hey," he called, "my chair, you!"

Andrew turned, and the newcomer stopped, as though he had received a blow in the face.

"I made a mistake," he said.

"Take your chair," replied Andrew gravely. "There are plenty more."

The other moistened his white lips. "I don't want it," he said unevenly. "Besides, I'm going right back inside."

Before Andrew could speak again, the latter had turned and gone hastily through the door. Lanning sat down, buried in gloom. Dead silence reigned along the veranda now. He knew what was in their thoughts—that twice they had come within the verge of seeing gunplay. And he writhed at the thought. Did they think he was a professional bully to take advantage of them? He knew, as well as they knew, that an ordinary man had no ghost of a chance against his trained speed of hand and steadiness of nerve and lightning accuracy of eye. Did they think he would force issues on them? Yet he felt bitterly that, sooner or later, they would actually herd him into a mortal fight. Indeed one of these boys would not wait to ask questions. If he crossed the path of Lanning by chance, he would take it for granted that guns were the order of the day and draw his weapon. And then what was the chance of Andy, except to kill, or be killed?

Decidedly the marshal was right. He must get onto the Hulan Ranch and let Martindale grow more gradually acclimated to the changed Andrew Lanning. He knew that this position of his was one that many a bullying gunfighter had labored years to attain and had gloried in, but to him it was a horror. He wanted to stand up before them and tell them they were wrong. But he had tried that on the first day of his return to the town, and he had seen in every face the conviction that he lied.

He was glad when it came his turn to see Hulan, and as he stepped through the door into the inner hall, he heard the murmur of voices break out again on the veranda in subdued whispers, and he knew that they were talking of him.

Old Si Hulan greeted him with amazing warmth. He was a stringy, old man who had once been bulkily strong and was still active. Age had diminished him, but it had not crippled him. His lean, much-wrinkled face lighted, and he came out from behind the table to grip the hand of Andrew.

"Why, son," he said, "are you hunting for work on my ranch?"

"That's it," said Andy. He had never known the old man well, and this generous greeting warmed his heart.

"You are? Then I'll tell a man that this is my lucky day. I been looking for your make of a man for a long time. Sit down, lad. Sit down and lemme look you over." He pushed Andrew into a chair. "In the old days they didn't think much of you. I've heard 'em talk, the idiots! But I knowed that a Lanning was always a Lanning, same as a hawk is always a hawk, even if a chicken does the hatching."

He kept grinning and chuckling to himself in the pauses of his talk.

"You go back and get your blankets," he said, "and get ready to come along with me this evening. Or, if you ain't got blankets, it don't make any difference. I'll fix you up like a king. I'll give you an outfit any rider on the range would be proud of."

"That's mighty fine," returned Andy, amazed by this cordiality. "About the wages . . . you can fix your own price. I'm pretty green at ranch work."

"We'll agree on wages," said the old man. "Ain't any trouble on that head."

"Another thing you ought to know before you take me on. My horse ain't very good at working cattle. Matter of fact, I wouldn't even train her for that job. But if it's just riding the range, she'll be fine for that. But not for a lot of roping and heavy work."

It seemed that Si Hulan was daunted by these remarks.

"Roping?" he demanded. "Roping? You? Why, boy, d'you think I'm going to use a mountain lion to pull a wagon? Cow work! Ride the range!" He rocked back on his heels, tucked his thumbs into the armholes of his vest, and burst into a roar of laughter.

"Son," he said, when he found his voice again, "you hark to me. The job I got for you is right in your own line." He lowered his tone, and his eyes twinkled discreetly. "Up yonder in the hills I got the finest little layout for moonshining that ever you see. I raise my own grain, you see, and I feed it into my own still. Nothing easier. And I got the still cached away where the best fox in the police service would never find it. Well, Andy, what I'm going to use you for is running that moonshine over the hills and down to the river. That's where I market it. I got a tough gang of boys working the run for me now, but what I need is a leader that'll keep 'em in order. And you're the man for me. I guess they ain't any of 'em so hard but what they'll soften up when Andy Lanning gives 'em an order. As for the wages, they ain't going to be none. You and me will just split up the profit, almost any reasonable way you say. I furnish the goods, and you take what little risk they is. It ain't really no big risk. It's for running the men that I want you."

He had kept up his harangue so closely and with such a hot enthusiasm that Andrew could not interrupt him until he reached this point, and he interrupted by rising from the chair into which Si Hulan had thrust him.

"Mister Hulan," he said slowly, "you got me all wrong. I'm going straight. I'm staying inside the law as long as the law will let me. Run your own still. It's nothing to me, but I'll have no hand in it."

Hulan gasped. Then he nodded. "I see," he said. "Trying me out? I don't blame you for being mistrustful of folks after what you've been doing the past few years, but . . ."

"First and last and all the time," said Andrew, "I mean what I say. I'm going straight, Hulan. I can't take that job. But, if you got an honest job running cattle on the range, let me take a try at it, and I'll thank you for the chance. I don't care what the wages are."

Hulan snorted, a flush growing up his withered face.

"That's the song, is it?" he asked. "D'you think I'm a fool, Lanning? D'you think you have anybody in this town fooled? Don't you suppose everybody knows that you're in here on some crooked job?" His voice became a growl. "I'll tell you one thing that may surprise you. You wonder why nobody has asked you to step out of town, why we've been so simple we've let you stay and make your plans and your plots, whatever they may be. But we ain't been sleeping, Andy. Not by a long sight. They's five of the best men in this town has got together and sworn to keep a hoss saddled night and day, ready to jump on your trail and run you down the minute you make your break. And we got other towns all posted, so we can get in touch with them *pronto*, the minute you tear loose.

"Why am I telling you all this? Simply to show you where you stand. No, Lanning, once wrong always wrong, and we know it. That's why I make you my offer. Come out with me, and I'll cover up your tracks. If you stay down here and try to work your game, we'll get you the minute you step crooked. Why, you fool, we been holding our breath ever since you come in, waiting for a chance to nail you!"

Andrew Lanning watched him gloomily. It was all in line with the attitude of the younger men on the veranda of the hotel. It was perfectly plain now. They hated him; they feared him, and they would get him if they dared. They would bide their time. If appearances were against him for a moment, they would make their play. The governor of the state had pardoned him, but society had not forgiven him, would not forgive him. With a breaking heart, he saw the vision of Anne Withero, the happiness of which he had dreamed, grow dim and flicker out into complete darkness.

He turned slowly away from Hulan and stepped into the hall, and then slowly down the stairs. As he went, anger rose in him and swelled his heart. It was unfair, cruelly unfair. In some way they should be made to pay for their stupidity. He hated them all.

At the bottom of the stairs he came upon a knotted little group, standing with their heads together, listening to some jest or gossip.

"Get out of the way!" said Andy Lanning angrily.

They jerked their heads aside, saw him, and then melted back from his path. Andrew strode through them without deigning a glance in either direction. He detested them as much as they feared him. If they wanted war, let it be war. He heard the whisper stir behind him, but he strode on through the door and went slowly down the steps to the ground. War, indeed, had been declared.

VII

Through the little town of Martindale a single whisper traveled as distinctly and as swiftly as the report of cannon down a small gorge. Hal Dozier heard of the first outbreak of the ex-outlaw ten minutes after it happened. He went straight to the hotel and found a grave conclave deliberating on the veranda. There was no sign of the usual jesting or the usual tales. They crowded their heads close together and talked with frowns. The marshal knew that serious trouble was in the air.

He was more alarmed than ever when they fell silent at his approach. He singled out Si Hulan, who was among the rest, and put the question to him.

"What's wrong with Andy Lanning?"

"What's wrong? Everything's wrong with him. He's no good," said the old rancher with deliberation. "I offer him a job with me . . . a regular, honest job at good pay," continued Hulan, lying smoothly, "and the infernal young hound asked me what he got on the side. I asked him what he meant by that. He said I ought to know that he wasn't interested in small-fry talk. He wanted action and big pay, and he didn't care for the danger. That's the sort of talk he gave me. I told him to get out of my room and never let me see his face again. And he went, growling."

Hal Dozier scented the lie under this talk. He had known Hulan for a long time as a man of dubious life, but now it was impossible for him directly to challenge the statement. All he could say was: "It doesn't sound like Andy. He doesn't talk that way, Hulan."

"Not to you. Sure he don't talk that way to you," said Hulan. "He's pulled the wool over your eyes and made a fool of you, Hal. Everybody in town knows it except you, and it's time that you be told. That kid comes to you and makes good talk, says he's going to reform. The rest of us know that he's gone wrong. Once wrong always wrong. He's going to the bad, and you're a fool to let him take you in."

A younger man could not have talked quite so frankly to the formidable marshal. But Si Hulan was too old to be in danger of physical attack, and he spoke his mind outright to Dozier.

He went on: "You've made a pet out of this man killer, Hal. That's bad enough for you, because one of these days he'll turn and sink his teeth in you. But it's particular bad for us in this here town, because you ain't the only one he's apt to muss up. I say it wasn't square to bring him in."

There was a gloomy murmur from the others, and Hal Dozier studied them in despair. One by one they told the story of how Lanning had come down the stairs and ordered the crowd to separate so that he could walk through. They told the tale profanely and expressively, and they assured the marshal that the next time such a thing happened they would not stand upon the order of procedure, they would fall upon young Andrew Lanning and teach him manners.

"Boys," said the marshal gravely, "I know how you feel. You think that Lanning is taking advantage of you, because he's a proved gunfighter. Maybe it looks that way, but if I could get close to this trouble, I know I could show you that you'd badgered Andy into it. He ain't a bully. He never was, and he never will be. But they's some around this town that's been treating him like he was a bear to be baited. Well, boys, if you ever tease Andy to the point when he breaks loose, he'll turn out the worst rampaging bear you ever see. Keep that under your hat, but give Andy a chance to make good, which he can do."

With this mixture of cajoling and warning, Hal left the hotel and sought Lanning. He found his young protégé buried in gloom in the silent blacksmith shop. Andrew lifted his head slowly and greeted his friend with a lackluster eye.

"Keep your heart up," advised the marshal. "Work will begin to come in to you, son. This old shop will be full of business all day long, as soon as the boys in town are sure you mean to settle down. You were a good blacksmith in the old days, and they know it. But no more busting out like you done today."

It was proof of the despair of Andrew that even to Hal Dozier he did not offer the true explanation of that affair. He let it go.

"Hal," he said sadly, "the main trouble is that I don't think I want the work to come in. I was a blacksmith in the old days. I liked it, and I liked to make things. But it doesn't interest me any more."

"What in the world are you, then?"

"I dunno, Hal. I can't find out. Maybe I'm what they figure me to be . . . no good."

The marshal found that he had no answer ready, and he could only make one suggestion. "If you can't make a go of the black-smith work, come with me. I'll make you a deputy. They's a big bunch of cash right now over in the bank, and they have been asking me for a good man to guard it. Will you let me give them your name?"

But Andy shook his head. "They wouldn't take me. Besides, I'm not ready to give up yet."

Hal Dozier went straight to the telegraph office and wired to Anne Withero: COME QUICK, OR NOT AT ALL.

In the evening he received an answer from Anne Withero, saying she was coming on the next train. That telegram gave him heart. But would Andrew Lanning hold out until the arrival of this great ally?

The marshal did not know it, but the great temptation was coming to Andrew even at that very moment. He sat in the old shack that his uncle, Jasper Lanning, had owned before him. Never had it seemed more dreary, more deserted. As he was coming home from the shop at the end of the idle day, little Judy had crossed the street to avoid passing close to him, and that told Andy more than the curses of a crowd of grown men what the town thought of him.

He felt the blight of it cold in his heart all the time that he was cooking his supper, and then he sat down to the meal without appetite. The bacon was cold, the flapjacks soggy, the potatoes half cooked. He forced himself to eat.

All the windows were open, for the night was coming on close and windless, and he wished to take advantage of every stir of the air. It was very hot, and it seemed to have grown hotter since the coming of the darkness. The little flame of the lantern seemed to add to it. He could feel the glow against his face, and there was the nauseating odor of kerosene and the foul-burning wick. But he had not heart enough to trim the wick and freshen the light.

When he had finished his meal, there was the doubly disagreeable duty of washing the dishes. The water was greasy to the touch, nauseating again. The walls of the kitchen were hung with shadows, memories of the old days, and those old days seemed cramped and disagreeable. He was returning to that life, and there was no glamour to it. It was like crawling into a hole and waiting for death.

He finished his task by banging the dishpan onto its nail on the rough-finished boards of the wall and strode slowly back to the other room. There he sat down with a book, but the print would not take hold of his eye. He found the book falling to his lap, while his mind wandered through the past. He had lived greater things than were in these romantic pages. He had been part and parcel and the prime mover in deeds that had stirred the length and the breadth of the mountain desert. And a faint, grim smile played and grew and died on his lips, as he remembered some of them.

He was recalled from his dreaming sharply, as though by a voice. All at once, although he did not change from his position, he was tinglingly alert. Another person had entered the room and stood at the door behind him. An added sense, which only men who have been hunted possess, informed him of that fact. Someone was there. His mind flashed over a score of possibilities of men who hated him, men who might have trailed him to the town to wreak vengeance. Any one of them would be capable of shooting him in the back without warning.

All this went through his mind in the least part of a second. Then in a flash he whirled out of his chair, slipping into the dense shadow on the floor with the speed of a snake that twists and strikes. As he fell, the long gun, which never left his hip, was gleaming in his hand.

The man at the door jerked both empty hands above his head and cursed softly. He was a handsome fellow with a rather colorless face, bright eyes, and an alert, straight carriage.

"Don't shoot!" he called. "Don't shoot, Andy!"

<del>45</del>

The latter came softly to his feet, but still crouched, panting and savage under the urge of that swift impulse to fight. He kept low in the shadow that washed across the room, below the level of the table on which the squat lantern sat. In this shadow Andy slipped to the farther corner of the room. There he was in a position that neither the two windows nor the open door commanded. Here he straightened, still with the revolver ready.

"You can drop your hands now, Scottie," he ordered.

Scottie had turned slowly to follow the movements of Lanning, always with his arms stiffly above his head.

"Whispering winds!" he exclaimed, as he brought his hands down. "Fast as ever, eh? Thought you'd be slowed up a little by the quiet life, but you're not."

"What's up?" demanded Andrew Lanning. "And what d'you want, Scottie? Is there anyone outside?"

"Nobody that means you any harm. Suspicious, aren't you, these days? How does that come, Andy? Living among these fine, quiet, honest men in Martindale, I should think that your life would be like a smooth-flowing river." He grinned impishly at Lanning.

"You've said enough," said Andy. It was a new man who faced Scottie, a dangerous, cunning, agile man whose eyes never ceased roving from door to window to the face of his guest. "Why are you here?"

Scottie sauntered to a chair and dropped into it, his hands folded behind his head. In this fashion, with a slow and lordly turning of the eyes, he surveyed the house.

"Not a lot to boast of as a house, Andy. Why am I here? Why, just for a chat. Dropped in to chat about old days, you know, Andy. The way you sat there, with your book upside down and your eye looking at nothing, I thought you might be thinking of the same thing. What about it?"

Andy watched him carefully, but he dropped the gun back in the holster.

"Well, Scottie?"

The latter refused to be pinned down to reasons and purposes. He rambled on. "Any of our camps could beat this, eh? In the old days when Allister led us around? Those were free times, Andy. Money, liquor, good cigars, best chuck on the range. Can you come over that here in Martindale?"

Andy was silent. Into his mind had flashed a picture of the campfire and the circle of faces bathed in yellow light and carved from black shadow.

"But I suppose you got friends down here who more than make up for what you miss, eh?"

There was a flash and twinkle in his bright eyes. How unlike the eyes of any man Lanning had seen in Martindale since his return. For the wolf light was in them, and as his heart leaped in response, he knew that the wolf light was in his own eyes. He knew that if he lived a long and peaceful life to the very end, that light would gleam from time to time in his face, and the fierce, free, joyous urge would pulse and rush through his veins. It was in him, and it was part of him. When he spoke to Scottie, like spoke to like. One word between them might mean more than a whole conversation with the men of Martindale. Two glances were question and reply.

"Leave out my Martindale friends," said Andy dryly. "Why are you here? And who came with you?"

"I came alone."

Andy smiled.

"You're right, chief," said Scottie. "You know I wouldn't risk coming down here alone."

"Who's with you?"

"Ask."

Andy whistled a prolonged, low note that traveled far and quavered up at the end weirdly. After a moment there came a still-softer answer.

"Larry la Roche and Clune, eh? Where's the big fellow?"

Scottie made a careless gesture of lighting a match and blowing it out.

"Dead?" asked Andy huskily.

"Dead."

"How?"

"They cornered him at Old Willow, Jordan and his two cubs of kids. Jordan came up and talked to him. His kids sneaked around behind and drilled him."

Andy began to pace up and down lightly, swiftly, soundlessly. "I wish I'd been there!" he said. "Jordan, eh?"

"I wish you'd been there," replied Scottie. "The big fellow would never have dropped out if you'd been there to lead. But the rest of us couldn't handle him, and now he's done for. As a matter of fact, chief, the three of us have come down here to make a little proposition to you." He leaned forward, his elbows sprawling out on the table. "Lanning, will you listen?"

Andrew hesitated, and before he could answer, Scottie struck smoothly into his talk.

"Chief, we need you back. I admit that we did a dirty trick. I admit that you've reason not to trust us. Particularly me. But you were getting Hal Dozier off free, and every one of us hates Hal Dozier like poison, and has reason to. We couldn't stand it. I couldn't stand it. I made a mistake and tried to get Dozier, whether you wanted to or not. Well, I didn't do it. You turned out faster in the head and stronger than the whole lot of us. I admit it, Andy. I'm older than you are. I've followed the game a lot longer than you've followed it, but I'll freely admit that, next to Allister, you're the best leader that ever rode the mountains. And time will give you as much or more than Allister had.

"Clune and Larry la Roche and I are three good men. You know that. But, without a leader, we play lone hands, and we get poor results. And what leader can we get? I tried to hold the boys together. I couldn't do it. I'm ashamed to admit it, but it's true. Then we agreed to follow Larry, but he's too hotheaded, just as you told us a long time ago. Matter of fact we thought you were too young to know much. It's taken the last few months to teach us that you knew a lot more than we gave you credit for. In short, we agree that we have to have you back.

"Allister picked you to follow him in the lead, and Allister was right. You were the next best man to him. We see that now. If you come to us, you'll be the chief, just as Allister was, and you'll settle the disputes, decide on the plans, and take two shares for yourself every time we split the pot. How does that sound to you, Andy?"

Lanning opened his lips to speak and then sank into a chair, with something like a groan. "No!" he declared.

"Lad, we need you."

"Clear out, Scottie," said Andrew.

"But I'm coming back," said Scottie, rising, but smiling in the face of Andrew. "I'm coming back, and when I come back, I'll get another answer. Remember, Andy, we're three who can do more than three things, and with you to organize and keep us together we'll live like kings, free kings, Andy. You're not cut out for life in a dump like this. Don't forget, I'm coming back."

"Don't do it," replied Andrew. "I've given you my answer. Stay away."

But Scottie laughed mockingly, waved from the doorway, and disappeared into the deep, hot black of the night.

Andrew stared after him with trembling lips, and his deep agitation showed in his face. He had to fight hard to keep from following.

VIII

There had been strange men in Martindale, but none stranger than the man who arrived the next morning. It would have been hard to imagine one less in tune and in touch with his surroundings. The slouching, loose-dressed careless cowpunchers on the hotel veranda stared at him askance, as he came up the steps. He wore a little, low-crowned, narrow-brimmed derby, a low collar, very tight for the bull-like neck, close-fitting clothes, through which the rolling muscles of his shoulders bulged under the coat, rubber-heeled shoes, square and comfortably blunt of toe.

When he signed his name on the register, he seemed to be trying to dig the pen through the paper, and the name sprawled huge and legible at a great distance: *J. J. Gruger.* While he waited to be taken to his room, he snapped a tailor-made cigarette out of a box and lighted it with singular dexterity.

He was the sort of man the cowboys would ordinarily have laughed at, almost openly. But there was something muscularly intense about the bulldog face of J. J. Gruger that discouraged laughter, and his eyes had a way of jerking from place to place and lingering a piercing instant, wherever they fell.

He was only a moment in his room upstairs, and then he came down. With short, springy steps he proceeded to the dining room and ate hugely. After that he came out onto the veranda, not to lounge about, but as one on business bent. He did not approve of Martindale any more than Martindale approved of him, and he was not at all eager to disguise his emotions. Having surveyed the white-hot, dusty street he turned with a characteristic suddenness upon one of the loungers who was no less a person than Si Hulan.

But the address of Lefty Gruger was not nearly so jerky and blunt as one would have expected from his demeanor. He drew up a chair beside Si, who eyed him curiously, and leaned a little toward the crafty old rancher. In his manner there was a sort of confiding interest, as though he were imparting a secret of great value. And he talked rather from the side of his mouth, gauging his voice so accurately that the sound traveled as far as the ear of Si Hulan and not an inch farther.

"Name's Gruger," he said by way of introduction. "I'm up here looking for a bird called Lanning. Got any dope on him, or is he a stranger to you?"

"More or less," said Si. "He's twenty-five or twenty-six years old, and I've knowed him along about twenty-four years, I reckon. But I wouldn't say we was ever familiar-like."

There was a little glint in the quick eyes of Lefty as they traveled over the face of his companion. In some subtle way the two came to an understanding on the spot.

"If you mean you ain't a friend of this guy," said Lefty, "it don't bother me none. I ain't his brother myself. But can you tell me anything about him?"

Si Hulan cleared his throat and paused, as if making up his mind how far he could go. Then he felt his way as he spoke. "Lanning was a nice, quiet kid around town," he said. "Nobody had nothing ag'in him, thought he was kind of spineless, as a matter of fact. All at once he busted loose. Got to be a regular fighter, a gunfighter!"

He waited to see if this shot had taken effect.

"You don't say," said Lefty with polite interest.

"Maybe you don't know what a gunfighter is, friend," observed Hulan.

"Maybe not," said Lefty guilelessly.

"It means a gent who lives with his gun day and night and never lets it get more than an inch or so out of his hand. He practices all the time. Tries the draw, tries himself at a mark, and gets ready to use that gun in a fight to kill. And the usual windup is that he gets so blamed skillful that he ends by trying himself out and picking fights till he drops somebody. Then he's outlawed and goes to the devil."

"But I sort of get it that young Lanning ain't gone to the devil yet."

"Son," said Si Hulan, who now seemed to feel at ease with the stranger, "that boy is rapping at Satan's door, and he'll get inside pretty *pronto*."

"Uhn-huh," said Lefty Gruger.

"Yesterday he made a little bust," said Si Hulan. "He's been here with us a few days, trying to make out that he figures on living real quiet. But yesterday he sort of busted loose. And now we're sitting around waiting for him to make a play. And the minute he pulls a gun, he'll be salted down. He's no good. Once wrong always wrong."

"You've said a mouthful, pal," observed Lefty Gruger.

His little eyes twinkled with thought for a moment. Then he sat up and hailed a freckle-faced youngster passing the veranda.

"Son," he said, "will you go find Andrew Lanning for me and tell him there's a man waiting for him at the hotel."

He followed the request with the bright arc of a quarter that spun into the clutching hand of the boy. The latter stared at the generous stranger for a moment, then dug his bare toes inches deep in the dust and gave himself a flying start down the street.

Lefty Gruger watched him thoughtfully. An idea had come to him that he considered, for its simplicity and its effectiveness, to be the equal of any he had ever had in his entire criminal career. A glow of satisfaction with himself spread through him. It was a conclusive proof that the enforced idleness of his career in the prison had not dulled his wits a particle.

Presently he eluded a question of Si Hulan, slipped out of his chair, and began to walk up and down in front of the veranda, gradually increasing his distance until he was out of earshot of the men on the verandah—out of earshot as long as only a conversational tone was used. This was the strategic point that he wished to attain, and when the voices on the veranda had faded to a blur behind him, he halted, settled his hat more firmly to shade his eyes, and waited, cursing the dazzling flare of the sunlight from the dust of the street.

He had hardly reached this position when he saw his quarry coming. He knew the man as well as if a herald had gone before, announcing that this was Andrew Lanning. The bold, free step, the well-poised head, and something, moreover, of hair-trigger alertness about the man convinced him that this was the gunfighter; this was certainly the man of action.

Lefty slipped his hand into his coat pocket and ran the tips of his fingers lovingly over the familiar outlines of the automatic. He withdrew his hand, bringing out a cigarette box, and took out and lighted his smoke with his usual speed. He had snapped the match away, and it was fuming in the dust when Andrew Lanning came close.

Lefty surveyed him with a practiced eye. The promise from the distance was more than borne out in the details that he observed at close hand. Here was a man among many men. Here was a foeman worthy, almost, of his own steel. A sort of honest enthusiasm welled up in the heart of Lefty Gruger, just as the boxer feels a savage joy when his own first blow of the battle is deftly blocked, and a jarring return thuds home against head and breast. Lefty Gruger measured his enemy and felt that the battle might well be close.

"You're Lanning," he said smilingly, and held out his stubby hand.

It was very essential that he should be seen by the veranda crowd to greet Andrew Lanning amiably. He could not resist the temptation, however, and allowed some of his bull strength to go into the grip. There was an amazing reaction. His own bulky hand had hardly begun to tighten before the lithe, long fingers of Andrew curled up and became so many bands of contracting steel, cutting into flesh and grinding sinews against bone. It was only a moment. Then their hands fell apart, and Lefty Gruger felt the life slowly return to his numbed muscles.

He maintained his smile for the benefit of those on the veranda. Then he shifted his position as to bring Andrew facing the veranda, while he kept his own back turned.

"I'm Gruger," he said, continuing the introduction. "I've dropped out here on a little piece of business with you. A sort of private business, Lanning. I didn't know how to tackle it, but I got a couple of hints from the birds on the veranda. They sure love you a lot in this burg, Lanning."

"They seem to," said Andy coldly. "What did they tell you about me?"

"Not much, but enough. Tipped me that you were a gun-fighter and a fire-eater and that they were just sitting around waiting for you to bust loose, which played right into my hand. Gives me a chance to do what I want to do, right in public. It's about the first time that I've ever had an audience. And say, bo, I sure love applause."

"I don't understand," said Andrew, falling back a pace, the better to study the half-grinning, half-ugly face of Gruger.

"Why, kid," continued Lefty, "I've come out here to bump you off, and I find that I can do the job and get a vote of thanks and my traveling expenses out of the town. That's easy, ain't it?"

Andrew blinked. It seemed that the chunky stranger must be either mad or jesting.

"I'm talking straight," said Lefty, dropping his voice to an ominous purr. "Kid, go for your gat. I've showed the folks that I've met you peaceable and all that. Now you got to go for your gat, and I'll do my best to drop you."

"I understand," said Andrew huskily. "They worked up the job, eh? Found a man killer to fit my case and now . . . but it won't work, Gruger. I've made up my mind to see this thing through. I'm going to live without gunfights. One gunfight is ruin for me. One more gunfight makes me what you are."

"You lie!" said Lefty, letting his voice ring out suddenly. "I tell you, you lie!" He added in a murmur: "Now get the gun, you fool. Get the gun, or I'll shame you, so you won't be able to show your face around this town again as long as you live."

The voices on the veranda had ceased. Men had scattered to shelter. From shelter they watched and listened. If someone had offered $5 for the life of the stranger, the offer would have been received with ardent laughter. But still there was no gunplay, even after Andy Lanning had been given the lie. They could see, also, that his face was white.

"It doesn't work," he was saying huskily. "Gruger, I won't fight."

"Take this then!" said Lefty, and his sturdy arm flicked out. The clap of his open hand against the face of Lanning was plainly audible to the listeners and the watchers, and their muscles tightened against the coming report of the guns.

But a miracle happened. While Lefty shot his hand back into his pocket and twitched up the muzzle of his automatic, prepared to send out that spurt of fire and lead with the touch of his forefinger, the hand of Andy Lanning had darted down to the butt of his gun and stayed there. He maintained the struggle for an instant, fighting bitterly against himself, and then he conquered. He turned on his heel and strode back down the street, his cheek tingling where the fingers of Lefty had struck him.

Lefty went back to the hotel as one stunned. He was greeted with a clamor of frank awe and applause.

"By heaven," said Si Hulan, "they all got a yaller streak, all these gunfighters, and it took this nervy little bulldog to bring it out. Son, come up to my room. I got a bottle to set out for you *pronto*, best in the land."

Lefty Gruger accompanied him thoughtfully, saying not a word

IX

Dazed, sick with longing to turn back and find the man again, Andy Lanning fought his way home. All the wolf that Scottie had wakened in him the night before came back to him with redoubled force.

He hurried to the shop, and there he frantically smashed a big bar of iron into useless shapes with the blows of a twelve-pound sledge. All his rage went into that labor. When it was ended, he was weak, but his spirit was quieter, and he dragged himself slowly toward his home. He passed the open door of the rival smith's shop and saw his competitor leaning there, filling a pipe at the end of a prosperous day. At sight of Andy, he nodded carelessly, and Andy suspected that the sudden frown with which the big, sooty fellow looked down at his fuming pipe was for the purpose of veiling a smile.

No doubt he had heard of the disgrace of Andrew Lanning earlier in the day. Now that he had once been braved, others would probably try it. How long could he endure? How long?

He was trembling with the mental struggle when he reached his shack and flung himself down on his bunk, his head in his hands. How long he remained there he could not tell, fighting always against that terrific impulse to rise and hunt out his persecutor. But, when a hand touched his shoulder, he lifted himself to a sitting posture. It was so dark that he could barely make out the face of Scottie.

"I've heard," said Scottie, "and I've understood. But is it worth the gaff, Andy?"

The words fell like a blessing on Lanning. Scottie was more or less of a gentleman in training, more or less educated. His trained mind had understood. But how many more would?

"The rest of 'em," said Scottie, "are saying that you've showed yellow . . . the fools."

"La Roche and Clune are saying that?" asked Andrew, rising.

"They? Of course not! They saw you go down to face Hal Dozier. I mean the rest of the town. They're laughing at you, Andy, and you're a butt and a joke among 'em. Now, partner, the time has come. Sally is ready and waiting outside. Come on with me, Andy. The best of it is that our first job, after you come to us, is in this town, this night. They'll curse themselves before the morning comes for having turned down Andrew Lanning."

Andy went hastily to the door. Sally, from the shed, saw the outline of his form and neighed very softly.

"Ah, Sally girl," exclaimed poor Andy, "are you asking me to go, too?"

"Because you'd be a fool not to go. It's fate, Andy. You can't get away from that."

A child's voice began singing down the street, a shrill, sweet, eager voice, breaking and trembling on the high notes. Little Judy was coming, singing "Annie Laurie" with all her heart.

"Hush," said Andy, and raised his hand.

The outlaw remained silent, frowning in the gloom of the twilight. He knew that that child's song was fighting against him and saving Andy from temptation. The voice passed and died away down the street.

"No," declared Andy at last. "I thank you for trusting me and asking me to lead you, Scottie, but I can't go."

"If it's for that girl," broke out Scottie, "I can tell you that she'll never think of . . ."

"That'll hold you now," said Andy warningly. "Leave her out of it."

"Lanning," began Scottie again, "if I go back without you, the boys will call me . . ."

"A fool," said Andy, "and maybe you are. Besides, you're a good deal of a snake, Scottie. I trusted you once, and you tried to get me. You'll have no second chance. No matter how I throw in, if I leave Martindale with every man's hand against me, I won't throw in with you and the rest of 'em. You played me dirt once, and I know well you would do it again in a pinch. Now get out."

Scottie, after hesitating through one moment of savage silence, turned and went.

Left to the darkness, Andy sank down on his bunk, his head between his hands. He had cut loose, it seemed, from every anchor. He had severed connections with the very outlaws who might have been his port of last refuge. Having already alienated the men of Martindale, he had also sacrificed the one thing that should have remained to him when all else was gone, his pride.

X

Scottie went hastily through the dark and, rounding the corner of Sally's shed, found two figures drawn back so as to melt into the shadow under the projecting roof.

"Well?"

"Missed, curse him," said Scottie.

A soft volley of invectives answered him.

"I knew you would," said the hard, nasal voice of Larry la Roche. "Stubborn as rock once he's made up his mind."

"You know a pile after a thing's done," declared Clune.

"Shut up," commanded Scottie. "The thing's settled. No fighting about it."

"But what'll we do for the fourth man? That's a four-man job we got on hand," declared Larry la Roche. "The fourth man, that's the first thing we got to get."

"The first thing is to get back at Lanning," said Scottie venomously. "He called us a lot of treacherous snakes. He cursed you, Larry la Roche. He said he might come back and lead us if it weren't for your ugly face. He says he hates the thought of you. I told him if he didn't want you, we didn't want him."

"Did he say that?" demanded la Roche, his tall body swaying back and forth in an ecstasy of repressed rage.

"And he said Clune was a cowardly fox, not worth having."

"I'll cut his throat to stop his gabble," declared Clune. "How come you to stand for such talk?"

"Because I'm not a gunfighter," said Scottie, writhing as he remembered the remarks that Andy had leveled at him in person. "But let's forget Andy for a while and think about the job. We'll get Lanning later on."

"Do we have to have four men?"

"One to watch in front, one behind, two inside. Yep, we have to have four. Who'll the fourth man be?"

"It just pops into my head," said Scottie thoughtfully, "that the fellow who bluffed out Lanning today might be our man."

"Did you see him?"

"Just from a distance. I'm not advertising my face around town. But he looks like a tough mug. He's at the hotel. Suppose we nab him."

"In the hotel?"

"No, you fool. Am I going to walk through the hotel and take a chance on being recognized?"

"Then where'll we find him?"

"If he tried to get Lanning once, he'll try again. Maybe he's simply been waiting for the dark. I'll wait down the street and stop him on the way. You stay here."

They obeyed, and Scottie turned the corner of the shed and sauntered around to the front of the shack, taking his position leaning against a hitching post, a little distance down the street from the hotel.

His reasoning about Lefty had been simple enough, and being simple, it was also justified. He had not been waiting in the place for twenty minutes when he saw a burly, little figure come swaying through the twilight with short, choppy steps. Scottie stopped him with a soft hiss as he passed.

"One minute, partner."

"Eh?"

"Gruger," he said, "my name's Scottie. I know where you're going, and I'm here to stop you."

"Oh," murmured Lefty Gruger. "You think you'll stop me?"

"Because I hate to see a good man wasted. Gruger, he'll kill you if you force him to make a gunplay."

"Say," asked Lefty, stepping close, "who are you, and what makes you think I'm going to force a gunplay on anybody? Where do you come in?"

"By needing you for another job that'll pay more."

"Hmm," said Lefty Gruger, peering through the shadows, apparently more or less satisfied by what he saw.

"I'll undertake," said Scottie, "to prove that Lanning is a better man than you are with a gun. And then I'll prove that my job is worth more than the Lanning job."

"And suppose all this chatter meant something . . . suppose I was really after Lanning . . . how would doing your job help me to get rid of Lanning?"

"I have an idea," said Scottie smoothly, "of a way we can ruin Lanning with my job."

"Pal," said Lefty, after an instant of thought, "I like the sound of your talk. Start in by showing me how good Lanning is with a gat."

"Follow me," said Scottie.

He led the redoubtable Lefty Gruger around behind the shed and presently introduced him with a wave of the hand to Clune and Larry la Roche. Scottie then asked Lefty to accompany the trio over the hill and into the valley beyond. Lefty followed willingly enough, for there was sufficient mystery about this proceeding to attract him. They halted a full mile away in a broad, moonlit ravine, paved with pale-gray stones that gave the valley the brightness of twilight.

"Now," said Scottie to Larry la Roche, "I want you to get out your gun, Larry, and do a little shooting for us. You're the best of us with a gun."

"Thanks," replied Larry la Roche, "but I guess that don't make Clune none too happy. But what's there to shoot at? I'm willing."

"I'll give him a mark," suggested Lefty Gruger. He bent, picked up a piece of quartz, and shied it carelessly into the air. "Hit that."

As he spoke the gun came into the hand of Larry, and the glitter of the falling quartz went out as though it had fallen out of the moonshine into shadow. Lefty Gruger remained staring where the quartz had last been seen, flashing dimly down through the air.

This was marksmanship indeed. But Lefty was not yet convinced. As a snap shot, he was a rare man himself.

"Turn your back," he said to Larry huskily, almost angrily.

Larry shoved the weapon back in the holster and obediently turned his back.

Lefty picked up a smaller rock and threw it high in the air. Not until it had reached the crest of its rise and was beginning its glinting descent did he call: "Now nail her!"

Larry la Roche whirled, the gun conjured mysteriously into his hand before his long body was halfway writhed around. His eye wandered, and the muzzle of his gun wandered, also, as he searched for the target. Then he fired. The rock glanced down again and was dropping into the shadow of a boulder when Larry fired the second time, and the little rock puffed into dust, white and glittering with crystals in the moonlight.

"All right," said Larry. "That was a hard one. What next?"

"What next?" asked Lefty Gruger. He passed his finger beneath his stiff collar, as if to make his breathing easier. "There ain't any more."

He continued to stare at Larry la Roche for a moment and then suddenly approached and held out his hand. He wrung the long fingers of Larry.

"Pal," he said, "I've seen shooting, and I've done some, but you got me beat."

It was the hardest speech that Lefty Gruger had ever compelled himself to make, but there was a basic honesty in the bottom of the soul of the killer, and it rang in his voice. He made a secret reservation, however, that shooting at a falling rock was far different from shooting at a human target. The latter might strike back at unknown speed. But it was not only the exquisite nicety of the marksmanship that stirred him. It was the careless grace with which the heavy gun had slipped into the bony fingers of the tall man; it was that lightning speed of mind that, having missed his elusive target once, enabled him to readjust to a new direction and fire again in the split part of a second later. The bullets had followed one second later, almost as swiftly as though they had spat from the muzzle of his automatic, and each had been a placed shot. No wonder that Lefty Gruger stepped back with a chilly feeling of awe descending upon him.

"Boys," he said, continuing that frankness that only a truly formidable man can show, "I didn't know they grew like you out in this part of the woods. I'm glad I bumped into you. But what's this got to do with me and young Lanning? How does this prove that he's a better man than I am?"

Scottie rubbed his chin, then he turned to Larry la Roche. "Larry, you tell him."

Larry thought a moment, taking off his hat and turning it slowly in his hands, while his eyes wandered slowly along the back, sharp-cut line where the hills met the mysterious haze of the sky.

"I'll tell you," he said at length. "I been born and raised with a gun, and I took to it nacheral. It was a long time before I met a gent that was better'n me. But I met one. Yes, sir, he was sure a dandy with a gat. He could make a big gun talk to him like a pet. I can handle a gun pretty fair, but he didn't handle his gun. It was just a part of him. It growed into his hand . . . it growed into his mind. He just thought, and there was a dead man. Seemed like it, anyways. He was so fast with a gun and so straight that he didn't hardly ever shoot to kill. But he'd plug a gent in the arm or the leg and leave him behind."

Larry sighed.

"Say," said Lefty Gruger, tremendously impressed, "I'd have give ten years out of my life to seen him. I guess there never was a better'n him, eh?"

"There was," said Larry la Roche calmly. "Yep, there was a better man than Allister. We never thought his equal would come along, but he came, and the man that beat him and killed him was Hal Dozier. He wasn't so fancy as Allister. He wasn't so smooth. Allister was fast as a cat's paw, but Hal Dozier is like the strike of a snake. He just explodes powder all the time, and when he fights, they's a spark added, and he blows up. Well, he was faster than Allister and straighter with his gun, and he beat him fair and square."

"Boys," said Lefty Gruger, laughing uneasily, "I figure this ain't any country for me. This Hal Dozier is the champion of champions, eh? I'd hate to have him soft footing after me."

"He ain't the champion," said Larry la Roche, "not by a long sight he ain't. They's a gent that beat Hal bad. Met him clean, man to man, and dropped him, shooting in moonlight dimmer'n this. A snake strikes plumb fast, but the end of a whip when it cracks is a pile faster. And that's the way with this other gent. He beat Hal Dozier."

"And who's he?"

"Andy Lanning."

Lefty Gruger took off his hat. He had become suffocatingly hot, and the perspiration was stinging his eyes.

"You get me now," murmured Scottie. "You see why I called you off him? Pal, you'll quit Lanning's trail?"

"I can't," said Lefty doggedly. "I give my word, and I stick to my word. I drop Lanning, or he drops me."

"But suppose," suggested Scottie softly, "that I show you how you make a barrel of loose coin and tie up Lanning at the same time. How would that suit you?"

"We'll talk about it, pal." He reverted to the last fascinating subject. "But this Lanning, how could he be so fast?"

"Listen," said Scottie, "and I'll tip you off. Allister and Hal Dozier are brave, you see? At least, Allister was, and Dozier is. They're afraid of nothing. They're plumb confident every time they fight. So's Larry la Roche, there. So's almost every gent who has a record as a gunman. But Lanning is different. He isn't hard as steel. He's all of a tremble when it comes to fight. I've seen him turn white as a girl and shake like a leaf before he went into danger. And he's always sure the other fellow will get him. He thinks it all out. He feels that he's as slow as a wagon wheel turning. He feels the other fellow's slug tearing through his body. He goes through agony before he fights, but when the time comes for the pull of the gun, he's a bundle of nerves, and every nerve is like loaded electricity. Well, partner, there's one thing faster than anything else, and that's the jump of an electric spark. That's what Lanning is when he fights."

"But he's a coward?"

"Don't fool yourself. He's just enough of a coward to get a thrill out of every time he pulls a gun. What booze is to some and cards to others and money to the rest, that's what gunfighting is to Lanning. It's the lion, and he's the trainer. It's fear that brings the trainer into the cage every day, and it's fear that brings Lanning into trouble."

"But me and him . . ."

"He says he's trying to go straight, curse him. He wouldn't fight because of that. Because, no matter how the trouble started, he knew that he'd be blamed for it. But you've crossed him, Lefty, and sooner or later, you lay to this, he'll get you and fill you full of lead unless you get him first. And the rest of us, the three of us, we all crossed him, too. We made this play tonight to try to get him back on our side. He wouldn't come. So we know he's going to try to get us, and our scheme is just to get him first."

"How?"

"By standing all together and using the law. Sit down, and I'll tell you how."

While he talked, the moon slid high and higher and slipped into a cloud, and still the chief of the gang was outlining his plan. But, whatever that plan was, it did not develop that night. Martindale did not waken the next morning with the shudder that Scottie had planned for it the day before. It wakened calm and tired with the heat of the night and drifted into another blazing-hot day as peacefully as ever.

* * * * *

The night had been terrible for Andrew Lanning, and the day was more awful still, for he came to it physically exhausted, ragged nerves on edge. Sally came and put her head in at the window as he washed his breakfast things, and afterward she glided at his side as he went to the shop. But aside from Sally, there seemed no cheering note in all the universe, and the dark sense of defeat gathered more and more thickly in the corners of his brain.

That day dragged out, and another, with every waking hour filled with the suspicion of the men of Martindale and by Andrew's fear of himself. He had to fight to keep himself from hating these people for once that hate took him by the throat, he knew that the killing would swiftly follow. It was in the very late afternoon of the second day that Hal Dozier came hurriedly to his shop, Hal Dozier with a drawn face of excitement.

"I got a surprise for you, Andy," he said. "Come along."

Andrew followed sluggishly to the door of the marshal's office. The marshal here bent to do something to his right spur.

"Go on in, Andy. I'll follow right on as soon as I get this spur fixed."

Andy mechanically opened the office door and stood slouched against the wall. A full moment elapsed before he sensed another presence in the room and came suddenly erect, his nerves twitching. He turned, fighting himself to make the motion slow, and then he saw her. She was rising from her chair, big -eyed, as if she doubted her reception, half smiling, as if she hoped for happiness. She was more flower-like than ever, he thought, and her beauty struck him with a soul-stirring surprise, as something remembered, and yet with all the exquisite details forgotten. The difference between Anne Withero remembered and Anne Withero present was the difference between a dream and reality.

His eyes went down to the slender hand and the bending fingers that rested on the table. He found nothing to say, but he shut the door, always keeping his hungry eyes on her. And now Anne grew afraid, for she was looking at a new man, not the smooth-cheeked, careless, fire-eyed youth she remembered, but a man stamped with a starved look of suffering and dull, melancholy eyes.

At last she managed to say: "You wouldn't come to me, you know, and so I had to come to you, Andrew."

"Oh, Anne," he whispered, "are you real? Is it you?"

"Of course. But, Andy, you've been terribly sick."

"That's all past, and . . ."

They seemed to fumble their way around the table, as if they were walking in sleep.

"You've kept one touch of belief in me, Anne?"

"Kept it? Ah, don't you see that I've never doubted you even?"

This much the marshal heard, for he had stayed guiltily near the door, but at this point, he was mastered by a decent respect for the rights of lovers and walked reluctantly away. It was still terribly hot, but the sheriff took off his hat to the full blaze of the slant sun and smiled, as if a cool breeze were playing on his face.

Dozier came back, after what he thought was a painfully long time, and found them sitting close together, their dim, frightened eyes avoiding each other. The marshal was one of those lucky men who keep close to their youth, and his heart jumped at what he saw. He even understood when Andy Lanning rose and strode out of the room without a word to either of them.

The marshal closed the door after him and stood fanning himself with his hat and grinning shamelessly at Anne Withero. He liked her blush, and he liked her dignity, and he admired a poise that enabled her to smile back at him, as if she knew that he understood.

"If you knew," he said at last, "what it means to me. That kid has been a load that's nearly busted my back. And now it's settled."

"But it isn't, you know," said Anne Withero, growing anxious again.

"You mean to say that, after you've come, he doesn't know that he has to go straight?"

"You see," she explained, fully as worried as the marshal, but determined to make Andrew logical and plausible, "he feels that he hasn't gone through a sufficient test. There is a bit of wildness in him, you know, Mister Dozier."

"Not much more than there is in a hawk," said the marshal dryly. "But what mischief is he up to now?"

"I tried to make him feel that he has been tested sufficiently. I told him that I knew about his meeting with the terrible man who struck him, and what a glorious thing I thought it was that he had endured it, and he wouldn't agree. He says that he came within an inch of doing something terrible. And he wants a little time still, you see, to make these stupid people accept him. He says that if he could do something that would make half a dozen of these men about the village come to him and shake hands with him, then he'd feel that he had restored himself, and then he would be willing to go anywhere."

"Even East with you?" asked the marshal still dryly. "And do you agree with this infernal nonsense?"

"I think Andrew knows best," said Anne gravely.

XI

The existence of Martindale was peaceful enough, but it contained citizens who habitually slept with only one eye closed. Some of these men were wakened in the middle of the night by a dull, muffled noise, as if a vast volume of tightly compressed air had suddenly expanded to its full limits. The sound was strange enough to bring them out of bed, and among them was Hal

Dozier, buckling on his gun as he ran. Other figures scurried down the street, and presently an outcry guided him through the moonlight to the bank.

The door was open, and a dozen people were gathered in the room around the wrecked safe. The empty steel drawers were scattered here and there. The marshal cast one glance at it.

"Neat work," he murmured. "If it weren't for facts, I'd say Allister had a hand there. What've you found, boys?"

"This!" They threw a coat to him. "We found this in the corner."

The marshal looked it over carelessly, then stiffened. "This!" he exclaimed chokingly.

"That's Andy Lanning's coat," said Si Hulan importantly. "Murder will out, Hal. We've got your fine bird at last."

"Go look in his shack," said the marshal, sick at heart.

He could not understand it. More than once he had seen the impulse to break the law, dammed up in a man like water swelling in the banks of a stream, burst forth at the most unlooked-for moment. But Andrew Lanning had nothing in common with the criminally inclined lawbreaker. All the man's impulses were for honesty, and the marshal knew that Anne Withero alone, in any case, should have been a sufficient motive to have held the boy to his self-imposed discipline of moral regeneration. He shook his head in sad perplexity.

Two or three in the crowd had run down the street toward the Lanning house. The marshal trotted across to his office, firing orders that sent the rest of the crowd in haste for saddles and horses. It was the newly installed telephone that brought the marshal to his office, but with his hand on the receiver, he was stopped by a shouting farther up the street. The outcries shot down on the far side of the town and then veered up the valley.

Hal Dozier ran to his door to be met there by half a dozen excited men.

"We found him sitting on his bunk, pretending he'd just heard the noise and was dressing to go out to see what was the matter. Cool, eh? Hulan shoved a gun under his nose, and he put up his hands and looked dazed. Good actor, he is. Then we told him what had happened . . . that we'd found his coat, and that we had him dead to rights. He looks over at a chair by the window, as if he'd just missed the coat that minute.

"'That's what they've done to get even,' he says.

"We told him to lead us to the money first.

"'All right,'" he said. "'Right outside.'"

"Looked as though he was going along easy and peaceable. Then, as he turned for the door, he made a flick of his hand and knocked the gun out of Hulan's hand and dived into the rest of us. He went through us like an eel through water. I got my hands on him, but he busted loose, strong as steel.

"He ran out, and we jumped our hosses and started after. Looked easy to run him down while he was on foot, but he let out a whistle, and that mare of his come tearing out of the shed and run alongside of him. Up he jumps on her back, as easy as you please, and away down the valley. Two or three of the boys headed after him."

Dozier heard this with the pain slowly dying out of his face and a red rage coming in its place.

"Boys," he said at the conclusion of the tale, "this is the end of the great Andrew Lanning. He's taken the valley road with the fastest horse that ever ran in the mountains, but they's one thing faster than horseflesh." He tapped the shoulder of Si Hulan. "Hulan, you've got sense. Use it now. Get onto that telephone and ring Long Bridge. Tell them what's happened. Tell them that

71

I'm chasing Lanning with a half dozen men. I want Long Bridge to send me men if they please. Above all, I want good horses, and I want them ready and waiting before the morning, on the other side of the hills. They'll have lots of time to get them together. I want horses more'n I want men. You make sure you tell them that. I'm going to run Lanning down with relays.

"After we get the fresh horses from Long Bridge, we'll send a man with the played-out horses back to Long Bridge to wire on to Glenwood. He can tell them where the hunt is heading and where to meet us with a second relay. Sally is a great horse, but she can't outlast three sets of horses. We'll catch her this side of the Cumberlands. Now, the rest of you that want to follow, come along. We got to ride tonight as we never rode before, and the end of our trail is the end of Lanning."

The marshal had spoken the truth when he said that there was no horse in the mountains that could pace with Sally, and it was never shown so clearly as on this night. With her master riding bareback and without bridle, guided only by the touch of his hand on one side of her neck or the other, she went down the only easy way out of Martindale, the long, narrow gorge that shot north into the mountains. She flew along well within her strength, but it was a dizzy pace for the three staunch little cow ponies that followed, and they dropped rapidly to the rear. Lanning became a flickering shape in the moon haze ahead, and finally that shape went out.

After that, they drew their horses back to a canter to wait for the main body of the pursuit to overtake them. They were courageous men enough, but three-to-one was not sufficient odds when one man was Andrew Lanning.

The clatter of many hoofs down the ravine announced the coming of the marshal. The thick of the posse overtook the forerunners on a rise in the floor of the valley, and they told briefly of what they had seen and done.

The marshal cursed briefly and effectively. They should have pressed boldly on, for the respite they gave Lanning would enable him to pause at the first ranch house for a saddle and bridle and, worst of all, a rifle. When the first house loomed out of the night, Dozier urged his men on ahead and dropped back himself to exchange a word with the people of the house. He was well enough mounted to overtake the rest.

He had hardly tapped at the door without dismounting, when the rancher appeared, revolver in hand.

"And who now?" he asked furiously.

"Dozier," said the marshal. "Who's passed this way?"

"Lanning and four men ahead of him."

"Four men ahead of him! Who were they?"

"Don't know. They didn't stop, and they rode as if they was careless about what become of the horseflesh. But Lanning stopped long enough to grab my best saddle. Stuck me up with a gun and stood over me while I done the saddling for him, and then he got my rifle."

The marshal waited to hear no more, but rode on with a groan. Mounted on Sally bareback, with a revolver strapped to his hip, Lanning was formidable enough, but with a rifle in addition and a comfortable saddle beneath him, the difficulties of the task were doubled and redoubled.

Who the four men might be, he had no idea. It was not common for four men to be riding furiously through the night and the mountains, but he had no time to juggle ideas. Lanning rode ahead, and Lanning was his goal.

When he regained the posse, Lanning had still not been sighted. The mountains on either side of the ravine now dwindled away and grew small, and it was possible that Andrew might have turned aside at almost any place. But something told Dozier that the fugitive would hold on due north. That was the easiest way, and in that direction Sally's dazzling speed would most avail the rider. Accordingly the marshal urged his men to the fullest speed of their horses.

One thing at least was in his favor if he had guessed the route of Lanning. The fugitive would hold Sally back for a long chase, not thinking that the marshal would run his horses out in the first twenty miles, but that was exactly what Dozier would do. At the end of the twenty miles, the fresh mounts from Long Bridge would be waiting for his men.

The first light of dawn came when they labored over the crest of the range, and as they pitched down toward the plain below, he picked out his men with shrewd glances. No one had joined who was not sure of his endurance or of his ability with weapons, for men knew that the trail of Andrew Lanning would not be child's play, no matter what the odds. Dozier gauged them carefully and nodded his content.

A strange happiness rose in him. This was the continuation, after so long a gap, of the pursuit in which he had ridden Gray Peter to death in the chase of Sally and the outlaw. And this second time he could not fail. It was not man against man, or horse against horse, but the law against a criminal who must die.

If only he had been right in his guess as to Lanning's direction! When the dawn brightened, he saw, far away across the plain, a solitary dark spot. He fastened his glasses on the moving object and made sure. Then he swept the lower slopes of the hills and found the huddling group of fresh horses that had been sent out from Long Bridge.

The marshal communicated his tidings to the men, and with a yell, they spurred on the last of the first relay.

XII

They changed horses and saddles swiftly, eager to be off on the fresh run. The marshal sent back to Long Bridge a message to telephone ahead to Glenwood to send out a fresh relay that must wait anywhere under the foot of the Cumberlands. Then he spurred on after his men.

Freshly mounted, they were urging their horses on at a killing pace, and presently the small form of Lanning began to come back to them slowly and surely. Twenty weary miles were behind Sally, and she could not stand against this new challenge. Yet stand she did! A fabulous tale at which he had often laughed came back to the marshal's mind, a tale of some half-bred Arabian pony that had done a hundred miles through mountains between twilight and dawn. But the endurance of Sally seemed to make the tale possible.

By the time the day was bright and the light could be seen flashing on the silken flanks of Sally, they had drawn perilously close to her, but from that point on she began to increase her lead. Once or twice in the morning, the marshal stopped his own mount for a breath, and when he trained his glasses on the great mare, he could see her running smoothly, evenly, with none of the roll and lurch in her stride that tells of the weary horse. And then he called to his men and urged them to save the strength of their mounts. The greatest speed over the greatest distance, between that point and the first hills of the Cumberlands, that was what was wanted. There the second relay, which would surely run Lanning into the ground, would be waiting. That was fifteen miles away, and the blue Cumberlands were rolling vast and beautiful into the middle of the sky.

Toward the end of the stretch they had to send their ponies on at a killing pace, for Sally was slowly and surely drawing away. A sturdy gray dropped with a broken heart before that run was over, and still Sally went on to a greater lead and disappeared into the first hills of the Cumberlands.

But five minutes later the posse, weary, drawn-faced, ferociously determined, was on the fresh horses from Glenwood. They scattered out in a long line and charged the hills where Lanning had disappeared. Presently someone on the far left caught sight and drew in the others with a yell. That was the beginning of the hottest part of the struggle.

Nearly forty miles of running lay behind her, but Sally drew now on some mysterious reserve of strength that only those who know the generous hearts of fine horses can vaguely understand. The hilly country, too, was in her favor, and she took short cuts as nimbly as a goat. In spite of that, they pressed closer and closer. Before the middle of the morning came the crisis. Hal Dozier came in distant range, halted his horse, pitched his rifle to his shoulder, and tried three shots.

They fell wide of the mark. After half an hour more of riding, he called for a volley. It was given with a will. Dozier, watching through his glass like a general directing artillery fire, saw the hat jump and fall lopsided on the head of Lanning, and yet he did not fall, but turned in his saddle. Three times his rifle spoke in quick succession, and three little puffs of rock dust jumped before three of the men of the posse. Dozier cursed in admiration.

"It's his way of telling us that he could have potted the three of you if he had wanted," he said. "Now spread out and ride like the wind."

They spread out and spurred obediently, fighting their horses up the slopes, which increased in difficulty, for they were nearing the heart of the Cumberlands. Sally still drifted just outside of close rifle fire. And eventually, about noon, she began to gain again. Hal Dozier shook his head in despair. Plainly the gallant mare must be traveling on her nerve strength alone, but how long it would last no one could tell.

He called his men back to a steady pace. They could only hope to get at Lanning now by wearing him down and reaching him by night. Certainly Sally would not last so long as that.

The afternoon came unendurably hot, with the men drooping and drowsy in their saddles from the long ride. It was at this time that they were jerked erect by the clang of three rapid shots, echoing a little distance ahead of them. They rounded the shoulder of the next hill hastily and saw the glistening form of Sally disappearing over a crest beyond, but in the hollow beneath them stood a horse with empty saddle, and the rider was lying prone beside it, his face exposed to the burning of the sun. Hal Dozier headed the rush into the hollow and dismounted.

It was Scottie who lay there, and Scottie had ridden his last ride. He begged for water feebly, but after it was given to him, he spoke more clearly, and they made a futile pretext of binding his wounds. One bullet had smashed his right shoulder. The other had pierced his body below the lungs, and he was in agony from it, but he made no complaint. Death was coming quickly on him. Hal Dozier hurried the posse on and remained holding the head of the dying man.

"It was Lanning," murmured Scottie. "We blew the safe, Hal, and we planted Lanning's coat there to fix the blame on him. Then we started out."

"You were the four men on horses," said the marshal. "But how did you keep ahead of Sally? And why did Lanning take after you?"

"We used Allister's old gag," said Scottie. "We planted relays before we turned the trick. Then we lit out in a semicircle. But Lanning . . . he must have known that we turned that trick and threw the blame on him . . . remembered that we had an old meeting place up yonder in the Cumberlands. And while we rode in an arc, he cut across in a straight line from Martindale, and Sally brought him up to us.

"We saw him following. We could see you following Andy. A game of tag, eh? The devil played against us, however. I cursed Sally till my throat was dry. There's no wear -out to that mare. She kept coming on at us. Finally we drew up and gave our nags a breath and drew straws to see who should go back and try to pot Lanning. I got the short straw, and I went back. Well, it was a game of tag, and I'm it." He added after a moment: "But while it lasted . . . a great game. S'long, Hal."

He died without a murmur of pain, without a convulsion of face or body, and to the very end, he kept an iron grip on himself.

Hal Dozier rode like mad to the posse and communicated his tidings. The real criminals rode far beyond. The man they chased was acting the part of a skirmisher. They must ride now, not to kill Lanning, but to keep him from being overpowered by the numbers.

It was a singular goal for that posse, but they were sharpened by the phrase: "The last of old Allister's gang."

They rode hard, using the last strength of their horses. Two hours wore on, but there was no sight of Sally again. It was a strange predicament. The more they pressed on Lanning, the more he would struggle to escape and close on the real criminals. And yet they could not desist and leave odds of three-to-one against him.

At last they were riding over gravel and hard rock that gave no trail to follow. Suddenly a second fusillade made them spur their horses on. The crackling of guns had been far away, only a gust of wind had blown the sound to them, showing how hopelessly they had been distanced. They urged their sweating horses on in the ominous silence that followed the firing. Then the neighing of a horse guided them.

They climbed to a ridge, and on the shoulder below them, in a natural theater rimmed by great rocks, they saw the picture. The gaunt, horrible body of Larry la Roche lay propped against the rocks, his long arms spread out beside him. Clune was curled up on his side nearby, with the gravel scuffed away where he had struggled in the death agony. In the center of the terrible little stage lay no less a person than Lefty Gruger, gaping at the sky, and across him lay the body of him who had worked all this death, Andrew Lanning. Above him, trembling with weariness, stood beautiful Sally, neighing for help till the mountainside reechoed.

Not a man spoke as they went down the slope.

The whole thing was perfectly clear. The gang, hard pressed by their terrible antagonist, had turned back and waylaid him, taking ambush behind these rocks. When he came down, they had shot him from his horse. It was while he was falling, perhaps, and while he lay on the ground that they had rushed him, but the revolver of Lanning had come out, and this was its work. The first bullet had slain the grim la Roche, and the second had curled up Clune. The head of Lefty Gruger had been smashed with a stroke of the butt as he came running to close quarters.

They lifted the form of the conqueror from the body of Lefty Gruger, and the marshal, with his face pressed to the breast of Andy, caught the faint flutter of the heart.

Only then they set about the work of first aid, and they started with a sort of fierce determination, hard- eyed and drawn- lipped. The marshal cursed them as they worked, telling them briefly the true story of Andrew Lanning, which they would never believe before. And now, it seemed, he had given his life for them.

It was a dubious matter indeed. The bullet that had knocked him from his horse had whipped through his thigh. Another had broken his left arm, and a third—and this was the dangerous one—had plowed straight through his body. When his breathing became perceptible, a red bubble rose to his lips. Somewhere that bullet had touched the lungs, and now the matter of life or death was as uncertain as the flip of a coin.

They could not dream of removing him. He must be brought back to life or die on the spot, and they worked like madmen, throwing a shelter against sun and wind above him, bedding him soft in saddle blankets and fir boughs, washing the wounds and bandaging them.

"Get the doctor from Glenwood," said Hal Dozier to his messengers, "and get Anne Withero . . . she's in Martindale. Let the doc come as fast as he can, but make Anne Withero come like the wind."

* * * * *

The doctor was there before dark, and he shook his head.

Anne Withero was there before midnight, and she set her teeth.

At dawn the doctor admitted there was a ghost of a hope. At noon he declared for a fighting chance. In the twilight Andy Lanning parted his stained lips and whispered into the ear of Anne Withero: "The bad strain, dear . . . I think they've let it out."

The Two-Handed Man

With the exception of two serials, all of Frederick Faust's published output in 1932—twenty-three short novels and fourteen serials—appeared in Street & Smith's *Western Story Magazine*, his primary market from 1921 through 1933. "The Two-Handed Man" was published in the issue dated December 3, 1932, under Faust's George Owen Baxter byline. The story deals with the theme of the redeemed outlaw, one of Faust's favorites.

I

When Jimmy reached the top of the hill, the wind and rain came at him across the valley with such a roar that his horse turned, cowering, but Jimmy squinted his eyes against the stinging and beating of the rain and stared down into the hollow. Like water, the pale evening and the storm filled the ravine.

Through the twilight he could see the glimmer of a town down there, and suddenly a craving struck him mightily for hotcakes and maple syrup, and coffee with real milk in it. He knew that he would be a fool to go into the town. Its name might be unknown to him, but he was probably well enough known to it. Men with a money reward hanging over their heads are quickly enough recognized. The newspapers see to that, and placards in post offices and other public buildings.

When money is hard to come by, why shouldn't the active fellows who are quick on the trigger look out for the odd chance? A bullet costs very little. In the case of Jimmy Bristol, it would bring home a reward of just over $5,000, to say nothing of the fame.

That was why Jimmy Bristol waited there with the rain volleying to smoke against the rubber face of his slicker. He dreaded the force of the law. He feared the many hands that might serve it down there where the lights were twinkling. But his craving for hotcakes and syrup, and coffee with real milk in it, was altogether too much for him.

For three months he had cooked his own food and boiled his own coffee. A good deal of that food had been toasted rabbit and mountain grouse. Tempting fare, you say. But that's because you have not been forced to live on it.

Now he turned the chestnut suddenly down into the valley and jogged it into the town. The ruts were full of water that was flung up from the cup of a forehoof now and then and splashed as high as the knee. Once a pair of riders went crashing by him, suddenly appearing and suddenly disappearing through the penciled grayness of rain that filled the air.

He passed windows that were covered with ten thousand little, starry eyes, where the lamplight inside was broken up by the drops that adhered to the glass panes. It was the supper hour, and many odors of cookery came out to him.

Far away and long ago, centuries distant from him, he had known the sweetness of ginger cookies. He knew how they breathed forth fragrance from a deep tin pan where they were kept in the pantry. It made him think of the taste of them as he sensed that odor again now. Tell me, what is as good as cold, fresh milk and ginger cookies?

There was many a flavor of bacon on the air, too. There always is, in Western cookery. Bacon runs through the kitchen work more than prayer runs through the air of a church. And he knew the smell of frying steaks, too, with some of the grease burning and the rest bubbling in the hot pan. Other scents were strong, such as cabbage boiling, onions frying. They all drew out in the heart of Jimmy Bristol various stops of emotion and great, crashing chords of desire.

Well, the safe, honest men, they could remain at home and enjoy such delicacies as liver and bacon—strange how he always had hated that estimable dish—but he, Jimmy Bristol, had time in this town for no more than hotcakes and coffee—with real milk in it.

He found two desired opportunities close to one another— one was a livery stable, and the other was a lunch counter. So he rode straight in through the big double doors of the stable and heard the hoofbeats of his horse sound muffled on the floor, made pulpy by the treading of countless iron shoes. The rain roared on the roof, high up and far away, and the rain crashed in the street, nearer at hand.

When he dismounted, the fall and the upsplash of that rain made a shining mist before the eyes of Jimmy Bristol.

A stable attendant came toward him, wearing rubber boots, a shirt with the sleeves cut off at the shoulders, and the suspenders holding his trousers worn outside the shirt. He held a big sponge in his hand, as though he had just come from washing down some buggy or buckboard. Jimmy Bristol looked curiously at him. He never could quite understand what made men work for wages—certainly he never could comprehend how a fellow would be willing to take on the night shift in a livery stable.

"Yeah?" greeted the man with the sponge.

"This horse of mine is tuckered out a little," said Bristol.

"Yeah." The stableman nodded.

"And I've got to be moving on before long. Got any good horses for sale here?"

"Yeah," said the stableman.

"Show me the three best, beginning with the best of the three," said Jimmy Bristol.

"Yeah," said the stableman.

He led the way to a box stall and opened the door. There was a brown mare inside, with dark points all around.

But Bristol did not even step into the stall to make a closer examination. His knowing eye had looked for and found the faults immediately.

"That's a good mare," he said. "That mare can carry weight, and she can run fast. But she can't go far. There's not much room for a heart in her under the cinches."

The stableman looked askance at him. He started toward the next box, but Jimmy Bristol called him back.

"If that's your best, I'll take your word for it and not look at the second best. You can start in working on this chestnut, will you?"

"Yeah," said the stableman.

"I'll be back here in about fifteen minutes. Give her a swallow of water, put her in a stall, and pass out a feed of oats. You have some good, clean oats?"

"Yeah," said the stableman. He hooked a thumb under his suspenders and snapped the elastic against his swelling chest.

"While she's eating those oats, never stop working on her. Rub her down. Do you know how to rub a horse down?"

"Yeah," said the stableman.

"And really work your thumb under the muscles?"

"Yeah," said the stableman. And this time there was a faint glint of interest in his eyes.

"Well, start working now, and keep on working," said Jimmy Bristol. "Peel the saddle right off her, and start in working hard on her. Here's a dollar for your work. I'll pay the other bill when I come for her."

"Yeah," said the stableman.

Jimmy Bristol went out into the rain and let it whip on his face. He smiled at the cold and the wet and the sting of it. There were few places where the water had not already soaked through to his skin, but that made small difference. Better to be wet by rain than by the melting snow and hail of a blizzard, as he had been three days before this.

He walked into the lunch counter and leaned on the rail. There was nobody else in the place, but it was an old, established eating house to judge by the greasy, battered look of the bill of fare that was written against the wall, and to judge, also, by the way the linoleum on the floor was worn into paths with holes in them.

"Have you got some hotcake batter all mixed?"

The cook was a man of importance. The lower part of his body and the lower part of his face bulged out into dignified curves. He had a drooping mustache, too, and he caught hold of one glistening, steam-dampened end of this mustache as he answered: "I got hotcake batter mixed."

"I don't mean just dough. I don't mean self-rising, either. I mean honest hotcakes, not leathery flapjacks."

"You mean something that comes apart in your mouth, eh?"

"That's what I mean."

"Look at that," said the cook. He pulled out a deep crockery bowl and showed to the eager eyes of Jimmy Bristol a yellowish, liquid mass whose surface was roughened by many bubblings of effervescence, a slow and sticky working of the whole.

"That's it," said Jimmy Bristol. The cook smiled at him, and he smiled at the cook.

"Slap a couple of dozen of those on the fire," said Jimmy Bristol. "Is that stove clean?"

"Look," said the cook.

He swabbed his steamy hand over a part of it and offered the tips of his fingers to Bristol's eyes—and nose, for that matter.

"All right. It's clean," said Bristol. "Cover that stove with flap-jacks. *Pronto!* But wait a minute . . . have you got some maple syrup?"

"You mean maple syrup or maple syrup?" asked the cook.

"I mean maple syrup."

"It's ten cents a plate extra."

"That's the kind of maple syrup I mean."

A positive fire of enthusiasm came upon the cook. "Taste it first," he said. "Let the taste of it start working in on you while I start them flapjacks cooking." He offered a battered can.

Jimmy Bristol took it, uncorked it, sniffed it as though it were a wine of vintage, and set it down with a sigh. "It's real," he said. "One more thing."

The cook was ladling out hotcakes all over the stove. "You bet it's real," he said.

"And maybe," said Bristol tenderly, "maybe you have some real coffee here? I don't mean that Mocha and Java that costs twenty-three cents a pound. I mean real coffee."

"What kind? What brand?" asked the cook.

"The kind that you like," said Jimmy Bristol.

It was an inspiration. The cook smiled a coy and greasy smile over the shoulder. Then he winked. Then he said: "All right, brother. You'll have it."

"And maybe," went on Jimmy Bristol, "you've got real milk from the inside of a cow instead of from the inside of a can?"

The cook turned around on him. "Me," he said, stabbing his breast with his thumb, "I keep cows. I keep Jersey cows. You know what I mean?"

"I'm trying to believe you, brother," said Jimmy Bristol.

"Look," said the cook. He raised a large, glass pitcher. At the top was a yellow stain of cream that ran through the upper strata of the milk. But, even so, there remained a rich tinting of yellow through the whole mass of the liquid.

Before Jimmy Bristol could speak, however, a boy who looked like the cook without the curves of the face and the stomach came running in and gasped across the counter: "Pop, the sheriff's been looking in through the back window!"

II

When the cook heard this, he put his lips all on one side of his mouth and then bit the hard-drawn, opposite corner.

"Whatcha mean?" he asked of the lad. "Get out of here. Whatcha mean?"

"I mean, I seen him," said the lad. "Jiminy, and didn't I. I seen him give the glass a swab with his hand and look through." Saying this, he fled out of the room the way he had come in.

"Thunder," said the cook, "what would that mean?"

Jimmy Bristol saw that the hotcakes were apt to be spoiled. He said: "The sheriff is looking around the town, and maybe he's looking for me."

At this the cook leaned suddenly nearer across the bar. He leaned so near that his glance was able to reach down across the farther edge of the counter and so find the big holster that was strapped to the thigh of Bristol's right leg. It had been black leather once, but now it was worn in many places to a slimy gray.

"*Ugh!*" grunted the cook, and opened his eyes.

"My name is Jimmy Bristol," said the outlaw. "There's five thousand dollars on my head. I came into this town not to shoot it up, but to get hotcakes and maple syrup, and coffee with real milk in it."

The cook licked his lips. Slowly color began to return to his blanched face. Although as a flapjack maker he was a man of parts, it was evident that he had no ambition to become an outlaw catcher.

"How long you been out?" he asked finally.

"Three months," said Bristol.

Suddenly the cook grinned. "I was out once myself. It wasn't nothing much . . . but I had to leave a town once. I was only out three days . . . but it was the biggest half of my life, them three days was."

He turned, suddenly twitched back to the stove by a sense of duty, and at that moment, the sheriff entered—the very moment when the cook began to shovel the first hotcakes onto a platter. For such a patron as Jimmy Bristol, he disdained to offer a mere plate.

The sheriff of that town was almost as fat as the cook at the lunch counter, but under his puffy body extended a pair of long, wiry legs that looked capable of mastering the toughest bronco on the range. He wore a gun on each side of him. His hat was on the side of his head.

The cook saw him coming as he shoved the platter before Bristol, between the half roll of butter and the can of syrup.

"That's him," whispered the cook.

"All right," said Bristol. "It's not time for me to move yet."

The sheriff came up and paused four feet away.

"I'm Tom Denton," he said. "I'm the sheriff."

"Hello, Sheriff," said Bristol. "Anything biting you?" He turned his young, handsome face on the sheriff and smiled straight into his eyes. The sun had burned Bristol to a golden brown, and that color set off the blue-gray of his eyes. It was only now and then that too much light crowded into the pupils of those eyes and made them blaze without any color.

"Nothing's biting me," said the sheriff. "I just wondered what your hurry was?"

"You mean, getting on through town?"

"That's what I mean," said the sheriff, running his eyes slowly over the big shoulders of Bristol and then down to the spoon-handled spurs that arched out from the heels of his boots. "You only got fifteen minutes in town, eh?"

Bristol smiled and hooked a thumb over his shoulder.

"That dummy in the stables had an idea, did he?" he asked.

"Yeah," said the sheriff. "Maybe he did, at that."

"Well, I'll tell you," said Bristol. "I've been working on the Jerry Comfort place, and Jerry laid me off the other day. I've got a cousin upcountry, working on the other side of the Kennisaw Gap, over near Milton. He wrote me a long time ago it was a good layout, and they fed well. So I thought I'd ramble up that way. I aimed to get up closer to the gap tonight and stop over at some ranch house. Tomorrow they're taking on three new men where my cousin works, and I aim to be one of the three, but even if I put on ten more miles tonight, I'll still be forty miles short of Milton. Isn't that about right?"

"But why the fifteen minutes? Why not an hour?" asked the sheriff.

"And let the chestnut get cold?" asked Bristol, smiling and shaking his head.

"There's something in that," agreed the sheriff, pursing his lips in doubt. Then he added: "Stand up and turn your back to me."

Rather slowly Bristol obeyed.

"Now," said the sheriff, "pull a gun with your left hand and aim it at that doorknob . . . that back doorknob."

Bristol hitched up the holster on his right thigh, reached across his body with his left hand, and drew out the revolver. He balanced the gun carefully, but still the muzzle of it wavered from side to side. He did not squint down the barrel with his left eye, but with his right eye, holding the gun well toward that side of his body.

Suddenly the sheriff laughed. "All right," he said. "Put up that gun and feed your face. Sorry I bothered you, son. But I had an idea."

Bristol put up the gun and buckled down the flap of the holster over it again. He sat down on the stool in front of the lunch counter and began to lay slabs of butter between the strata of the pile of hotcakes.

"What idea did you have?" he asked.

"There's a fellow named Jimmy Bristol that's riding not a thousand miles from here," said the sheriff. "From what I hear, I guess that he's a bigger man than you are. But just the same . . . well, I thought I'd see."

"See how big I am?" asked Bristol, apparently amazed.

"Jimmy Bristol's a two-handed man," said the sheriff. "He's a little faster and a little better with the left than he is with the right. But it's easy to see that you're no two-handed man." He laughed again. "You took hold of that gun with your left like an old woman," he added. "Well, so long. It's all right, son. I just had an idea . . . that was all."

He left the place, and the cook sighed. He seemed to be deflating, although his dimensions grew no less.

"My Jiminy," said the cook. "And you *are* Jimmy Bristol?"

"These," said Bristol, "are the best hotcakes that I ever laid a lip over. And this," he added, raising the cup of coffee and hot milk, "is the best coffee and the finest milk that I ever set a tooth in. Brother, here's to you, and bottom's up."

He was as good as his word. When he put down the cup, he saw that the cook was mopping his forehead with a towel, and still the perspiration gleamed again and again on his brow.

"You've finished that platter of hotcakes," said the cook. "Maybe you better drift along, son. I wouldn't want . . ."

"It's not time to go," said Bristol. "It's nowhere near time to go. Let's have some more. The next row of 'em are beginning to smoke. Look at the beauties puff up, will you?"

"Yeah. They're made, that's what they are," said the cook. And he stacked them on the platter once more. He laid his hands on the edge of the counter and smiled with a frightened admiration upon Bristol. "You got the cold-steel nerve," he declared. "I never seen nothing like it." He added: "What they want you for?"

"Not much," said Jimmy Bristol. "There was a fellow in Tombstone who felt like four of a kind when he was only holding three tens, and so he borrowed one out of his sleeve. When I saw it, he started to draw, but I beat him to it. And I took the pot and went away. But a lot of people at the burying of that *hombre* didn't know about the cards up the sleeve or him going for his gun, and they thought that they'd better inquire into the business. So they came and asked me a few questions, which I answered over my shoulder as I was cutting the wind, because I saw too many guns and too many ropes in that crowd, and I've got a right tender neck when it comes to stretching hemp. And when my own horse wore out, I borrowed another. And that made me a horse thief. You see how the landslide starts?" He laughed a little. "That was three months ago," he said.

"My Jiminy," said the cook.

Jimmy Bristol looked at a far corner of the ceiling. "I'll tell you, partner," he said. "I spent too much time learning how to shoot with both hands. I was riding for a fall, and I got it. Besides, these three months have been fun. The best in my life. Except that I got pretty hungry for hotcakes and maple syrup."

The back door of the room opened, and there entered a quick-stepping fellow with a set face and blazing eyes.

The cook saw that, and saw the flash of the man's gun. But he hardly followed the whiplash movement by which Jimmy Bristol produced a gun from inside his slicker. With his left hand, he produced it and fired. The stranger dropped his own gun and caught at his right shoulder with his left hand.

"I'm sorry, Bob," said Jimmy Bristol. "I only trimmed the wick, though. I didn't put out the light. The cook, here, will put a bandage on you."

"Damn you!" said the wounded man. "You murdering hoss thief . . . you . . ."

"Tie up his shoulder, cook, will you?" requested Jimmy Bristol.

"You better get out," said the cook in a hoarse whisper.

"There's still time," said Jimmy Bristol, putting up his gun. "I can finish this platter. Fill up my cup again before you start working on him, will you?"

He continued eating, while the cook ran around to the wounded man and made him sit in a chair.

"Go raise the town, you danged fool!" shouted the stranger. "That's Jimmy Bristol, and there's five thousand bucks on his murdering head!"

Bristol continued to eat. "The fact is, Bob," he said, "that your friend McNamara borrowed a card out of his sleeve that day."

"You lie!" shouted Bob. "There were three others at the table. They didn't say nothing about that."

"Sure, they didn't," answered Bristol. "They all had reasons for getting me out of town. That's why that game was started . . . to squeeze me out of Tombstone. So long, Bob."

"Help! Murder! Jimmy Bristol's here!" yelled Bob.

Bristol rang a $10 gold piece on the counter and stood up. "Here's to your health, Bob," he said. And he drained the coffee.

A stream of men poured through the front door as he walked toward it.

"Get a doctor," said Bristol. "There's a fellow back there raving, and he needs help. He's tried to kill himself."

He passed into the street.

III

He reached the livery stable, walking close to the wall of it and suddenly stepping into the open doorway. There was the man with the sponge, gaping round-eyed and listening to sounds of excited shouting that streamed out of the lunch counter not far away.

Bristol took him by the fat of his chin. "I told you to keep working on that chestnut," he said.

"I was working . . . only . . . except . . ." said the man with the sponge.

"Get the saddle and bridle back on it," said Bristol.

Standing in the doorway, he could watch the liveryman saddle the chestnut; he could also watch the street, and as the horse was led up, he saw a sudden rush of men boil out from the front of the lunch counter, like steam out of the spout of a kettle. He knew that in every one of those men, there was a passionate hunger for $5,000 worth of Jimmy Bristol.

The chestnut was led up to him on the run by the stableman.

"I kind of thought . . ." he said.

Bristol looked him fairly between the eyes. Then he exclaimed: "You're a poor devil! Here's another dollar." He flung the money on the floor, leaped into the saddle, and raced the chestnut up the street.

He heard shots behind him. The shooting ended as he turned a corner, and half a minute later he was out of that town and heading again toward Kennisaw Gap. And the loneliness of the rain, which is only less than the loneliness of the sea, gathered around him and cupped him in with his own soul.

He got off and ran when he reached the sweep of the hills and the grama grass that covered them. The chestnut was tired, and he needed to put miles between him and that town.

He mounted and rode again at a steady jog until, far away, he saw the shattered starlight of a lamp shining through a wet windowpane.

Presently he was in front of a small ranch house. The roof sloped down over the shed-like back of the house, where the lamp was burning from the kitchen window. Dismounting, he looked through that window. The rain had fallen away to a thin drizzle, and through the misted window, he could see the details of the small kitchen and the girl washing dishes. She was as brown as the back of a cowpuncher's hand, and the darkness of her sunburned skin gave an extra flash to her teeth and her eyes. She was washing dishes and singing, and the words or the music of the song, which he could scarcely hear, kept her laughing.

Jimmy Bristol began to smile in turn. In fact, he had ridden all the way from the last town with a smile on his lips, fed from a source of upwelling, inward contentment.

He led his horse past the back of the house and out toward the looming shapes of great barns.

He pulled open the door of the first one. The moon had risen behind the rain, and since Bristol was looking east, he was able to see the naked skeleton of the barn, the huge beams, and the joists. There were no animals here; there was no bay in the mow. Through a gap in the roof, he could hear the patter of the lonely rain inside the building.

He closed the door and went on to the next barn gloomily. There were four of those huge barns dimly outlined through the rain and lying about a great corral. And beyond the corral, there was a forest of entangled fencing, such as one finds on a place equipped for the handling of thousands of cattle.

However, when he pulled open the door of the next barn, he heard a jangle of tin close beside him. He guessed that it must be a lantern hung on a nail, and when he lighted a match, he found it. By the light of the lantern he looked upon a barn whose interior was as vast as the other, which he had dimly beheld in its nakedness against that pale moonshine that made the rain luminous outside the great upper door of the haymow. In this mow, there was a small stack of hay at the farther end. Tethered to the manger and lying down were an old gray mule and a brown mustang.

He tied his chestnut to the nearest stall. Then he stripped saddle and bridle from it and held the lantern close. The knees of the chestnut were trembling.

"I thought so," said Bristol to himself. He ran his fingers under the belly of the horse and found the muscles drawn hard. The gelding was badly gaunted by the long labor it had passed through.

He took wisps of hay and fell to work, laboring earnestly until the horse was dry and glowing. Then he put out the lantern, left the barn, and went back to the house.

The girl was still in the kitchen. He looked through the dining-room window and saw an elderly man in his shirtsleeves reading a newspaper.

He held the edges of the sheets between thumb and finger of one hand and between the first two fingers of the right hand, for the good reason that his right hand lacked a thumb. By the red of the scar, Bristol judged that the wound was not many years old.

He went to the door that opened from the dining room onto the little, black veranda.

"Come in," said a voice.

He pulled open the door and stepped in.

The girl came to the open door of the kitchen and looked at him. "Hello," she said.

"Take off your coat and sit down," said the elderly man.

Bristol had pulled off his hat, and the water from it leaked in rapid drops onto the floor.

"I've tied a horse in your barn out there," he said. "Is that all right?"

"Sure, it's all right," said the host.

He stood up and extended his thumbless hand. Bristol took it.

"I'm Joe Graney. Here's my girl, Margaret."

"I'm Jimmy Bristol." He waited for that name to take effect, like an acid, but there was no shadow of a response on their faces—merely a polite interest. He shook hands with the girl, too, and saw that her eyes were pure, unwatered blue. She used them not like a pretty girl, reaching for admiration, but straight and true, as a man does who knows what hard work means. And she, like a man, measured his height, his shoulders, his weight.

These are honest people, he thought to himself, and he felt a little uneasy.

Graney was ordering him to sit down, telling the girl to put some food on the stove.

But Bristol said: "Never mind. I had two platters of hotcakes in a town not more'n eight or ten miles back."

"Richtown?" asked Graney.

"I don't know the name."

Graney took off his spectacles and looked at his guest, not offensively, but with open curiosity. "You say you didn't know the name?"

"I was passing through fast," said Bristol. He hung his slicker on a nail. Water still ran down from it to the floor as Bristol sat down. "I'll go out and tuck myself up in the hay," he suggested.

"There's an extra bed here in the house," said the girl.

"Sure. You'll sleep in here," said Graney. "Won't you take a cup of coffee?"

Bristol shook his head. He felt more uneasy than ever. It seemed to him that these people would hardly be able to afford even as much as a cup of coffee to a stranger. The house was clean, so were the clothes they wore, but faded and patched to the last degree. Good people who had fallen in the world, who had missed their chances. He half wished that he had ridden on and left the place, for he could feel a silent and insistent demand being made on his conscience.

He asked suddenly: "Look here . . . not long ago those barns were filled with hay."

"How long ago would you say?" asked Graney.

"Two years. I saw the bits of hay high up on the sides of the walls. And the spiders hadn't built many cobwebs. Those barns have been in use not so long ago."

"No, it's just two years," admitted Graney. "Two years ago Dirk van Wey stepped in, and everything stepped off the place except the two of us." He smiled faintly and nodded.

"Who's Dirk van Wey?" asked Bristol.

"Dirk van Wey? You don't know him?"

"I come from pretty far south," said Bristol.

"Dirk van Wey," said the girl, "liked the look of Kennisaw Gap and decided to settle in it two years ago. But he didn't like to have neighbors too close to him. So little by little our cows began to wander off . . . hundreds of 'em. There's only a handful left now. And when they're gone, I suppose that we'll move along, just as Dirk wants us to."

"No," said Graney calmly, steadily. "You know that I'll never move along, Margie. I'll eat grass first."

"Van Wey is a rustler, is he?" asked Bristol.

"Van Wey is anything that makes money without work."

The lips of Bristol twitched, and not with mirth. He felt the eyes of the girl on his face and knew that she had seen him wince.

"Van Wey," said Graney, "lives in an old house of ours up in the gap, and there he'll stay, like an eagle on a rock, king of everything in sight."

"Why doesn't the sheriff take a hand with him?" asked Bristol.

"One sheriff did, and he never came back. Then a deputy sheriff took a big posse up there. They found the house empty. They scattered through the woods and the rocks. And three of them never came back. Since then, hunting down van Wey hasn't been popular. Eh, Margie?"

The girl did not answer. Instead, she remarked: "You're tired. You'd better go to bed. I'll show you the room."

She led the way before Bristol, when he had said good night to the broken rancher, and ushered him into a small room that had a clean rug on the floor, a bed of enameled iron, and the first big mirror he had seen in three months. She pulled back the curtains and opened the window.

Outside, the rain had stopped, but he could hear the crinkling sound of the soil, still drinking.

"Look," said Bristol. "Is anything going to be done about van Wey?"

"Nothing," said the girl.

"And your father's going to stay here with his lost cause?"

"It's a horse that keeps him here. I'll tell you in the morning, if you want to know. Good night. Sleep well." She smiled at him from the door and closed it softly after her.

She sees through me, he said to himself. And he sat down in a chair with his head bowed, regardless of the clammy cold that began to steal slowly through him from his wet clothes.

IV

In the gray of the morning, Jimmy Bristol was at the barn, where he found the chestnut in a cold sweat, with knees still trembling. He rubbed down the horse again, but it was clearly folly to take the gelding out for another journey that day.

He stood for a time in the doorway of the barn, looking across the great tangle of fencing, wondering how many hundreds of cattle could be worked with ease with such accommodations. Then he went back to the house, remembering every step of the way that Tom Denton, although he might be a fat sheriff, had the lean legs of a good rider. And how long might it be before Sheriff Tom Denton picked up his trail?

When he came to the house, he found the girl up, with a white streaking of smoke in the kitchen air. The half-thin, half-choking smell of burned paper dominated. But the stove was already humming. The draft was open. The chimney trembled with the strength of the flames that were shaking their heads inside it. And Margaret Graney was swiftly rolling out a slab of biscuit dough. He went out to the woodpile, split some chunks into size for the firebox, and brought the load back to fill the woodbox. Then he retired to the pump, filled the granite wash basin, washed, and shaved.

He came inside once more with a face somewhat red and tender from the quick work with the razor, and leaning in the kitchen door, he said: "Let's have it, will you?"

She was cutting out the biscuits, dipping the round cutter in flour every time. Then she began to lay the limp little rounds of dough rapidly in the greased pan.

"It's not a long yarn," she said. "Father was doing well with everything until two years ago, when Dirk van Wey appeared and asked to rent the old house in the gap. He took the house, but of course, he never paid the rent. It's his headquarters for his gang of thieves. They've cleaned out Father, but he won't leave."

"There was something about a horse, too," Bristol suggested.

"Father had bought a stallion called Pringle, a long, drawn-out, shambly sort of a creature to look at, but Pringle can carry weight all day long and go like the wind. Father's idea was to build up the quality of the horse herd for the ranch. He wanted them all half-bred, or three-quarter-bred, or still better. He was ambitious. That was just before van Wey came, and of course,

Pringle was the very first animal that Dirk van Wey stole from us. And the thought of Pringle sticks in the mind of Father. He doesn't mind so much the empty barns and corrals. He doesn't mind the loss of the thumb that one of Dirk's men shot off a year ago. It's the loss of Pringle that really matters."

Joe Graney came out—smiling, cheerful—and talked until breakfast was ready about deer hunting in the gap. But all during breakfast Jimmy Bristol was silent, trying to lift from his mind the weight that lay redoubled upon it every time he looked at Margaret Graney. She had the calmness of one who understands. And he felt that above all, she understood Jimmy Bristol and had put him down for a rascal.

So he said suddenly, at the end of the meal: "Give me the right, and let me ride up through the gap and try to get Pringle and the back rent."

"Yeah, and that would be a joke," murmured Graney. "A whole posse has tried that trick, partner!"

"Crowds are not much good with fellows like Dirk van Wey," said Jimmy Bristol. "But let me try my own hand and my own shuffle with him, will you? I'll have to trade my chestnut horse for your brown one to get there. That's all."

He saw the girl frown, very faintly, and saw her eyes look with warning at her father. And, for that matter, it was true that the chestnut was a stolen horse; so were all the horses that he had ridden during the last three months, except the first one, the best one of all. As for Graney, he seemed more irritated than suspicious by the offer, as though it angered him to have a young braggart attempt the impossible.

"You start now, if you want to," said Graney, frowning.

Yet it was chiefly to escape the cold, clear eyes of the girl that Bristol hurried from the table. There was neither disgust nor contempt in her face, but an amused understanding that was more humiliating than anything else could have been. It made Jimmy Bristol want to slay armies or cleave mountains. And always that newly awakened sense of guilt worked like a poison in him.

In two minutes, Bristol sat on the brown mustang before the small ranch house, waving good-bye to the faint smile of the girl and the gloomy frown of Graney, then he turned and rode over the wet hills toward Kennisaw Gap, an axe cleft between Kennisaw Mountain and Downey Peak.

He found a creek lined with cottonwoods, and the valley lifted to lodgepole pines, then to big trees, until he came into the gap itself. It was a place of the utmost confusion. Vast boulders had dropped from the mountainsides above, and here and there were groves and clusters of big yellow pines, to show that the soil was deep and good. Through the middle ran a trickle of water, flashing and dodging here and there among the rocks. That lonely mountain quiet gave him second thoughts. He camped for half the day, telling himself he was a fool to go on. But in the late afternoon he was in the saddle again.

Bristol heard the occasional tinkling of a bell, the sound growing louder and louder. Then he saw a scattering of sheep, but not the goat or the wether that carried the bell, when a voice said, close beside him: "Hello, partner."

He turned and saw a little man seated in the lap of a great rock that offered a natural seat. He was a fellow of middle age, wearing old, battered leather chaps, and he had a rifle across his knees. His face was very thin and brown, but he had the smooth brow of a mountaineer, as distinguished from the puckered forehead and the squinting eyes of a man of the desert.

"Hello," said Jimmy Bristol, reining in his horse. "Looking for something?" He nodded toward the rifle.

"Yeah. Wolves . . . and coyotes," said the other. "Seen any?"

"You're the shepherd, eh?"

"That's me. The doggone coyotes, they'll be down among the rocks and trees trying to sneak a lamb if they get a chance. The coyotes make more trouble than the wolves."

"You're the shepherd, eh?" repeated Jimmy Bristol, hooking his right leg over the horn of the saddle and making a cigarette.

"Yeah. What are you, brother?"

"I'm an ace full on a pair of kings," said Jimmy Bristol, smiling gently.

The little man did not smile, however. "That's a pretty big hand," he said, "but you can lose money on it in some games."

"It takes four of a kind to beat it," answered Bristol.

"They can be found, brother . . . they can be found," said the shepherd. "Did I see a streak of yellow over there?" He stood up, the rifle at the ready.

And, turning his head a little, Jimmy Bristol actually saw the yellow-gray fur of a coyote as it flashed among the rocks, some fifty yards away. "There's a coyote over there," agreed Bristol.

"There's more'n one coyote in this gap," said the other man. "And they know how to use cover and sneak up close on the sheep, too, day or night. There . . ."

He jerked the rifle to his shoulder and fired. The coyote, either that which Bristol had just seen or another, had appeared suddenly on top of a rock that was not far off. It had barely pointed its head into the wind when it saw the flash of the rifle. At the clang of the gun, it made a leap into the air and, landing, sprang for safety among the boulders.

This had taken a full second, perhaps, and a full second was a very long time for Jimmy Bristol. His revolver exploded. The coyote twisted sidewise in the air and disappeared.

"That was pretty smooth," said the little man, calmly as ever. "Maybe you been up here in the gap before?"

"No. It's my first trip," answered Jimmy Bristol. "But I like the scenery and the air. I wouldn't mind staying a while in this sort of a neck of the woods."

The little man walked away among the rocks and came back carrying by the scruff of the neck the limp body of a dead coyote.

"Right behind the shoulder," he said. "You nailed him clean. He didn't suffer any. He must have died in the air. Want the skin?"

"No," said Jimmy Bristol. "I'm heading for Dirk van Wey's place. Know where it is?"

The other stared earnestly at him. "You know Dirk van Wey?" he asked at last.

"By reputation. Not by sight."

"There's quite a lot to know about him, take him either way. Well, I'm about ready to go in. I'll take the skin off this coyote and go in with you and show you the way. I'll introduce you."

Bristol did not offer to help in the skinning of the dead coyote. There was little need, for the mountaineer seemed to know perfectly how the skin was fitted over the supple body, and the edge of his knife seemed to have eyes and a separate sense of touch. All in a moment the skin was off, and the slender, naked, little carcass lay on the ground, white streaked with slashes of red.

The pelt was folded, the knife cleaned, and the man of the rifle walked away, with Bristol riding behind him.

"What about the sheep and the coyotes?" asked Bristol.

"What about 'em? The coyotes'll keep away when they see their pal lying dead there. What's your moniker, brother?"

"Bristol. Jim Bristol. Who are you?"

"I'm Dan Miller."

"Been in the sheep business a long time?"

"Quite a spell."

"That's what I guessed," said Bristol, "by the look of the chaps."

Dan Miller turned his sharp, brown face and spoke over his shoulder. "It's easy to see too much up here," he said gravely.

"Because of the altitude, eh?" asked Jimmy Bristol.

"Yes," said Dan Miller. "A lot of fellows get up here and find it so high that they think they can see over the whole world, pretty near."

"That must make 'em dizzy," suggested Bristol.

"It does," said Miller. "And a lot of 'em get bad falls, too."

After these cryptic remarks, he led the way through a tangle of trees and rocks until they came out suddenly into a clearing, where a rambling house of rough-stone masonry and logs stood beside a blue pool, into which the sunset was beginning to drop embers of red and gold. A big spruce grew before the house, and under the tree stood a table built up from the ground, meant to stay there in all weather. Tin plates and cups had been laid out on it, and one man already sat at the head of the board. On a blanket in front of the door of the house sat a broken-nosed, swarthy fellow rolling dice with a handsome, golden-haired youth of twenty.

That pair at the side would have taken the eye ordinarily, but they were nothing compared with the fellow who sat at the table. Dark by nature and still darker from exposure to all weather, he sat with his great arms folded on top of the table, the might of his shoulders thrown loosely forward, and in the wide slit of his mouth, a pipe was gripped savagely, as though he intended to bite through the stem at once.

That was the air of him, at once brooding, and ready for instant action. There was such a bright spark in his eyes that Jimmy Bristol could hardly conceive of eyelids that could cover and shut out entirely that uneasy light.

Dan Miller, the pair who rolled the dice, the ragged old cabin, the big mountains around them, the flaming western sky, all became a blank before the mind of Jimmy Bristol, and he saw only the face of this man.

It was Dirk van Wey; he knew at once.

"Here's a fellow wants to see you," said Dan Miller. "He's by name of Jimmy Bristol . . . and he snagged a coyote down the way. I missed with a rifle, and he snagged it with his Colt."

"That's the right kind of a Colt to have," said the big man at the table.

"Hello, Mister van Wey," said Bristol, and held out his hand.

It was seized with a pressure that turned his arm numb to the elbow and made him into a helpless child.

V

He was aware that the two who rolled dice had turned their heads to watch him.

From the corner of his eye, he saw that they were grinning and knew at once that the grip of the giant must be a famous thing among them.

"How d'you know my face? I never saw you before," said the man at the table.

Jimmy Bristol maintained his smile. The quality of it had changed a little, but it was still a smile.

"When you see the cubs and the father together," said Jimmy Bristol, "it's very easy to pick out the old bear."

The mouth of van Wey widened on either side of the pipe stem, but the grimace was not a smile. He did not relax, but freshened his grip, and although Bristol strove with all his might, until his arm shook with the effort, he could not make an impression on the iron grasp. Yet he managed to continue his smile and keep his face unexpressive of pain.

"You can pick out bears, eh?" said van Wey. "Well, to know that is a lot better than to know nothing. You know a Colt, too, do you?"

"I know it partly."

"Lemme see how well you know a gun," said van Wey. "There's a fool of a squirrel over there at the edge of the pool. Pick it off for me." He relaxed his grip.

The right hand of Jimmy Bristol was as white as a stone and his wrist crimson. It was his left hand, however, that flicked out the shining length of a revolver and fired. The red squirrel, which had been sitting up on a small stone at the edge of the glowing water, disappeared. A splash of blood remained on the stone for a sign of the life that had been there the moment before.

Dirk van Wey puffed on his pipe and let a stream of smoke squirt out from each corner of his mouth.

"You're a two-handed man," he said. "Or are you a lefty?"

"I have two hands," agreed Jimmy Bristol, putting up the gun.

"Two hands are better'n one," reasoned Dirk van Wey. "Sit down."

There were immovable stools of stone or wood driven into the ground around the table. Jimmy Bristol sat down on the nearest one and faced van Wey. He saw the golden-haired youth leave the dice game, step to the edge of the standing water, and pick up from the margin a pitiful little rag of bloodstained fur. He looked at it, then tossed it toward his gambling companion. Last, he turned and stared steadily at Jimmy Bristol, as a cat stares at a bird.

"What brought you up here?" asked Dirk van Wey.

"I was sashaying through the country," said Jimmy Bristol, "and I ran into a ranch down the valley that's owned by Joe Graney."

"Yeah. He's an old friend of mine. He's my landlord. I got no complaints about him for a landlord, neither." A flash came in his eyes.

Dan Miller began to chuckle.

"Shut up, Dan," said Dirk van Wey. "Ain't Joe Graney a fine landlord?"

"Sure he is," said Miller.

"Then shut up, and lemme talk to this two-handed man. Bristol, go on. What happened at the Graney place?"

"My horse went lame," said Jimmy Bristol. "And when Graney heard that I was aiming for the Kennisaw Gap, he told me that he'd keep my horse and let me have a fresh one if I'd do him a favor."

"Aye," said Dirk van Wey, "and what was that favor?"

"Just to drop by up here and ask Dirk van Wey for the rent he owed and to bring back with me a bay stallion called Pringle, which is on pasture with you here."

"How much is the rent?" asked Dirk van Wey.

"A thousand dollars for the year."

"And how many years?"

"One year's rent is enough for me to take away."

Dirk van Wey puffed steadily at his pipe and, by the trick of his mouth, still squirted out the smoke in two separate streams.

Around the stem of the pipe he spoke, as before: "How'll you have the money? Gold or bills?"

"I'll have it the easiest way," said Jimmy Bristol.

"All right," said Dirk van Wey. "Take it in greenbacks." He pulled out a wallet, thumbed some bills in it, and then rapidly counted out a stack of ten hundreds. "There's a year's rent. Times are kind of hard, Bristol. You tell Joe Graney that."

Bristol fingered the money for an instant. "It's a fair joke, but bad money," he said.

"Why is it bad?"

"The stuff is all queer."

Dirk van Wey stared, then snatched up the money and held one of the bills toward the western light. He grunted suddenly, balled the apparent greenbacks in his hand, and hurled them at the head of Dan Miller.

"That's what you bring in . . . counterfeit?" said van Wey.

"It ain't possible," groaned Miller. "Nobody could make a sucker out of me like that." He had put up one of the bills to the light in his turn by this time, and now he broke off his talking and began to curse in a subdued rumble.

Van Wey silently unbuckled a money belt. In the pause, Jimmy Bristol heard the golden-haired young man saying: "I'm tired of this dice business, Lefty."

"All right, Harry," said the man of the broken nose. "Anything you please."

"I'll bet you there ain't a bill in this lot of the queer that Dan Miller is swearing at that has a corner torn off."

"That's a fool bet. There's always a corner torn off."

"If I'm a fool, I'll bet you a hundred bucks on it."

"All right. Or two hundred."

"Make it five hundred and be danged!" exclaimed Harry heartily.

"Five hundred it is. Dan, come let us look at that stuff."

"Take it and eat it, for all I care. I'm going to have the hide of the gent that shoved that queer on me!" exclaimed Miller, balling the paper into a wad again and tossing it to the pair on the blanket.

Dirk van Wey had stacked up fifty $20 gold pieces in two piles. "Here's the money," he said.

There was something electric in the air, and Jimmy Bristol felt the prickling of it down his spine. He took up the money, counted it with a rapid chinking of the coins, and pocketed the gold. Only now was the circulation returning to his right hand.

"About the horse," said Dirk. "Come along."

He led the way into a wide shed where half a dozen horses were tied to the mangers, on either side of a mow in which the hay had sunk lower than breast-high. Van Wey pointed at the animals on the farther side of the mow.

"Pringle is over there. Pick him out," he said.

And again that sense of electric suspense swept through Jimmy Bristol. Something very important depended on the correctness of his judgment, something more than the mere possession of the stallion.

The light was dull, also. The sun was down, and although both the western doors of the shed were open, only a reddish haze was flowing into the shed. Big Jimmy Bristol shaded his eyes and stared.

Of the six horses, three were bays that faced him. The high mangers shut them off at the breast. One was a big, noble creature, with the gloss of polished bronze. That could hardly be Pringle, the stallion, which had been described as a lean and ugly horse. There were two of the bays, in fact, which looked from the head, like long-eared, long-legged rambleshacks. The temples of one were rather sunken, as though by many years.

Jimmy Bristol hissed suddenly like a snake, and every horse in the shed jumped and threw up its head. All, that is, except the bay with the sunken temples.

"I'll take that fellow to be Pringle," said Bristol.

Dirk van Wey grunted. "All right," he said. "You picked him. And you picked a good one. He can carry a ton all day long, and I need a horse that can pack a ton."

He did, in fact. He was hardly taller than Jimmy Bristol, but he was a square chunk of power from head to heels. When he moved his arms, his muscles filled his shirtsleeves.

"It's a pile better for you to pick out Pringle than to pick out . . . bad luck," said Dirk van Wey suddenly. "Know that?" He clapped his hand on the shoulder of Bristol and let the grip of it remain there, bruising the flesh against the bone.

"I know something else," said Jimmy Bristol, "that if you don't take your hand off my shoulder, I'll split your wishbone for you. And if you ever put a hand on me again, I'll do the same thing."

"Will you?" said Dirk van Wey. And he kept his grip intact.

VI

In the pause they stared solemnly at one another. Fear leaped like a cold snake up the back of Jimmy Bristol, as he saw the eyes of Dirk van Wey apparently draw nearer to him. But suddenly the hand that gripped his shoulder was withdrawn.

"It's all right, brother," said van Wey. "I won't lean on you ag'in unless I have to. There goes the dinner bell. Let's go."

It was the roar of the cook, bellowing—"Come and get it! Come and get it!"—and banging on a tin pan.

Van Wey led the way back to the table, where a fellow with a ship tattooed on one arm and the rather blurred face of a pretty girl on the other forearm was shoveling fried steaks onto the plates. In the center of the table, on a platter, rose a great mound of potatoes, fried to a golden brown. That and pone and black coffee were all of supper.

As they settled themselves around the table, the cook began to pour coffee into the cups, and golden-haired Harry said: "I want two hundred bucks, chief. I've just lost a bet."

"*I* ain't got two hundred bucks," said van Wey. "Dan paid me with some queer . . . and Bristol, here, has just collected the rent for the landlord. I'm pretty near cleaned out. You had better go fishing for that two hundred bucks if you want it, Weston."

Harry Weston nodded. And his blue eyes flashed once toward Jimmy Bristol.

"And me pulling out in the morning," said the man with the broken nose, "it kind of rushed Harry a little to raise that money."

"You pulling out in the morning, Parr?" asked van Wey.

"Yeah. You know I got an engagement over the hills and far away."

Dan Miller said nothing. He lowered his head until his sharp nose was almost touching his food and ate in a thoughtful silence. But for some reason Jimmy Bristol felt that the thoughts of Dan Miller were fixed firmly upon him.

"It's a darkish sort of night for a ride through the gap," said van Wey to Bristol. "You better put up here tonight."

"Got an extra blanket?"

"Yeah. And an extra bed. And an extra room," said van Wey. "There's a lot of space in the old shack. It was built by a man that had a big family. What's his name, Dan?"

"Gresham," said Dan Miller. "Oliver Gresham built it. He had three thousand head of cows running here in the gap and down in the valley. He done pretty well for a long while."

"Yeah," said van Wey. "He done pretty well. He kind of went to pieces before the end, though." And as he finished speaking, his mouth stretched.

Bristol at last recognized the grimace as a smile, or the nearest that van Wey could come to an expression of mirth.

"What happened to him?" asked Bristol.

"His girl married Joe Graney. The cows still grew fat. But then the rustlers, they sort of edged in and skimmed the cream off the pan. There's been a terrible lot of rustlers around these parts," said Dan Miller solemnly.

Lefty Parr rubbed his broken nose. His eyes shone. At last his mirth grew greater than his self-control, and he burst into hearty laughter.

"Whatcha laughing at?" demanded van Wey.

"Nothing. I just thought of a joke. Nothing much to tell," said Lefty Parr, and concealed his face behind the upward tipping of his tin coffee cup.

The cook came to the table and took a place, reaching his greasy hands for what he wanted. They called him Rance. He looked like a low-grade Scandinavian with a great, flat slab of a face, a mouth that was a brother to the mouth of van Wey, and a pair of faded-blue eyes. He never looked a man in the face, but always askance. When he talked, he kept turning his head from side to side, as though he were searching for a hidden thing in the background.

Van Wey filled and emptied his plate three times, poured a fourth cup of steaming coffee down his throat, filled and lighted his pipe, and rose from the table.

"Where you going, chief?" asked Harry Weston.

"For a walk," said van Wey.

"Far?"

"Far enough," answered the chief, and turning his back on them, he strode away, letting the rumble of his voice come back over his shoulder. "The three of you and Rance can take care of Bristol. Make him mighty comfortable, I hope."

There was an odd accent on the last words, and Bristol heard it. He did not need to see the glances that were covertly exchanged between Harry Weston and broken-nosed Lefty Parr in order to understand that the mode of their entertaining might be distinctly original.

"What about a game?" asked Weston gently, at the end of supper.

"I'm flat broke," said Jimmy Bristol. "I haven't a penny on me."

"I told you he was a high-stepper," said Lefty Parr dryly. "He don't call a thousand bucks a penny. He's one of these gents that picks his teeth with diamonds maybe, and washes his hands in rose water, eh?"

He leered across the table at Jimmy Bristol, and the quiet, steady smile of Jimmy Bristol answered him.

"We'll play for fun," said Harry Weston. "I'm broke, too. We'll play for matches. Poker, eh?"

"I'm tired," answered Jimmy Bristol. "One of you fellows tell me where to find a blanket and a spare bed?"

They looked at one another.

"I'll show you," said Rance, the cook, who was shoveling the last of the fried potatoes into his vast mouth. He rose, took a swallow of coffee standing, and led the way to the house. And behind him, Bristol felt three pairs of sharp eyes, following and probing.

By the door hung a lantern, which the cook lighted and then led the way through the open door and across a big room with a low ceiling. The flooring was broken. Some of the masonry of the fireplace at the farther end of the room had fallen down on the hearth. And it was plain that, for van Wey and his followers, the house was no more than a strongly covered camp, a place to sleep in rather than a place to live in.

Rance led the way up creaking stairs, humming a song in the guttural depths of his throat. Down the upper hall, he turned until he came to the end of it, and kicked open a door.

"How does this sound to you, brother?" he asked.

It was a good-size room, with a single cot stowed in a corner and a tousled blanket heaped on the foot of that bed. There was no other furniture, not a washstand or a chair or any rag of a rug.

"Regular palace hotel," said Jimmy Bristol with his smile. "Bath with every room, telephone, hot and cold running water. A regular home, eh?"

Rance held up the lantern and slowly turned around. "It's better than a forecastle on an old hooker off the Horn, laying her nose ag'in the westerlies for six weeks, like I've seen," he said.

"It'll do for me," agreed Bristol. "Can you leave me that lantern?"

"Sure," said the cook. "I can find my way around by dark in this place."

"Makings?" asked Bristol, holding out a battered, little sack of tobacco and wheat-straw papers.

The cook hesitated. Then, with an almost imperceptible shrug of his shoulders, he accepted the makings, tore off a paper with his greasy fingers, and built a smoke. He returned the makings to Jimmy Bristol and was fumbling for a match when Bristol held a lighted one before him. The faded-blue eyes of Rance shifted up uncomfortably toward Bristol's face. He nodded a little apologetically as he used the proffered flame.

And then, standing back with a worried frown on his fleshy forehead, he puffed on the cigarette, turned toward the door, and now turned back again.

"What's the matter, Rance?" asked Bristol. "Anything on your mind?"

"No," muttered the cook. He came a stride nearer to Bristol and looked earnestly into his face, as though seeing him for the first time. "Well," said Rance, "what I was just wondering was . . . *er* . . . I dunno . . . It's all right, I guess."

He went back toward the door. His baffled eyes stared again at Bristol, but in another moment he had stepped out and closed the door with a grunted: "Good night."

Bristol listened to the muffled tread of the footfalls going down the hall. He heard the squeaking of the stairs as the cook descended. A lonely feeling came over him, as though a friend had just departed.

"Murder," whispered Bristol to himself. "Murder is what it all means."

VII

The heart of Rance had been touched by the small courtesies that Jimmy Bristol had showed him. Rance had been stirred to the very verge of speech—yet he had not spoken. He had gone as from a death chamber.

It seemed to Jimmy Bristol that he had been the greatest fool in the world to allow himself to be herded into the house, when all the while he had known that the money that Dirk van Wey had given him was not intended to be kept in his pocket for long. It was simply a jest on the part of that man, van Wey, a brutal jest, to appear to give merely for the sake of taking away again. He said that he had gone for a walk and did not know when he would return. In the meantime, his inference was perfectly clear. He had four men there. If they were worth their salt, they would handle Jimmy Bristol in a manner that he would never forget and either bury him or send him packing as fast as he could go. To a brute like Dirk van Wey, such a scheme would be a very clever way of testing his men, keeping them up on their metal.

Bristol went to the window of the room and looked out. The wall of the house dropped sheerly down without a break. And below the foundations, a steep bank continued the fall. It was a full sixty feet from the sill of his window to the level. Suppose that he made a rope out of the blanket and his own clothes, still he would never be able to get to the ground without broken bones.

As for going out the door, not even a ghost could walk down that hallway or those stairs without making the warped boards creak like an empty wagon on a rough road.

A scratching sound made him jump. It was an old, gray tiger cat, which reached up from the floor to sharpen its claws on the edge of the canvas tick of the bed.

Bristol sat down on the edge of the bed, picked up the cat, and let it stretch out on his thigh. The cat accepted the position at once, closed its eyes, and, purring with content, began to work its claws into the tough cloth that covered his knees. The cat was very old and very ill cared for. Its whiskers were white as silver. With the tip of a finger, he could count its vertebrae from behind its ears to the root of its tail, and its poor old ribs were obvious through the thin mist of its fur. Plainly the animal was not fed, but had to hunt for its living, and increasing age made this more and more difficult. He could see it waiting for death at last under the lee of a southern bank, its paws tucked under its body, purring for gratitude because of the warmth of the sun.

But the cat was a poor beast incapable of reason, and therefore trapped by circumstance, and Bristol was a human creature with a brain, yet from the moment he met Dan Miller in the gap, he had allowed himself to drift on from one point to another until he found himself closed in this impasse. He had done such things before. He was a wine taster, and danger always had been the wine that he loved. The danger that thickened around him in the gap had been a glorious delight to him. There had only been one moment of real fear, and that was when Dirk van Wey gripped his shoulder in the barn. But now there was fear again, real fear. The breath of it was in the cold damp of the room.

He had one consolation. If it were impossible for him to get out of the room unnoticed, it would also be impossible for the men of the house to get into the room without waking him.

There was a key in the door. He got up and turned that key, and felt the rusty bolt slide home. They would have to beat down that door to get at him. And they were not apt to do that. Morning might bring him new ideas. So he pulled off his boots, opened the window, blew out the lantern, and lay down in his clothes to be ready for any alarm. The old, gray cat curled up against his breast, and the hoarse music of its purring put him to sleep. The last he remembered was the secret voice of the wind through the foliage of the big tree outside the house.

* * * * *

He wakened with a start and in another world. Pale moonlight streamed before him, and a monstrous tiger, striped with dim, gray stripes, was before him. Only gradually he realized that he was lying in the bed in the house of Dirk van Wey and that the moonshine was streaking through the window. The huge tiger that stood with ears laid savagely back and with tail lashing its sides, was no other than the old, gray cat that had awakened him by its sudden start and that now stood on the edge of the bed, staring toward a corner of the room.

Bristol turned his head in that direction and almost exclaimed aloud. For a whole section of the ceiling now hung down, a big square section of the boards. And now, into the dimness, dropped what seemed the limber length of a snake, but turned out to be a swaying rope ladder. It began to swing and sway more violently. The boots and spurs of a man appeared, then his knees, his hips, his head and shoulders.

Bristol drew a revolver and leveled it.

Having reached the floor, the intruder waved his hand. The rope ladder gradually ascended; the trap door closed on soundless hinges. And peering through the gloom, Bristol made out the profile of that broken-nosed man, Lefty Parr.

The head of Lefty had turned only once toward the bed. Now, as though perfectly assured that his victim slept, he raised his face and watched the soundless closing of the trap. In that moment the gray cat couched itself as if for a spring, and big Jimmy Bristol glided from the bed and across the floor. Moonlight bathed him to the knees, and as though the flash of it struck the corner of Lefty's eye, he whirled suddenly, gun in hand.

The leveled Colt in the hand of Bristol made Lefty's own weapon waver. Then it hung at his side at the length of a limp arm. Yet there was little or no fear in his face.

"Walk over to the bed and put the gun on it," said Jimmy Bristol.

Lefty Parr obeyed. He laid down the gun with a sort of reverence and, straightening, turned to Bristol again.

"Now stand over in the moonlight," said Bristol softly. "And take care of your hands. No quick moves, Lefty."

"All right," said Lefty.

He stood back into the moonlight until the bright current of it cut across his face at the sag in his nose. Still he seemed perfectly calm.

"Now, what's up, brother?" asked Bristol.

Lefty made a gesture with both hands, palms up, inviting Bristol to see for himself.

"A thousand bucks is a whole lot of money. Is that it?" asked Bristol.

"Yeah," said Lefty, "it's too much to throw away."

"On rent, eh? Van Wey left it up to you fellows to get it?"

"Something like that," muttered Lefty Parr.

"Where are the rest of 'em? Who elected you? I mean, for the dirty work."

"We drew for the first black ace. I collected it," said Parr. "I wasn't going to bump you off. I was just going to stick you up and take the dough."

"Tap me on the head, maybe, for a settler?"

"Well, maybe. I dunno." His casual attitude remained.

"Where are the rest of 'em, Lefty?" asked Bristol.

"I dunno. That's their business."

"I like a man that talks up," suggested Bristol. He got up and crossed the floor. The muzzle of his revolver he laid on the square chin of Lefty Parr.

"That's no good," said Parr. "It wouldn't buy you anything to blow my head off."

"It would make me a lot happier, though," said Bristol. "It's worth dying for, Lefty, to put away a rat of your size."

Lefty considered him with a sudden squinting of the eyes. He said nothing.

"Tell me where those fellows are . . . all of 'em!"

Lefty moistened his lips. The tip of his tongue glistened in the moonshine. "Dan Miller was up in the attic, handling the trap and the ladder for me," he said. "And out in the hall is Harry Weston."

"Where's Rance?"

"I dunno, exactly. Maybe outside the house."

His tone inferred that the whereabouts of Rance did not greatly matter.

"Has van Wey come back?"

"Maybe. I dunno. I ain't seen him."

"You lie," said Bristol.

The first real sign of fear was the shudder of Lefty's body. "I'm telling you straight!" he gasped.

Bristol considered for an instant. It might well be that Dan Miller was still working his way quietly down from the attic. And in that case, it was time to move at once. He merely paused to ask: "Ever use this room this way before?"

"No," said Lefty Parr.

"That's a louder lie than the rest," said Bristol. "You keep the hinges of it oiled. That shows it's always ready for use."

He saw the Adam's apple work up and down in the throat of his captive as Lefty swallowed. It was confession enough.

"Walk to the door," commanded Bristol.

Lefty obeyed. He stood at the door, whispering: "What's the idea going to be, Bristol?"

Bristol laid the muzzle of the Colt against the small of Lefty's back, reached past him with the other hand, and turned the key.

Then he fastened the grip of his left hand on Parr's neck from behind.

"Pull the door open and walk out," he ordered.

"Hey, wait a minute," argued Parr, whispering. "If I walk out there, you know that that snaky devil of a Weston is out there."

"That's all right. You'll be walking first."

"He wouldn't let up because I went first. He'd shoot me to get at you. He ain't human. He'd do a murder for ten dollars. He'd do it for fun!"

And Bristol remembered the handsome, cold face of Harry Weston and knew that what he heard was true. He merely answered: "Better take your chance with him. You've got no chance with me. If I have to leave the room without you, I'll leave you dead behind me, Lefty. Killing snakes is not murder, Parr. Open that door."

The head of Lefty Parr dropped weakly back with a groan. But he pulled the door open, nevertheless, and before them was the velvet blackness of the hallway.

VIII

The voice of Lefty Parr went before them, whining, appealing, with the same shiver in the sound that there was in his body.

"Harry, don't shoot! Harry, you ain't going to shoot, boy. He's got me. He tricked me, and he got me."

Out of the darkness down the hallway a voice laughed softly. "You used up all your luck tonight, Lefty. I'm sorry for you. Are you walking ahead of the big boy?"

"I'm right ahead of him," said Lefty Parr, stepping slowly into the blackness, with his arms stretched out before him. "He's got me by the neck. He's got a gun rammed into the small of my back. Harry, don't shoot, for God's sake."

"No, I won't shoot," said Harry Weston. "I'll let the big shoemaker walk right out of the house and never try to stop him. I'll let him walk away with the coin just because I don't want to hurt your feelings, eh?"

Bristol, straining his eyes through the blackness, could make out nothing, but the hallway was so narrow that few bullets could fly at random. Besides, since Weston had been in the hall for some time, his eyes had probably grown accustomed to the blackness.

"He's going to do it. He's going to kill me," breathed Lefty Parr to himself. "Bristol, you see how it is. It ain't any good . . . it ain't going to help you . . ."

"The best way with rats is to let 'em kill one another," said Bristol. "Stop squirming and walk straight ahead. Faster!"

Lefty cried: "Harry, will you listen?"

"Yeah, I'll listen, if listening will do you any good."

"I always liked you, Harry. You was always about my best friend. It's going to be a murder if you shoot me. Harry, if things was different, I never would pull a trigger on you. You know that, don't you?"

"I know what you'd do," said the voice of Harry Weston. "Stop your whining and take it like a man."

"Then shoot low!" screamed Lefty. "Don't shoot breast-high or head-high. Shoot low. Maybe you'll snag his legs as well as mine. Don't go and murder me, Harry. Don't shoot for the breast . . ."

"Shut your mouth, you cur!" snarled Weston. "You've never been a whole man. You've never been more than half a man. Now you take your chances the way you find 'em. This ain't a pack of cards that you can stack."

He laughed as he said it, and suddenly big Jimmy Bristol could endure the thing no more. The direction of that voice seemed to him to come rather high and to the right, as though Weston were standing with his back to the wall, thus giving greater clearance for bullets to go by him. As for poor Lefty Parr, he was squeezing himself to nothing against the left-hand wall. And now Bristol tried a snap shot in the direction of his guess.

The gun raised a thunder in his ears. There was an instant flash and report in response. By the flash he saw that all his guessing had been wrong, for the golden-headed youth lay flat on the floor of the hall with his gun stretched out before him.

As Weston fired, Parr shrieked, then doubled up in the hands of Bristol.

Bristol let the writhing body fall and bounded ahead. He could thank his stockinged feet and the screeching of the wounded man for making his coming silent.

Again the gun flashed, this time not from the floor, but higher up and to the left, for Weston had moved between shots. He was kneeling, and as the flash of his gun showed him, Bristol fired at the dimly revealed body, the white glimpse of the face. He knew that he had missed, but he was not a stride away, and through the darkness he reached out and struck with the length of his Colt.

The weight of the blow fell on metal, and the sudden force of that shock knocked his own gun out of his hand. He was disarmed!

Then sinewy arms were cast about him. It seemed that a lithe python had cast a coil around him and was striking his body with sledge-hammer blows. And yet this was that slender fellow, Harry Weston. Amazement stunned Bristol's brain. He would have given his word that he could break the man in two like a brittle stick, and yet he found himself fighting in the darkness for his life.

Down the hallway, Lefty Parr had stopped shrieking. He was merely drawing out terrible groans, for he was sick with his wound. He kept moaning: "Lemme have some light. I don't wanna die in the dark. Lemme have some light. Gimme a candle, even. I gotta have light."

Jimmy Bristol heard the groaning clearly. He was working for a proper hold or a place where he could plant a telling blow, but still it was like struggling with an active snake that continually shifts its grip.

A fist like the steel face of a hammer struck the side of his head. It struck again, lower down, and thudded against his cheek-bone. He ducked his head down and struck. His blow glanced from a muscular body, and his fist hammered against the wall, numbing his arm.

Footfalls were racing up the stairs. The voice of Dan Miller shouted: "Where are you? What's up?"

"I got him here. I don't need you. I'm going to tear the big hunk of cheese in two!" gasped Harry Weston. "I'm going to strangle him. Leave me alone!"

And it seemed to big Jimmy Bristol that, in fact, he soon might be helpless against this tigerish fighter. The fellow had the strength of a wildcat. He never paused for a breathing space. Then, hooking his left hand down and striking hard, Bristol felt his fist drive through between the arm and the ribs of Weston. He jerked his arm up until it fitted under the other's armpit. Then, bending his hand over the shoulder, he reached Weston's face. He was promptly bitten through the palm of his hand. That agony did not matter. He fumbled lower down and curled the steel-hard tips of his fingers around Weston's chin. Golden-haired Harry cursed. For now, with a mighty leverage in his favor, Bristol put forth all his strength and felt Weston's head go back by jerks, little by little.

"What's up, Harry?" cried Dan Miller through the choking darkness.

"Dan! Oh, Danny!" screamed the voice of Parr. "He murdered me. Harry murdered me! Gimme water! Gimme a light! Oh, please, don't let me die in the dark like this!"

"He . . . he's got me," gasped Weston.

Bristol, with a desperate effort, snapped back the head of Harry Weston at that moment. The whole body of the man gave, and into the body Bristol struck with all his might. The expelled breath of Weston gasped at his ear.

He raised his hand and struck three hammer blows against the side of Weston's head.

And at last Harry Weston dropped like a limp rag to the floor of the hall.

Bristol was free barely in time. Dan Miller, bewildered by the darkness, had fired a bullet over his head to give himself one flash of light. That flash, however, found Bristol with his hands free. He saw Miller clearly and the slanting well of the stairs behind him. At that thin wedge of a face, he struck with all his might. And his fist struck a glancing blow. The revolver exploded again, and the bullet ripped through the wall beside Bristol as he sprang in, reaching for the gun.

He found the wrist that held it, lurched on, and toppled down the slope of the stairs head over heels, with Dan Miller's arms and legs entangled in his own. They regained footing for an instant almost at the first landing, but they fell again.

The head and shoulders of Bristol struck against the closed shutters of the window that was meant to light the stairway and knocked those shutters wide, so that for an instant a blinding stream of moonlight poured over them.

The grasp of Bristol luckily found Miller's gun hand and closed on it. He lurched forward to tear himself free from the clinging grip of Miller. But the little man was almost as tenacious as Harry Weston. And in the effort that Bristol was making, he merely sent them both staggering down the lower flight of the stairs. Strangely enough, they did not fall until they struck the level of the big room beneath, and above them they could hear Lefty Parr screeching: "Boys, don't leave me! Don't leave me! Don't lemme die alone!"

Then they hit the floor and tumbled head over heels across it. The shaft of moonlight followed and fell upon them and the large form of Rance, the cook.

He had an axe in his hands, and he came toward them with the weapon gripped and held high over his head. His face was convulsed. Jimmy Bristol could see the desperate crime in it by the moonshine.

And little Dan Miller, with incredible strength, was grappling at the hands of Bristol, snarling the while at Rance: "Strike, Rance! Sink the axe into him! Kill him, the big devil! Now, now, now!"

For an instant, as they rolled and struggled, Miller was on top, and Bristol's head was clearly exposed for a blow. To that purpose Rance sprang closer and swung up the axe again. Death glimmered on the chisel edge of it, and Bristol, looking up in agony, clearly saw the glimmering of the danger.

But something staggered Rance as though a club had struck him. His head jerked back. His whole body wavered. The axe shuddered wildly back and forth in his grasp.

Prison shakes! Bristol had heard of them before, but never seen them—the terrible and utter unnerving of a man who has felt the grasp of the law too long. In the last emergency, in the moment of utter need, strength goes out of those poor victims, and fear takes its place. So Rance shuddered now, helplessly.

That moment of delay was enough for Bristol.

Above him he heard the wounded man groaning in the sickness of his pain again; he heard the voice of that wildcat, Harry Weston, calling hollowly: "Hold him, Danny. I'm coming!"

But now Bristol managed to tear the gun from Miller's hand at last. He struck with the barrel; the warding hand of Miller checked the blow.

He could pull the trigger, of course—but that was a killing almost in cold blood, and he had no appetite for such a slaughter.

He struck again, harder, and part of the length of the steel barrel rang on the skull of Miller.

That game, little man twisted his legs together, kicked out once, and lay still.

IX

There was Rance, the ex-sailor, between him and the door, still, as Bristol came to his feet, charging. The axe was raised again on high, but when Rance saw the leveled revolver, he shrank back against the wall with a groan and threw up a hand before his face.

Bristol, disdaining to touch a man so helpless, ran past him into the open.

Dirk van Wey—where was he? The rest had fought hard enough, but where was Dirk van Wey? It seemed to Bristol that the giant was about to step out from behind the trunk of the big tree. And as the door of the horse shed was torn open, surely Dirk van Wey would spring upon him with his irresistible hands—or a straight tongue of flame would dart at him from the muzzle of van Wey's gun.

He reached the place of the stallion and found Pringle just lurching to his feet, the last of the horses to rise. A saddle and a bridle hung from the peg on the wall. There was no time for the saddle. Even the seconds used for pulling the bridle over the head of the horse were moments in which all the blood in Bristol's heart seemed to flow away. He blessed the stallion for parting its teeth to receive the bit, and with the throatlatch still unfastened, he ran toward the door of the shed again, with the horse trotting willingly behind him.

He saw the form of Harry Weston come running through the doorway of the house opposite him, with a rifle in his hands. And as Bristol swung onto the back of the stallion, he saw the rifle go to Weston's shoulder.

Twice the gun barked, but the bullets sang nowhere near Bristol. As he straightened out the stallion to full speed up the gap, he saw Weston rub a hand across his forehead, as though trying to wipe away the cloud that hung over his eyes. No doubt he was still more than half stunned by the blows that he had received from powerful fists.

Again and again the rifle barked, and this time the bullets stung the air close to Bristol's head. Then the maze of trees and great rocks received him and shut him off from danger.

But where was Dirk van Wey? That question haunted him on the way down the pass. Every moment he seemed to hear the beating of the hoofs of horses behind him. The wind rose and howled through the gap. And it was to Bristol the voice of the giant.

Yet no van Wey appeared.

The stallion went under him like silk. One hardly needed a saddle. For though withers and backbone thrust up, the gait of this daisy cutter was like the motion of a boat down a smooth current.

Leaving the steep descent, he opened up Pringle to a sweeping gallop that poured the hills behind them like moving waves of the sea. With hardly a break, the tall horse maintained that gait until, far before them, Bristol saw the old, squat outline of the ranch house of Joe Graney. The moon was far up the sky now, whitening the hills, and when he came close to the house, he saw the hoof-marked dust in front of it as bright as water under that steady light, with little shadows as black as ink outlining the hollows where horses had stamped at the hitch rack.

There he dismounted and threw the reins. At once the ugly head of Pringle dropped low. He pointed a back hoof and seemed instantly to fall asleep on his feet.

At the door of the house, Jimmy Bristol paused and looked over the sweep of the landscape. The hills swept away in steady succession, and the mountains were half hidden in the moon haze. It seemed impossible that he had started not many hours ago toward the Kennisaw Gap. That must have been in another life, or in a dream.

Yet he could feel a lump on the side of his head and another on his cheek, where the hard fists of Harry Weston had gone home. His whole body was bruised and sore from that tumble down the stairs, and where the grip of Dan Miller had lain on his flesh, it burned as though it had been scorched.

Then he tried the latch, found the door open, and walked into the dimness of the house.

It was not like the damp cold of the stone-and-log building in the Kennisaw Gap. A faint, half-stale odor of cookery hung in the air of the hall. There was a gentle hush, as of sleep. He could almost hear the breathing of the sleepers.

He thought of the girl then and smiled. Weariness could be permitted to come over him now. He could relax for a few moments—although not for long.

Dirk van Wey by this time must know what had happened to his money, his horse, and his men. And Dirk van Wey would follow him around the world to be quits for the defeat. It was only the first trick of a long game that Bristol felt he had won.

In the meantime, he was hungry. He would get to the kitchen, start the fire, and heat some coffee. After that he would have to waken Joe Graney. It would be worthwhile to see the face of the rancher when he looked again on Pringle.

He was almost at the end of the narrow hallway when a door opened. It was the girl.

"Hush, Margaret. It's Bristol," he whispered.

"Ah, thank God," he heard her answer softly. "This will make Dad the happiest man in the world. Look . . ." She pushed open the door to the dining room. A lamp was burning, and through the doorway, big Jimmy Bristol saw the rancher sitting with his head bowed upon one arm, asleep. His mutilated hand was extended before him, palm up. It was like the last act of one in despair, asking alms from an unheeding world.

Something pinched the heart of Jimmy Bristol.

"He wouldn't go to bed," said the girl. "He was in misery. He wanted to ride after you and make you come back. I told him it was too late . . . that he'd never overtake you. And here you are . . . safe." She called: "Father!"

He groaned in his sleep. It was like an echo, to the ear of Bristol, of the sick moaning he had heard from the wounded Lefty Parr on that same night.

The girl rounded the table and touched the shoulder of Graney.

He wakened with a start, jumping to his feet, exclaiming, still half in his dream: "Don't go, Bristol! Don't . . ."

"He's back. He's safe," said the girl.

He rubbed his eyes in confusion, and she began to laugh with such a happiness in her eyes that Bristol seemed invited to join in the mirth.

Joe Graney came to him and gripped him with that deformed hand of his. "Well, this is pretty good. This is pretty good," he said. "I half thought that I'd never . . . Margie, she thought that you wouldn't have the nerve to go right on ahead . . . but I was sure you would. I'm glad that she was right. I kind of thought that I'd sent you off to be murdered. That was the way I felt . . . like a murderer. And here you are back, son."

He blinked his eyes, and there was a moisture in them that stung the heart of Bristol again. But he muttered: "Margie thought I wouldn't go, eh?" He looked at the girl, and she frowned a little, shaking her head.

"No one man could do it. No one man could walk in on them. I knew that, Jimmy."

"Anyway," said Jimmy Bristol, "I brought back some luck for you, Graney. Here's a part of it."

"Hush," said the girl, "or you'll wake him. The stranger."

"Who?" asked Bristol, with his hand in his pocket.

"A man dropped in last evening. We put him up, of course, for the night."

It was on the tip of Bristol's tongue to ask what man it might be, or a description of him, but the act he was engaged in was too important for that. He pulled out the gold pieces and spilled them on the table. "That's only one year's rent," he said. "Van Wey didn't seem to be able to spare any more than that for the moment."

Joe Graney picked up one of the coins, turned it in his hand, and stared helplessly at it.

Then Margaret Graney caught Bristol's arm and shook it a little. Her eyes were starting out. There were white patches of fear in her face. "You went . . . into the Kennisaw Gap?" she breathed.

"Sure," said Bristol, "and Dirk van Wey was glad to see me. I suppose he'd been anxious to pay that rent for a long time. He forked it right out. And the horse, too."

She looked carefully into his face. "There's been a fight!" she gasped. "You've been hurt! Father, do you see that?"

"Wait a minute," said Graney. "Did you say the horse, too?"

"Yes."

"You brought back Pringle with you?"

"He's out at the hitch rack in front of the house."

"Great Moses," murmured Joe Graney. He shook his head, but could not seem to clear the cloud of astonishment that possessed it.

"We'll go out and see the horse," said the girl. There was no joy in her face—only trouble and anxiety.

That was the woman of it, thought Bristol. The terror of the unknown was on her and would take many words to dispel.

"We'll go out and see Pringle. I don't know how you did it, Bristol. I can't even ask yet. But maybe it's the turning point. Maybe it's the beginning of a change . . ." He turned, as he spoke toward the door into the hall, but paused. "We've waked him up. That's too bad," muttered Joe Graney. "Here he comes now."

All that Bristol saw at first was a dim shape that moved among the dense shadows of the hall, obscure as a fish that stirs in dusky waters.

But now the form of the man crossed the doorway into the light of the dining-room lamp, and Bristol recognized the battered face of Sheriff Tom Denton, who stood there with a gun in his hand.

X

What Jimmy Bristol was aware of later was that neither the girl nor her father uttered a single exclamation. But all he was conscious of at the time was the thunderclap in his own brain as he saw the sheriff emerge from the shadows, carrying the gun that was pointed at Bristol's body.

"Just stick 'em up, Jimmy," he said.

And Jimmy Bristol, inch by inch, fought with his hands to make them rise as high as his head.

"Is this right?" said Graney suddenly. "It's in my own house, man."

"It's in your house, but it's in my county," said Denton. "I'm the sheriff, Graney. I didn't tell you when I came, because this gent is the kind that makes friends and keeps them. It's a good thing for the law that I didn't talk too much, either, by the look of things. Bristol, turn your face to the wall."

Jim Bristol obeyed. In the despair that came over him, he pressed his forehead and the flat of his hands against the wall, while he felt the muzzle of the sheriff's gun lodge against the small of his back. All was of the recognized procedure. A large revolver was taken from Bristol's person, to say nothing of a very capable jackknife.

The sheriff stepped back a little. "Turn around, Jimmy," he ordered.

Jimmy, turning, saw the revolver still covering him closely, while in the sheriff's left hand dangled a pair of manacles.

"Hold out one wrist," commanded Tom Denton.

Jimmy Bristol did not move. And now the color was gone from his eyes, and they were a blaze of light.

"You're helpless, and the sheriff means business," said the girl calmly.

He looked suddenly at Margaret Graney and saw that the white of her face denied the smoothness of her voice.

"I mean business, all right, son," said Tom Denton. "I don't wanna do you no harm, but you know what you're wanted for."

Jimmy Bristol held out his wrists, and the handcuffs were rapidly snapped in place.

"That's that," said the sheriff. "And now I guess you're as good as in the death house, Bristol, and God help your soul. I'm sorry for you, at that."

"Death house?" cried Joe Graney. He reached for the arm of the sheriff, who exclaimed: "Don't touch me, Graney! I can see that the boy's done you a good turn. But don't touch me. I belong to the law, just now, and so does he. I've got my job to do, and I'm going to do it."

"Yes," said Bristol bitterly. "Five thousand dollars' worth of a job."

"It ain't the money so much," answered the sheriff, flushing, "but it's the way you made fools of us back there in the town. Beginning with me, you made fools of us all. You might've known that we'd do some riding to get onto your trail."

"I knew. I took the wrong chance," admitted Bristol.

"You knew," said the girl, "and yet you came back here, when you might have ridden on?"

Bristol made a sudden gesture that caused the manacles to clank musically. "Sooner or later my sort of a trail comes to this windup," he told her. "I'm not so sorry."

"That's what you say," said Joe Graney. "But what I know is that I've been the bait in the trap for you. And God forgive me. Sheriff, what's this boy charged with?"

"Murder," said the sheriff bluntly. "The shooting of a gent in Tombstone about three months ago. After that, stealing a few hosses to help him along his way. That's about all." He smiled sourly and added: "Winged a fellow back in town yesterday. Fellow that had trailed him all the way from Tombstone. And made a fool of me, too. The biggest fool that I've ever been. How come you to drill that gent in Tombstone, Bristol?"

"Poker," said Bristol. "The deck of cards on the table wasn't enough for him. He helped himself to extra deals out of his sleeve."

"That so?" murmured the sheriff. "Well, in this part of the world, shooting comes to folks that fool too much with the deal in a poker game. Too bad for you, Bristol. But maybe the jury will do some considering."

"Maybe," said Bristol shortly. "But I'll tell you who'll have to do the considering for all of us if we stay here long."

"Who?" asked the sheriff.

"The coroner," answered Bristol. "That money comes from Dirk van Wey. And outside the door is the horse that Dirk likes better than anything else in this world. Dirk left me to be trimmed by some of his boys. He was testing the lot of 'em. But the test went bad, and I had the luck. He won't let the stuff go, though. If he can guess my back trail, he'll be here before long, and he won't be alone."

"We'll see that horse," said the sheriff.

The whole group moved out into the moonlight, with Bristol marched at the head of the line, the sheriff at his back. So they came into view of the stallion, which stood with hanging head still, and pendulous lower lip.

"That nag?" said the sheriff.

"It's Pringle!" exclaimed Joe Graney. "Pringle, d'you know me, boy?"

The stallion lifted its head suddenly, tilted its long ears forward, and actually whinnied a faint greeting to its master.

Joe Graney began to laugh aloud. "He knows me, Margaret!" he called to the girl.

"Aye," said the sheriff, standing at the side of Pringle and looking over the long lines, the whipcord muscles. "I can get the idea of him better, now. No wonder that van Wey liked him."

"He's ridden nothing but Pringle for two years," said Graney.

"If van Wey's in danger of coming down here, we gotta move," said Tom Denton. "Graney, will you saddle that chestnut and that mule in the barn . . . and my horse? You'll have Pringle, here, and Bristol can take the mule."

The girl ran with her father toward the barn, and the sheriff muttered to Bristol: "I'm sorry about this, son. A low hound of a yaller-toothed coyote that cheats at poker deserves being salted away with lead. I'm mighty sorry. Never heard anything about the crooked poker at the start of your trail."

"There were four of them framing me," said Bristol calmly. "Nothing can be done about it now. They'll all swear black's white. They have to, to save their own hides."

"If you've been up and fronted that thug, van Wey, it'll tell in your favor."

"Of course it will. Life instead of the rope. That's about all the good that it will do me."

"You saw van Wey face to face?"

"I shook hands with him."

The sheriff whistled. "How many went with you?" he asked.

"I went alone."

"Well," said Tom Denton, "either you're a cut above the rest of us, or you're a little light in the head. I've tried three times to get a posse together and clean out that devil of a van Wey. But I never managed to raise three men at a time. It's because everybody knows that van Wey isn't in the game for the money he makes, but for the number of his killings. It's hard to go ag'in a fellow who kills for the fun of it. Here come the horses. Maybe we'll all be glad when we reach town, eh?"

Bristol looked up at the brilliance of the moon and said nothing. He was considering that the moon already had moved forward in the sky since he arrived at the house of Joe Graney, and if Dirk van Wey was the man and the brain that Bristol felt him to be, the outlaw might ride over the nearest hill at any time.

"How many men would he have with him?" asked the sheriff.

"Three, I suppose, or perhaps only two. One of his crowd is sick, and another one has the prison shakes. Here are the horses."

They mounted at once, Bristol on the mule, whose bridle was tied to the horn of the sheriff's saddle, and Graney on the back of the stallion. The girl rode the chestnut, and the sheriff his own low-built, powerful mustang.

The girl passed close to the side of Bristol and whispered: "Do you want to face a trial or to escape tonight on the way?"

He looked closely at her. There was hardly a chance to answer, unless he had been able to think like lightning. So he merely replied with a shake of the head. Whatever happened, he wanted her hands to remain clean.

They went off at a canter, from which the mule continually broke down into the sort of a trot that comes from straight shoulders and the stiffness of age, so that Bristol was continually lagging to the rear. The sheriff kept beside him and urged the mule along with an occasional lash from the quirt. The two Graneys rode ahead on the dim trail.

But the whole party had not gone two miles when Bristol felt, rather than heard, a vibration of hoofs in the distance.

"Somebody's coming, and coming fast," he told the sheriff. "Keep your eyes open. Not many people are likely to be in the saddle at this time of the night."

They dipped from the top of a low hill into a wide hollow, and so climbed the side of a higher eminence beyond. As they angled up the shoulder of it, they gained a wider view of the rolling land behind them, only rarely broken by patches of trees and groups of rocks that glistened in the moonlight. And now, not a mile behind them, they saw three riders come over the brow of a hill, clearly outlined for an instant against the sky, and then lost in the next hollow.

The Graneys had seen the trio. The girl's cry came needle-sharp, and she reined suddenly back beside the sheriff.

"It's Dirk van Wey and two of his men!" she exclaimed. "Take the chestnut for yourself. Give Pringle to Jimmy Bristol. You'll have a fair chance to get into town ahead of them then. And as for father and me, they won't harm us. We're not afraid!"

"It's the one way!" cried Joe Graney. "Dirk van Wey will have the blood of both of you unless you take the best horses and ride like mad for it!"

"And he's likely to have the blood of you two if we leave you behind," said the sheriff. "Heaven knows what's best to do. We're no faster than the slowest horse in the lot."

"You can do one thing," said Bristol. "Take my word of honor to ride into town freely and give myself up after this brawl is over . . . and let me have my parole and my free hands for tonight."

The sheriff groaned. "Graney," he said, "can you handle a rifle?"

"I've lost a thumb from my right hand," said Graney. "I can shoot a rifle, but I only hit a target now and then."

"Ride on. Ride like the devil," said the sheriff. "I'll try to think. The devil's behind this. I never saw worse luck. The devil's in it all." He groaned again as he said it and lashed the mule that carried Bristol.

They topped the hill and swung recklessly down into the small swale beyond it. Again they reached a crest, and looking back, they saw that the three pursuers were near and gaining with a bewildering speed at every moment.

"Make your choice, Sheriff!" shouted Graney. "Make a choice now, or you'll be the death of all of us . . . and free hands for Jimmy Bristol could save us, maybe."

But the sheriff was totally bewildered. He looked at Jimmy Bristol and saw in him a prisoner of price, a captive who would give him fame. He looked behind and saw ruin sweeping up on them.

Finally, with a shout of despair, he drew a key from his pocket and leaned toward Bristol. "What your word of honor's worth, heaven knows, not me," said Tom Denton. "But I'll take it."

"I give you my word," said Bristol. "Fast, man! They're walking up on us."

The sheriff had barely turned the key that gave Bristol the freedom of his hands when they had terrible proof of the nearness of the pursuers. It could not have been more than a snap shot, a long chance taken, but a rifle bullet clipped through the head of Tom Denton's horse. The poor brute dropped and pitched down the slope, throwing its rider from the saddle. Far ahead of the mustang, the sheriff hit the ground and lay like a stone.

XI

"He's sure dead!" shouted Joe Graney. "Bristol, you ride with us! D'you hear me, Bristol?"

Jimmy Bristol had leaped to the ground while the mule was still cantering, and he raced forward to the spot where the sheriff lay.

If Tom Denton were dead, there was no harm in leaving him there on the ground behind them as they fled. But when he pressed his ear to the breast of the stunned body, he heard the faint beating of the heart. It was like a death warrant to Bristol.

"He's living!" he said, without rising from his knees.

"Then we've got to stay by him!" exclaimed Graney, jumping to the ground in turn. "Look yonder, Jimmy! There's a nest of rocks where we can hold 'em off. I'll help you carry him. Margie, slide onto Pringle and burn your way to town as fast as he can gallop!"

What girl, thought Bristol, could have failed to appeal wildly to her father to join her and ride for freedom, leaving the sheriff and the outlawed man to fight it out alone? But no such thought seemed to enter her mind.

Like an athletic boy, she was instantly off the chestnut and onto the rangy form of Pringle. There was no time for her even to touch their hands. She could only cry out a farewell to her father. But to Jimmy Bristol she suddenly threw out her hand, calling: "Jimmy . . . if we never meet again . . .!" Then the sweeping gallop of Pringle carried her away, riding for her own life and for theirs.

If they never met again, what was he to understand by that impulsive gesture? He knew what meaning he would put upon it, and a grim joy began to surge in his heart as he helped Graney lift the body of the senseless sheriff.

The rocks were not far away, an irregular outcropping of small boulders and large that had been exposed by the wash of water down the hollow during the heavy rains. In hard clay and gravel those big stones were embedded, and as the two got their burden to the center of this meager screen, they saw the three riders come over the top of the next hill and plunge at them.

Bristol, on his knees behind a rock, found Graney's rifle thrust into his hands. He fired at the central rider, for it had the great shoulders, the unhuman bulk of Dirk van Wey.

The bullet missed. The instinct of the true marksman told Bristol that he had fired a trifle high and to the right—that commonest of all faults. The second shot would not miss, however, he promised himself as he drew another bead for the same target.

Dirk van Wey and the others, at that first shot, had split their charge and were swerving off to the sides, yet Bristol caught the big outlaw fully in his sights, swung the gun with the target until he knew that the life of Dirk was in the crook of his forefinger, and pulled the trigger.

There was a muffled explosion. The gun jumped like a wounded thing in his hands, and he knew that that good Winchester was hopelessly jammed.

From under his eyes, the three riders swept off to present security and left him there with the injured man and poor Graney, half helpless with that mutilated hand.

He considered the condition of their shelter. There were enough big rocks scattered about to shield them fairly well from any fire directed at them from the level, but high over them towered the head of the hill, where even a child could take control of them, firing sharply angled shots until they were killed, one by one.

"The gun's gone, eh?" asked Graney.

"It's gone," said Bristol curtly. "And you could be off there on the edge of the horizon, riding safe and fast for town."

"Well," said Graney, deliberately taking out a pipe and beginning to load it, "I wouldn't mind living a while longer as a man, but I don't hanker to crawl around the face of the earth as a yellow dog. Taking things the way that they've come, I'd rather be here with you, Jimmy, than sitting on top of a throne with a crown on my head, kicking a couple of prime ministers in the face and ordering up champagne for supper."

Bristol looked at him with that involuntary smile of his that meant well-being of mind and of body.

"All right," he said. "All right." He meant more, far more, than the words said. He saw, in the small speech of Joe Graney, more of the character of the rancher than ten years of other acquaintanceship would have shown to him. That was why he smiled, for he saw that the whole soul of the man was clean, selfless, and sound to the core. He was a proper father of such a girl as Margaret Graney.

If we never meet again! she had cried, as the stallion swept her away to hunt for help in the town. Well, he would extract the best meaning possible from those words, since it was very highly probable that they never would meet again.

He kneeled by the body of the sheriff.

"If he comes to and gets to his feet again," said Bristol, "that will make two and a half of us, Joe Graney. And we can give Dirk van Wey some sort of a fight."

"He won't be getting on his feet again any too soon," said Joe Graney. "There's not much chance of that. Listen to his breathing. Listen to . . ."

The hurt man groaned out at this moment: "Put more wood on the fire, you lazy hounds. You want us all to freeze and . . . Where am I? Where are we, boys? Where . . . ?"

"You're flat on your back. They snicked a bullet through the head of your horse just after you set my hands free," said Jimmy Bristol to him. "We carried you in here among the rocks. Dirk van Wey and two of his thugs are somewhere out there trying to get a shooting position at us. How are you? Can you sit up?"

The sheriff tried to do so, propping himself with his hands until he was supported halfway from the ground. Then he gasped and fell back. "My back's gone," he said.

"His back's gone," said Bristol calmly to Graney, as though the rancher might not have heard. Then he added: "Sheriff, if you can lie on your face and use a rifle that way, you may help to save yourself and the rest of us. Can you manage it?"

"I can try anything," said the sheriff huskily, "as soon as the fireworks stop in front of my eyes." He began to edge himself over, but when he was lying on his side, he fainted and dropped back to his first, inert position.

"He's no more than a bag of sawdust now," said Jimmy Bristol.

"You and me will be the same before long," answered Joe Graney. "Look!" He had his pipe going by this time, and as he puffed at it, he pointed toward the brow of the hill that almost overhung the rocks among which they lay. Utterly black it rose against the brightness of that moonlit sky. And Jimmy Bristol saw a figure scurry from one bush to another.

A silence followed.

"No," said Bristol. "This is about the finish. Except for the sheriff, we might make a break for it and try to run down the hollow to those trees."

"Yes. *Except* for the sheriff, we might do that," said Graney, with an emphasis that Bristol did not miss.

"We're goners, then," remarked Bristol. He sat down beside the older man and made a cigarette. He felt a certainty that he was about to die, and he was more than sure that he could not die in better company.

"Margie . . . she's what I wonder about," said Joe Graney.

"She'll be all right," said Bristol.

"You think so?"

"I know so. A girl like that couldn't do the wrong thing. And any man with a brain in his head would want to marry her. She'll have the whole land to pick from."

"The pick of the land'll have to wait a while, then," said Graney. "You made a kind of an impression on her. She knows that you're back here with me, because you wouldn't ride on through the gap about your own business on the back of Pringle, with a thousand dollars in your pocket. And she's not a girl to forget. You saw her wave to you when she rode away?"

Bristol nodded.

"Well, she meant something by that. This is going to be a black night for us, Bristol. But it's a black night for her, too. She's going to lose a father she's fond of. She's going to lose a man that maybe she's fonder of still."

A rifle cracked above them, sounding strangely far away. At the same instant a bullet kicked up the dirt at their feet. Neither of them moved.

"No, there's no getting away," said Graney calmly.

"If I could get a fair crack at just one of 'em . . . if one of 'em would come inside revolver range," muttered Jimmy Bristol. He reached out and pulled a revolver from the holster at the thigh of the sheriff, and as at a signal, the sheriff roused himself again, groaning once more.

"They won't come in range," said Graney, "unless they keep in cover of those bushes. Instead of being whittled away, maybe it's better to stand up and let them clip us off quick."

"Maybe that's the best way," said Jimmy Bristol.

Another rifle bullet beat the ground.

"That's in the same place," said Graney. "I should think they could shoot a whole lot straighter than that."

"Oh, they can," agreed Bristol. "They mean something by it."

The meaning was announced suddenly from a point not far away and in the huge voice of Dirk van Wey.

"Hey, Jimmy Bristol!" that voice called.

"Here!" called Bristol instantly.

"I guess we got you bozos . . . all of you!" cried van Wey.

"You've got us, van Wey," agreed Bristol.

"Stand up, then."

Bristol rose slowly to his feet. He reached out his hand. Joe Graney mutely gripped it in farewell.

"Where you die don't matter, Bristol," said van Wey. "But if you come over here, I'll give you a favor before you kick out."

"What sort of a favor?"

"The life of either of those fellows that are with you. Either of 'em!"

"He lies," said Graney eagerly. "Don't do it, Jimmy. He wants to torture you before he finishes you. There's more devil in him than in any red Indian."

"Don't go, boy," said the sheriff faintly. "Graney's right. They'll devil you to death if you go there."

Bristol hesitated. If torture were in the mind of Dirk van Wey, there was no doubt that the man would be a consummate artist in his practice of the evil work. Merely to remember the gross, unhuman face of van Wey was enough to curdle his blood.

"You hear me?" shouted van Wey.

He was about halfway up the hill, hidden in deep brush.

"I hear you," said Bristol, still hesitant. "How am I to know that you'll let one of these fellows live?"

"Why, son," answered van Wey, "the fact is that you don't know. The fact is that all you can do is just to take the word of Dirk van Wey. If he don't feel like keeping his word, he ain't going to keep it. Understand?"

"I'm going up to you!" called Bristol.

"Good boy!" said van Wey. "I've got a kind of a reception committee waiting here, all ready for you." And he laughed, a brazen peal that thundered through the still air of the night.

Somewhere out of the distance, a cow began to low mournfully. It was like a ridiculous echo, at which Bristol could have laughed at any other time.

"Don't go, Jimmy," said the sheriff. "Stay here, and we'll both take our medicine with you. Besides, what he promises he won't keep. I *know* him."

But Bristol shook his head. "I've made up my mind," he said. "Any kind of a chance is better than no chance at all. Graney . . . Denton . . . so long, and good luck to you."

With that he stepped straight forward among the rocks and began to ascend the hill.

XII

The brush was taller than it appeared from the rocks below. He was soon swallowed up by bushes that rose as high as his head. And as he climbed, he was aware of a great form that stalked him from behind.

At the top of the hill he came out on a small platform that was so level it looked as though it had been shaved off by human masons. It was solid rock, except for a little sifting of soil that appeared here and there, scarcely deep enough to afford rootage for the grass. At one side of this little plateau rose a great tree, a single plume of the head of the hill. From where Bristol stood, the moon appeared exactly behind the tree, turning its leaves into black shadow and a silver luster.

Under that tree sat two forms, and he was able to recognize them presently as Dan Miller and that terrible, young fellow of the golden hair and the dark-blue eyes—Harry Weston.

And now, behind him, strode Dirk van Wey up the slope of the hill.

"I told you I'd get him, boys," said Dirk van Wey.

"I've got him covered," said Dan Miller from behind his rifle. "None of the rest of you have to worry none. I've got him ready to plant."

"We're going to take some time for that planting," said Harry Weston. "How does he come to be a big enough fool to come up here when you ask him, though? That's what I don't make out."

"Sit down or make yourself easy, son," said Dirk van Wey. "Smoke a cigarette, Jimmy Bristol. I'm kind of glad to see you ag'in."

"Thanks," said Bristol.

He was panting from the climb, but he noticed that the slow labor of the great chest of van Wey had hardly been increased in rhythm. There was no possibility of exhausting the brute, it appeared. His endurance was like his actual strength—extra-human.

"Who's down there behind you?" asked van Wey. He added: "I mean, besides old Joe Graney."

There was no point in hiding the truth.

"The sheriff is down there," said Bristol.

He expected a great outburst of rage. Instead, Dirk van Wey merely nodded his head.

"He's kind of a decent fellow, that Tom Denton is. Got plenty of nerve, too. Three more like him would run me out of the gap. How come you and him didn't join forces ag'in me, Bristol?"

"Because," said Jimmy Bristol, "he had handcuffs on me."

There was a deep shout from Dirk van Wey. It sounded almost like a yell of joy.

"Had 'em on *you?*"

"Yes," said Bristol.

"Wait a minute. Lemme get at something. He had the braces on you and . . ."

"I told you he shot too straight to be honest," said Harry Weston, approaching.

"What they want you for?" asked Dirk van Wey, his face working to an extra hideousness as he asked the question.

"Murder. Shooting a fellow in Tombstone three months ago."

"Good," said Dirk van Wey. "Doggone me, but that's pretty good, all right. I kind of guessed that there was something to you the minute that I laid eyes on you, and that's why I give you a chance to try out the four boys I had along with me. Men, they'd always seemed, to listen to their talk and their bragging. Men, and hard-boiled, was what they wanted to seem. But a lot of fresh-water clams was all that they turned out. Fresh-water clams!" He laughed, and his laughter was a snarl. Then he made a brief, ugly gesture toward the two.

"I banked on 'em . . . I left four of 'em, counting the cook, to trim you to the quick. And you went through 'em like nothing at all. It took Dirk van Wey to run you down. It took Dirk to handle you." He laughed again. The snarl was one of triumph now.

"How's Lefty Parr?" asked Bristol.

"Lefty? He thinks that he's going to die, and I wish he would. But he's going to live. Rance is taking care of him, and he's sure to live. You done him in proper."

"I didn't shoot him," protested Bristol.

"No. That's the howling beauty of it," said Dirk van Wey. "You held him up like a light and let one of his own partners put him out. I never seen such a fool as Weston is . . . and I used to think that he was a bright kid. I'm a fool, too. That's what I am."

"It was dark," said Harry Weston savagely. "It was dark, and there wasn't any fair chance to get at him. That's the only thing that saved his hide. I'd like to have a whirl at him now."

"Would you, now?" asked Dirk, with something almost plaintive in his voice.

"Yeah. I mean it. I'm not afraid of him. I'm not afraid of any man that walks except you, Dirk. And you're not human."

"What about you, Danny?" asked van Wey.

"It goes for me, too," said Dan Miller.

"You'd fight him ag'in, you would?"

"I'll fight him right now," said Miller.

Dirk van Wey pulled from his holsters two revolvers with barrels of an extra length—great guns that would have bent the wrists of most men, although they were mere toys to him.

"Well, boys, you're going to have your chance, and that's why I called Bristol from them rocks, where we could've snagged him dead easy, and no trouble to anybody. You're going to fight him, the pair of you. Understand?"

They blinked at him. There was no answer. Then they stared at one another, but still without comprehending. But the first grim flash of understanding came to Jimmy Bristol as he listened.

"Those two down there," said Dirk van Wey, "which of 'em is to live? Speak up, Bristol. One of 'em has to die, and one of 'em can live. I promised, and my promises go. I promised you the money and the hoss, didn't I? And you got 'em. I didn't say nothing, though, about taking 'em back ag'in." His mirthless grin stretched his mouth once more. He added: "Speak up. Which man is it to be . . . the sheriff or old Joe Graney?"

"Graney," said Bristol slowly. "I suppose it has to be Graney."

"Good," answered van Wey. "I'd kind of miss him if I didn't have him around to cuff now and ag'in. He's used to it, and I'm used to it. It's fine to have him on the old ranch." Then he turned to his two men. "Danny . . . and you, Harry . . . here's your chance. I got the idea when I come back and found him gone with my hoss and the money. Kind of a funny thing, Jimmy. I waited till I thought you'd never begin to bust loose, or the boys would never go after your hide. And then I took a walk, and while I was a ways off, doggone me, but I hear the guns and start back on the run. But I was too late. I only come up in time to hear Lefty Parr yelling and Harry and Dan Miller cussing a little. And so I says to myself right then and there that it's a pity I've missed watching such a good fight. I missed watching you open up them soft-shelled, fresh-water clams. And I says to myself that I'm going to take the first chance and put you together with 'em. Miller!"

Miller started. "Yeah, chief?" he said very mildly.

"You're pretty good with a rifle, ain't you?"

"I've handled a rifle now and then."

"You've kept us in venison, anyways. And now you're going to have a chance to shoot something better'n deer. Him!" He pointed toward Jimmy Bristol.

"Bristol," he added, "are you any good with a rifle?"

"I'm fair."

"Was it you that took the flying shot at me from the rocks?"

"Yes."

"You're good, then. It was an inch from my nose. Why didn't you shoot ag'in?"

"The rifle jammed."

"That's a better reason than no reason at all. Harry, give Jimmy your rifle."

Silently Harry extended the gun.

And then van Wey went on: "You two can have it out with rifles first of all. Then we'll see. Stand up there, back to back."

So they stood together, Dan Miller and Bristol, in the center of the little, moonlit plateau. Each had a Winchester rifle held in both hands, diagonally across the body.

"When I give the word," said Dirk van Wey, "you're going to start marching. I'm going to count to ten, and each of you is going to take a step every time I count. And if one of you tries to take them ten steps faster than I count, and if one of you tries to turn and start shooting before I reach the end of the count, I'm going to put a slug through the head of that fool. Y'understand?"

"I understand," said Jimmy Bristol.

"I understand," said the iron voice of Dan Miller. "Harry, I know this game. Put a bet down on me with the chief."

"I'll bet you a hundred," said Dirk.

"I wouldn't bet on the little runt," said Harry Weston, "except that he's too doggone small to be hit very easy. I'll bet a hundred with you."

"That's a go," answered Dirk. He began to laugh a little as he stood there, enormous, with his great shadow spilled behind him and the wind furling the brim of his hat, so that the moonlight could get at his ugly face.

"Look at the fun I show you, Harry," said Dirk van Wey. "Look at the game I show you. And maybe better stuff than this is going to come afterward. I've got my hundred on you,

Jimmy Bristol. Mind you, Dan Miller is sure a poison rat. You gotta move fast and shoot straight when I count to ten. Start in. One . . . two . . . three . . . four . . . five . . ."

It came to Jimmy Bristol, as he paced those grim steps through the moonlight, with his shadow sloping before him, that a rifle is not, after all, so very much heavier than a revolver. If it had been revolver play, he would hardly have feared for the outcome. He knew exactly what he would do. And if the rifle were longer and heavier, there was the stock that would fit under the forearm.

Suddenly he gripped the weapon in his right hand, alone, with his forefinger on the trigger and the stock extending up under the powerful cushion of his forearm.

"Ten!" shouted the thunderous voice of Dirk van Wey.

Jimmy Bristol whirled, leaping far to the side as he turned and swinging the rifle up like a revolver in his right hand.

Without aim, shooting only by the marksman's sense that he had learned in the handling of a revolver, he took a snap shot at the body of Dan Miller.

The speed of that firing quite eclipsed Miller's return shot. As it was, the sharp-faced little man merely pulled his trigger to fire a blind shot and then spun half around and dropped to one knee, groaning and cursing.

"Finish him!" yelled Harry Weston. "The dirty cur . . . he's double-crossed me and beat me out of a hundred bucks when I'm broke. Finish him, Bristol. Kill him like the dog he is."

"Go on!" shouted Dirk van Wey savagely. "Kill him like a pig, Bristol!"

With his two revolvers, he dominated the scene.

"No," said Jimmy Bristol. "He got that through the shoulder joint, I think . . . and that means he's never going to pull another gun in a fight as long as he walks."

Dirk van Wey shouted with glee. "That's better'n killing him! That means that every Chinaman can kick him in the face. I'm done with you, Miller. You can go rot, for all of me. Now I see what my men have been like. They're glass, is what they are. They're all glass. Nothing but glass." He cursed loudly and then cried: "Now it's your turn, Weston! Stand up and show us what you can do!"

XIII

Harry Weston was not dismayed. He merely smiled and threw back his head until the moon glimmered over his handsome face. He shied his sombrero to the ground.

"I want him!" cried Harry Weston. "Make it knives, chief!"

"Knives!" cried Dirk van Wey. "Why, you got a brain, after all. I ain't seen a knife fight since I was last in Mexico. This is going to be a show. Here, Jimmy. Here's a knife. This Weston is a hot trick with a knife. You wanna watch yourself."

"I'm going to carve him down to my size, and then cut him in two," said Weston, drawing a Bowie knife.

A knife of exactly the same pattern was tossed into the air and landed at the feet of Bristol. He picked it up.

"Down guns!" shouted van Wey. "Shell out, boys . . . on the ground with 'em!"

They laid their Colts on the ground.

"Now at it, wildcats! *Yow!*"

Harry Weston answered that yell with another. He hopped up a little, as though to test the limber speed of his legs. Then he came racing in, swerving a little from side to side, like a snipe flying down the wind. Bristol stood straight as a ramrod, so straight and still that Dirk van Wey yelled: "Watch out, Bristol! He'll cut your heart out!"

Only at the last instant Bristol sprang sidewise, bending his body to avoid the thrust and slashing for the throat. He missed in his turn. They swept in a circle around one another, crouching. Weston leaped in, stabbing and slashing, yelling like a fiend. Bristol gave ground again. He stabbed at the body with the knife in his right hand, but in midair he tossed the knife into his left hand and slashed for the face.

He felt the grit of the keen blade against the bone, and Harry Weston reeled back with a scream. The handsomeness of that face was ruined forever. A dark tide of blood flowed down over it from the forehead.

Dirk van Wey yelled with laughter. "A two-handed man! A two-handed man!" he shouted. "Get out of my sight, the pair of you sick rats. Miller . . . Weston . . . move on! I'm through with you. I've found a man!"

They got on their horses, the two of them, and rode off. The hands of Weston were covering his face as Bristol saw him last. And Miller, bent low in the saddle, gripping his wounded shoulder, was leading the way. So they dropped below the shoulder of the hill and out of sight.

"I've found a man," went on the booming voice of Dirk van Wey. "And a two-handed-man! Boy, I want you, and I'm going to have you. You and me do business together. You and me go halves. That's what I think of you! Halves!"

"Or else what?" asked Bristol.

"Or else," said the giant, "you drop that knife, and we have it out with bare hands." His laugh once more was thunder as he said it. For what hands could match his?

But it seemed to Bristol that he saw, in that instant, the calm face of Joe Graney as he had sat among the rocks, puffing at his pipe and waiting for death, resigned utterly. And he saw the girl throwing out her hand as she cried: "If we never meet again . . ." Well, if he joined Dirk, they would never meet again. He would never dare to stand before her. He hurled the knife from him as far as he could fling it. "Come on, van Wey!" he called.

Dirk van Wey nodded.

"Maybe it's better this way," he said. "Maybe I was a fool to think of anything else. Maybe it's better to have the feel of you in my hands. I'm going to break you, kid. I'm going to tear you and twist you in two . . . slow and easy."

He thrust his two revolvers into their holsters along his thighs as he strode in.

To flee was impossible. Those guns would be out and spitting death if Bristol ran. In a frenzy he leaped straight at van Wey, all his might going into the drive of his right arm. Fair and truly, he smote the corner of Dirk van Wey's chin. It was like striking a rock. There seemed no give in the head of the giant, but a sharp agony shot up the arm of Bristol, and he knew that he had broken the bones across the back of his hand. With the right he could not strike again in that battle.

He danced back, and Dirk van Wey followed, shouting, his face insane with the battle lust. His hat was off. His long, greasy hair flew back in the wind of his own running. He did not try to strike, but only to grasp with his hands, and once they secured their grip, the battle was ended, as Bristol well knew.

"Stand up to me, damn you, or I'll salt you first and tear you up afterward!" shouted Dirk van Wey. And one of his hands dropped for an instant toward a holster gun to emphasize the point of the threat.

That instant was used by Bristol to leap straight in and drive his left to the face. It found not the jaw, but the cheekbone, and split the flesh. The shock of the stroke merely turned the arm numb.

The great hand of the giant found a hold on the arm with which Bristol had struck. The fingers of van Wey seemed to find the bone through the flesh. Only by hurling himself wildly away could Bristol gain freedom, and the empty sleeve remained in the hands of van Wey.

He threw the rag from him and rushed on, bellowing. He was drunk with the fighting now. Fists were useless against that head of iron and that body of well-ribbed India rubber. Bristol flung his whole body at the knees of the giant.

Van Wey went down under the impact, his head hitting the ground with terrific force. For the first time Bristol was on top. At last the balance had tipped in his favor.

Desperately the giant clawed at the revolver whose butt appeared above the edge of the leather holster that was strapped to his thigh. But Bristol knocked aside his hand and grabbed the butt of van Wey's six-gun.

Dirk van Wey felt the drawing of the revolver and yelled with rage and fear. With a swing of his great shoulders, he flung Bristol from him, and as Bristol struck heavily and rolled, he saw van Wey stride after him, his other gun in hand, shooting as he came.

The stolen revolver was in the broken right hand of Bristol, but he could not waste time in shifting it to his left. The moon blazed against his eyes, but he could not even turn on his side to get a better light. He had to fire half blindly at the vast silhouette, and he knew, as he pulled the trigger, that he had fired lower than the body of the outlaw.

Yet van Wey, striding forward, at his next step crumbled suddenly and lay face downward on the rock.

It was as though a miraculous hand from the sky had struck him down. There was no sense of triumph in Bristol as he leaped to his feet and leveled his gun on the mark. There was only a profound sense of gratitude to—he knew not what. Fate, he might call it, or the great god of chance.

The giant propped himself up on both arms. He was quite calm. He seemed almost contented and happy as he boomed out: "Well, kid, you snagged me. I guess you busted the bone of the leg. Poison in both hands, eh? Oh, you're the real two-handed man."

And to the bewilderment of Bristol, Dirk van Wey began to laugh. It was as though the beast of him had been so contented by the battle that he cared not for his own defeat, his pain, or the death at the hands of the law that might now loom before him.

* * * * *

They put the wounded sheriff on a litter when the men from the town reached the place, with the girl on Pringle, showing them the way in the gray of the morning.

They made another horse litter, on which they heaved the bulk of Dirk van Wey.

Then they stood in consultation.

"This here is a wanted man," said the deputy sheriff to Tom Denton, pointing toward Jimmy Bristol. "They want him pretty bad, too, down there in Tombstone."

"They don't want him so bad, brother. They don't want him so bad," drawled the sheriff. "It was a card game, by what I've last heard. And down there in Tombstone they've likely found out a good deal about the kind of *hombres* that were playing against Bristol in that game. Murder was what Bristol was sitting with in that game."

"Five thousand dollars!" groaned the deputy. "Five thousand whole dollars locked up in that hide, and we gotta let it go?"

"We can keep that hide in jail," said the sheriff, "till he's wanted for trial, or out on bail. And when the gents in Tombstone hear what Bristol has done in this part of the world, they're going to hand him his freedom on a silver platter."

The other men grinned, and the rising sun gilded their lean, brown faces. The girl, who had brought all this power of the law to the place, drew closer to Bristol, watching him with the grave happiness of possession in her eyes.

"Come here, kid!" roared Dirk van Wey. "Come here, Jimmy."

Bristol stepped to the litter and looked down into the brutal mirth of that grinning face.

"What tickles me," said Dirk van Wey, "is that you done it with my own gun. I'm going to be laughing at that when the rope strangles me. Swipes my gun offen me and drops me with my own gat."

"You went for the Colt first," Bristol reminded him.

"Oh, yeah, yeah," said Dirk van Wey. "But why bring up the little things? It was a good fight, was what it was. So long, kid. See you in hell, if not sooner."

The horses that supported the litter of van Wey started on.

"Who's going to guard Bristol?" asked the efficient deputy sheriff.

The sheriff bellowed at the deputy: "Why, you fool, he doesn't need guarding, does he? D'you think he's going to try to run away from all the glory that newspapers and the whole West can give him? D'you think that he's half-wit enough to run away like that when a week in jail will make him free forever? But hold on . . . wait a minute. I'll give him a guard, at that. I'll give him a guard that looks as though she'll keep him in hand the rest of his days. Miss Graney, will you take hold of Jimmy Bristol and deliver him safe and sound at the jail?"

She laughed at the sheriff joyously and without shame. She and Bristol were already on their horses when Joe Graney shouted: "Wait a minute! I'll come along with you brats, so's you don't miss the way!"

They did not pause, but let their horses go on at the softest of dogtrots. Now and then, of a mutual impulse, the girl and Bristol would look at one another, but as a rule they stared straight before them, as though they were alone in a great space and had before them the longest journey in the world.

The Black Muldoon

When Frederick Faust's "The Black Muldoon" was first published in Street & Smith's *Western Story Magazine* in the issue for September 30, 1922, it was under the byline Peter Dawson. It is probable that Frank Blackwell, who edited the magazine, provided the Peter Dawson byline for Faust, and it was the only time in all of his publishing career that a Faust story ever appeared under this pseudonym, the name of a popular brand of Scotch whisky. Some fourteen years later, Jonathan H. Glidden was given the same pen- name by his agent, which he used throughout his career. "The Black Muldoon," under whatever byline, remains a gripping narrative in which Faust explored the urgent question of what ultimately takes precedence in a person's life: nurture, genetics, psychology, character, temperament, or fate.

I

His day had begun at 5:00 in the morning, but 11:00 at night found Jefferson Peters still at work over his ledger. Sometimes, out of the upper story and rear rooms of the old crossroads hotel and general merchandise store, a piercing, small rhythm of sound worked down to him. Whenever he heard it, Jefferson Peters dropped his pen and folded his hands with nervous fingers and looked into the future with a falling heart. Upstairs were new-born twins, small, pink bodies possessed of strangely lusty lungs.

Over them leaned Kate, his dear wife. Three lives depended upon young Jefferson Peters.

No wonder, then, that his stomach grew hollow and his throat dry. The day when the minister pronounced them man and wife had been bad enough, for on that day he had taken upon his not overly broad shoulders the responsibility of another life. But that day was nothing compared with this. Two lives, although so new, two mortal souls although so lately come into the world—it seemed to poor Jeff Peters that their smallness was a dreadful thing. Out of his work, their bodies must find the means to live and grow; out of his soul, their souls must have sustenance.

A wan ghost of his face suddenly stared out at him from the wall. He saw colorless lips, thin, pinched cheeks, hollow eyes. It was his image in the little mirror that hung on the opposite wall, but nevertheless, it seemed to Jeff Peters a ghost portentous of ruin and dismay. He stood up from his desk where he had labored so long and so futilely to make the figures for that month show a real profit, and lifting the lamp above his head, he looked eagerly about him.

It was a large room, filled with salable articles. He took heart at once. Yonder, blue and red and yellow rolls of ginghams and calicoes should clothe the figures of the women of the town of Custis sooner or later. There were sleek-barreled Colts to make the hearts of young cowpunchers jump, to say nothing of long, spoon-handled spurs, rifles, and shotguns, ropes, boots, and a thousand articles of saddlery. In a far corner glimmered the steel blades of hoes and spades and shovels for those who kept vegetable gardens. There were augers for digging postholes, saws, hammers, barrels of nails.

Adjoining this came the hardware department, where one could find anything from pairs of Dutch ovens to rolling pins.

Beyond this, again, was the colorful and shimmering department of the little pharmacy, rich in patent medicines—a thousand bottles, and each with contents of a different hue. Every inch of the floor space was crowded with the necessaries of cow-country life. And from the very ceiling hung a myriad other things. Yes, there was a plentiful stock on hand, and it would sell at handsome prices. But, alas, it would not sell at all until the gala days of the fall roundup. Could he hold out that long? He lowered the lamp with a sigh, while the shadows swept across all the colors in his store and illumined no more than the one, sharply defined circle upon the desk where he had been working.

There came a knock at the door, and Jeff Peters jerked up his head in surprise, for the men of Custis had various bad habits, such as taking goods and failing to pay for them until two or three years later, but they had never yet shown a fondness for late shopping hours. Red-eye was the only thing purchased after dark. It was probably someone who wanted a room for the night, and although this was not the entrance to the hotel section of the building, Jefferson Peters hurried to the door and unlocked and opened it, holding the lamp high, partly to illumine his smile of welcome and partly so that he could see the other.

He found himself looking up half a head higher than he would have looked for the average man. The stranger brushed past him into the room and, with a flirt of his heel, smashed the door shut. He was broad in proportion with his height, a man so large that, although he was hardly as old as the storekeeper, his bulk gave him great dignity. He was dressed in a cowpuncher's usual outfit, well-made boots covering his feet, while a great slicker, gleaming with rain, swept over the rest of his body and masked his arms, which seemed to be folded. The rain had soaked the brim of his sombrero until it drooped about his face—a wild and handsome face with sleek black mustaches and long black hair and black eyes, now glimmering at Jefferson Peters in the lamplight.

"Ah, Lord!" groaned the poor storekeeper as he looked upon the giant. "I'm done for." And, stepping back, he threw up his arms as far as he could strain them above his head. "Don't shoot, Muldoon," he began to gasp out. "Don't shoot. I'll show you where the cash . . ."

"Don't be a fool," said Muldoon. "I don't want your cash. You know me, then?"

"Of course I remember you, Bill," said the storekeeper, bringing down his hands by inches and keeping them in a quivering state of alertness to jerk them above his head at the first command. "I remember you at school, Bill, as well as I remember myself."

The other produced a hand from beneath the slicker and pushed back his mustaches until they glistened again and bared a smile that was half amusement and half pure contempt. There was a stir beneath the slicker and a faint sound. The smile of Muldoon vanished, and, tossing the oilcloth over his shoulder, he revealed that he carried in his left arm a young infant. It put out both tiny fists and began blinking at the light. Muldoon thrust an immense forefinger in front of the child, and the finger was instantly clutched.

"Got a fine grip," asserted Bill Muldoon. He lifted his head and grinned at Jeff. "Hangs on like a bulldog . . . hanged if he don't. He's going to have the grit, this kid."

"Most likely he will," said Jeff Peters flatteringly. "He sure will have it if he's got any of your blood in him, partner."

Muldoon received this communication with an undisguised sneer of scorn. "Peters," he said, "the kid'll be yapping in a minute or two more. And I got to be away before that happens. Listen to me! You remember two years back when you come down one morning and found the lock on your door busted?"

"I remember."

"That was laid to me. The fools! If I'd busted the lock, wouldn't I have gutted the store, no matter if the sheriff was in town that night? Sure I would. Matter of fact, the boys started to raid the store, but I recollected you at the school and the way you used to help me at arithmetic. Figures never done no good with me, anyhow. I say, I remembered you all at once, and I decided that the gang could get along without ruining you."

"That was mighty good of you, Muldoon. It sure was," said Jeff, his voice shaking under his effort to seem cordial. He did not believe a word of it, but it might mean death if he seemed to disagree.

"Well," said Muldoon, "you might say I done you that good turn, looking to the future for a time when maybe I'd have my back against the wall and would need a friend."

"Nobody would ever say that," said Jeff Peters, forcing a noise-less laugh. "What could I do for a gent like you, I want to know?"

"More than you ever thought of doing," said Muldoon. "Look at this here."

He moved his hand from the grip of the child and doubled it into an immense fist. Instantly the baby balled its own pudgy fists and struck at the hovering threat. Bill Muldoon chuckled softly at the sight.

"All nerve and fire," he declared, "that's what little Jerry is made of. Now step up and take a closer look at him."

"He's sure a buster," said Jeff, bending a little as though on rusted joints.

"Does he look like any other Muldoon you ever seen or heard tell of?" went on the big man.

"Why, come to think of it, he's got the same sort of look around the head."

Muldoon broke into hearty-but-controlled laughter. "There ain't any chance of the womenfolk coming down here, is there?" he asked, breaking off his laughter and frowning.

"I dunno . . . no, I hope not," said Jeff Peters, turning deadly pale. "Leastwise, they wouldn't tell nobody that they'd seen you here, Bill."

Muldoon cursed in a heavy whisper, as though a sudden rage half stifled him. "You little fool, Peters," he said when he could speak. "D'you think that I'd harm womenfolk? Man, ain't you got no sense?"

Jeff Peters was paralyzed by the dread of what his mistake might now bring forth. He could not speak.

"I ask you to look again," he said. "D'you ever hear of a Muldoon that didn't have black hair and black eyes?"

"I disrecollect," said Peters, choking. "I dunno that I ever have, now that you mention it."

"Lord," groaned the giant, "what a man to have the bringing up of a Muldoon! But look again. Ain't them eyes as blue as the sky in the evening, I ask you? Or blue as a lake in the mountains?"

"They sure are."

"Jeff," said the other suddenly, with such a change of voice that Jeff Peters for the first time had the courage to look up into the eyes of his guest, "old man . . . he's the son of Mary Conrad, that was my wife."

"That girl with the yaller hair that lived over to Coffeytown? I ain't heard that you married . . ."

"Nobody else ain't heard. And she died giving birth to Jerry, and so we can't prove to 'em, now, how happy we'd've been. I got the marriage certificate, though, and nailed it to the door of the church in Coffeytown. Then I stole Jerry, and I come away."

He began to breathe very heavily and walked up and down the room with a rapid and irregular step. Jeff Peters turned his head to glance after the outlaw, and he dared not speak. He winced away when Muldoon paused before him.

"Jeff, when I come riding through the night, I got to thinking that what kills the Muldoons is the knowing that they're Muldoons. There ain't been a one of 'em for nigh onto fifty years, now . . . not a single one of the menfolk of the Muldoons . . . that have died peaceable in bed like a man should. They've gone with their boots on, speaking by and large, and they've gone down hell-raising. But I ask you man-to-man, Jeff, is it the blood that does it, or ain't it just that they know they're Muldoons? And when they walk out with other gents, they're watched all the time like they were snakes about to strike. Yes, sir. When I was a little kid in the school, you remember how the whole tribe of the Saunders boys jumped you that day, and how I come running to help you? And, just because I was a Muldoon, not one of the Saunders tribe would stand to me. They all turned and run. Well, when a man grows up, feeling all the time that he's stronger than other men, the time is sure to come when he can take what he wants by might. D'you understand the drift of this, Jeff?"

"It's all clear, Bill."

"It does me a pile of good to hear you talk up like that, Jeff. Well, when I come riding through the night, I say with the wind in my face, and poor Mary . . . Lord bless her . . . lying dead behind me . . . and looking down on me out of heaven, if there is a heaven, d'you see? When I come through the night thinking to myself, Jeff, what I done was to say that

Jerry must change his name and live his life never dreaming that he's a Muldoon. Could that be done? It didn't look none too easy to work. And then I asked myself who would take the upbringing of him? Who would want to do a kindness to a black Muldoon? I says that to myself, and then I recollected your face, Jeff. I remembered some good turns that I'd done you in school, and I remembered some good turns I'd done you since . . . like the night when I kept the gang from cleaning up on your store . . . d'you see?"

Jeff Peters tried to speak. His throat was so dry that he could not utter a sound and only nodded.

"And so I've come to you, Jeff . . . and now that I'm here, tell me what you'll do?"

Still Jeff could not speak. Was he asked to raise a Muldoon? He hardly knew what was asked.

"Will you raise him as your own son, and tell nobody in the world where you got him, more'n that you found him on your steps?"

"Bill . . ."

"And here's something that would go along with him."

He tossed a thick bundle of bills into the hands of Jeff Peters. The glance of Peters, falling, clung upon the denomination of the outer bill . . . fifty dollars on that slip of paper, and so many other slips beneath.

"That whole roll . . . I dunno how much there is in it . . . if you swear to me that you'll raise him and not ever tell a soul who is his father."

"Kate . . ." began Jeff Peters.

"Not even your wife. She's a good woman, but there ain't no woman good enough to hear the secrets of a black Muldoon and keep 'em."

"Give me the boy," said Jeff Peters. "And, so help me heaven, I'll try to raise him like my own boy, by the name of Jerry Peters."

"And if it should come out that a story was to go about saying what his real name was, d'you know what I'd do, Peters?"

"But it'll never come out!"

"If it did, Jeff, I'd ask no questions, but I'd come gunning straight for you. D'you understand?"

"I understand, Bill."

"Then take Jerry."

The soft, warm bundle was placed in the arms of the storekeeper.

"Now swear, Jeff."

"I swear, Bill."

"May the money do you a pile of good," said the big man with a peculiar smile. That smile vanished as he leaned and looked closely into the face of the strangely cheerful and silent infant. "And may Jerry see little of me? Between now and the day I bump off, hang me if I don't hope, for Mary's sake, that he never lays them blue eyes on me."

He turned and strode out of the room. The instant the door was closed, the storekeeper, devoured with anxiety, placed the child on the desk. There he rolled unheeded, scattering the precious papers over which Jefferson Peters had been working so patiently.

With his hands free, the latter hurriedly opened the roll of bills that the outlaw had given to him. The wrapper bill, as he had seen before, was a wrinkled fifty . . . but the bills within were simply a sheaf of $1 notes. Even in so great a crisis of his life, a black Muldoon had been a rascal. The poor little storekeeper raised his despairing hands to the heavens. Here was an added mouth in the nest. And, besides, what earthly explanation could he offer to Kate?

II

Eight years showed Jeff Peters at exactly the same poundage, with exactly the same puckered and wistful brows. His hair had grown a little gray. His cheeks were a trifle more lean and wrinkled, but otherwise his face was the same. His back was somewhat bowed, now, but on the whole he seemed no nearer the breaking point than ever. For he was one of those men who anticipate the worst, always. And therefore, when the worst came, it was never a shock. It was impossible for him greatly to succeed, because he never dared greatly hope, but for the same reasons, more or less, he could not possibly be a complete failure. For eight years he had carried the burdens of a wife, his twin boys, and Jerry Muldoon who had been left to him, and who passed in the eyes of the world as an adopted son calling himself Jerry Peters. He was never given cause to doubt that his parentage was other than that of the two husky youngsters who played with him every day. So far no one in the village of Custis had taken upon himself to tell Jerry of his mysterious origin.

It was recess at the school, and Kate and Jeff Peters sat by the teacher's desk. She was the proper mate for her spouse. Her square and placid brow as yet showed no sign of a wrinkle. For his wasting form she made amends in a steadily increasing amplitude of the waistline. She was not yet exactly ponderous, but neither could she be termed active. She carried with her one remaining quality from her girlhood spent on a ranch, and that was a straight and piercing glance that, on occasion, thrust her husband through to the soul and made that soul tremble. But, although she understood her power, be it said in her favor that she rarely abused it. She exercised her strength not more than once a year, as a sort of secret holiday pleasure.

But she had no reticence about abashing the schoolteacher. The latter was newly out of normal school, a mere child, eager as a hawk and keen as a whip, but rather painfully conscious of her youth as a handicap placed between her and the accomplishment of great ambitions. And schoolteaching was to Elsie Dennis a great ambition accomplished. Three generations of drudgery lay in the immediate past of Elsie. If instinct is an inherited thing, all of Elsie's desires should have turned in the direction of scrubbing floors or, at most, cooking in ranch grub wagons. Instead, she had risen by force of detestation of all she found around her and had turned to a future of higher education. Had Elsie been equipped with a pretty face, her way would have been far easier.

As it was, Elsie's round, serious countenance was set on the end of a long, scrawny neck, along which the unfleshed tendons played in and out whenever she moved her head. Weak eyes, outworn by the labors of prodigious reading, blinked feebly behind the great lenses of her glasses. Her skin was sallow. Her forehead was wrinkled with the anguish of mental labor. Her bony hand was tremulous and cold. Her figure was chiefly a matter of lines running straight up and down.

In spite of appearance, Elsie Dennis had a soul of fire. She could speak of an example of arithmetic or a lesson in geography with a flaming enthusiasm that shortened the breath of her pupils. She felt her inward fires quenched, well nigh, by the presence of Mrs. Jeff Peters. That lady, knowing nothing of books, had fortified herself with a high disdain. As a matter of fact, she was afraid to praise the gaunt schoolteacher, because she feared that an expression of praise would be for the wrong thing and thereby expose her ignorance. But she knew, as many wiser persons have also learned, that it is easy to damn with criticism and appear intelligent.

"As for Harry and Jack," said Elsie Dennis, "I don't know which is the better." She was answering one of Mrs. Peters's very direct questions. "Harry is slower, but then, he works harder. Jack is much quicker, but he is a little lazy . . ."

"Miss Dennis," cried Mrs. Peters, "I dunno how you can talk about Jack being quicker! Anybody that's ever seen the two of 'em around horses . . ." She stopped, breathless with indignation.

"I've no doubt," said Elsie Dennis in her most gentle voice, "that Jack may be more apt with horses, but with books . . . you see, it isn't exactly the same with books and with horses. They're so different."

Mrs. Peters sat back with a superior sniff intended to indicate that no matter what the teacher said, she had her doubts about it.

"Well," said Mr. Peters, reverting to the immediate cause of their call at the school, "we want to know what can be done to bring up their standing. There ain't any natural reason, so far as I can see, why my boys shouldn't be right up with the leaders in their class."

"If they got the right sort of teaching," appended his better half.

Elsie Dennis confined her answer to the father. Somehow, it was always thrice as easy to talk to a man.

"The reason they don't lead . . . oh, it would be hard for any boy really to lead so long as Jerry Peters is in his class." Her eyes shone as she spoke. She threw back her head with a fine little outburst of enthusiasm, which for the instant, made her actually pretty. "Oh, what a boy he is," she cried softly. "Sometimes he stares at me so hard when I'm talking or reading to the class that I think the words are being printed on his brain."

She looked down to the parents. She found that their faces were utterly blank and cold. It was Elsie's first term at the little school. She had not yet learned that Jerry was only an adopted child. And poor Elsie, bewildered, stared at the two in amazement. She knew that parental likes and dislikes are often hard to understand, but how any human beings could prefer such children as Jack and Harry to that restless flame of a boy, Jerry Peters—that was indeed beyond her.

"But with a great deal of special care," she concluded lamely, "I think that Harry and Jack may be brought up in time. They've improved a lot over their last year's record already."

"If Jerry has been favored so much," said Mrs. Peters, fixing upon poor Elsie Dennis her frostiest glance, "it's no wonder that little Harry and Jack are backward. Children can't be expected to get on when they're neglected, Miss Dennis."

Elsie Dennis crimsoned. Her lips trembled.

"And as for even comparing Jack, for quickness, with Harry," said the mother, "why . . ."

She made an eloquent pause. Her spouse bit his lip and, stirring in his chair, cast anxious glances from one to the other. He foresaw a storm, and he almost equally dreaded the lightning cuts of Kate when they were directed at the head of another. He never knew when a random bolt would strike him.

"Dear little Jerry," went on Mrs. Peters, "is such a mischief . . . but, if you put up with that . . ." She paused again, sternly.

"I try to keep discipline," said Elsie Dennis. "Jerry is high-spirited . . . that is all." Her color was gone now. Her fighting instinct was aroused. Another side fling at Jerry would bring fire from her.

Here they were interrupted by a shrill clamor in the school-yard, followed by utter silence and then the scurry of many running feet converging to a point. One keen voice pierced the air: "Fight!"

Elsie and her two visitors ran to the door of the school. They were in time to see the slender form of Jerry bristling up to another boy of far-greater bulk. The other youngsters of the school were scampering to form a circle, the boys pressing to the center, the girls at the outer rim on tiptoe, terrified and delighted.

"William!" cried poor Elsie Dennis. "Don't you dare to strike Jerry Peters! William, do you hear me?"

As well call to a thundering storm. At that instant, big William smote in hearty earnest at the fire-red head of Jerry with such effect that Jerry tumbled head over heels in the dust, and there was a shout to witness the fall. Prominent among the rejoicers were Harry and Jack Peters, who saw many a downfall of their own now about to be requited with a vengeance.

But Jerry had come to his feet as by magic, and before William could follow his first advantage, he was assailed by a hail of fists. The air was thick with the showering blows. William, smiting in roundabout fashion, with eyes closed, struck nothing but utter emptiness, and all the time those hard, stinging little fists were cracking against his face. A trickle of red began to pour down from his nose. Both eyes and his mouth puffed. And then, retreating and raising a hand to his face, the fingers came away stained with gore. The sight completely unmanned him. A loud yell of terror issued from his lusty throat. Turning on his heel, he fled for safety.

He would have gained it, perhaps, had there not been that circle of witnesses. But they impeded his course, and before he had taken half a dozen steps, there was a red-headed fury upon his back. Down he went with a final shriek of mortal anguish and fear.

Elsie Dennis and the Peterses, in the meantime, had hurried down from the front door of the school. All this part of the brief fight they had seen to the point when stout William crashed to the ground, and now, as they went forward, the shrill shout of the onlookers turned to a cry of dismay in which the voices of the older boys predominated.

What Jeff Peters, brushing his way through the tangle, found was William lying flat on his back and making faint gurgling sounds, while the hands of Jerry were buried deeply in his throat. William was far gone. His eyes were wide and popping out, his face was purple, his mouth was distended as he gasped in vain for air that would not come, and the older boys, in alarm, were trying to tug the conqueror away from his victim. But he clung like a leech.

It required the entire force of Peters to tear Jerry away, and then it was to divert the force of the attack to himself. There was a wild and mighty flailing of little fists at him. At length, dismayed, he brushed them away and captured the warrior.

But by this time, the passion of Jerry had broken into outright grief. Suddenly he began to weep. He pointed with mingled rage and disdain at the prostrate and gasping form of William.

"He said," gasped out Jerry, "that I haven't any father or mother, and that I just happened along and you found me, Dad. And I . . . I'll kill him unless he takes it back!"

"Jefferson Peters!" called his wife. "I hope you'll thrash that young man within an inch of his life. Look at the condition of William Jones. Why, in another ten seconds there would have been a tragedy. Why . . ." She became speechless. The real nearness of the catastrophe stopped her usual flow of words.

But her husband had picked up Jerry and carried him to a little distance, and now he put him down with a suddenness that seemed to come from his weakness. His face was gray, and he was trembling.

"Mother," he said to Kate, "I guess this ain't the time for a thrashing. There'll have to be a talking first. Or maybe it's best not to talk, even. Blood will out. It ain't poor Jerry's fault. Blood will out." He took Jerry by the hand, silencing the clamor of Mrs. Peters with a single gesture. "I'll take this matter in hand," he declared. "Let me manage it. Miss Dennis, we'll take Jerry out and home for the day."

They left the poor schoolteacher, pale and trembling, with concern for her favorite. She followed them to the corner of the yard, saying over and over: "Something went wrong. We all have our outbursts. Oh, Mister Peters, you won't be too hard on him?"

Jerry cast a wan and unhappy look after Elsie Dennis as they departed, but he said not a word and walked, stiff and straight, down the street ahead of his foster parents.

"And now, Jefferson Peters," whispered his wife sternly, "I'd like to know about the real father and the real mother of that boy. How come you been telling me for eight years that you didn't know?"

"Kate," said her husband, "you got to take my plain word for it. If you learn who his father was, it'll scare you plumb to death. And . . . I wish to heaven that somebody, besides me, could tell him that you and me ain't his real father and his real mother."

III

The best way to make a secret delectable is to surround it with terrors if it is revealed. The one room we are forbidden is the one we truly desire to enter. And so it was with Mrs. Peters.

Yet fifteen years more passed, and the question that devoured her soul was never answered. Sometimes, to be sure, there came to her a poisonous doubt that Jeff Peters himself might be the father of the boy. But that doubt never endured long. She knew that her husband was not a good actor; the fear with which he referred to the true parent of Jerry could not have been assumed. Therefore, during the fifteen years, she held her council.

In fact, the knowledge that her husband had guarded a great secret all this length of time had established her respect for him upon a foundation of rock. Hitherto, she had felt rather contemptuous. But thereafter she came to believe that, no matter how weak he was in appearance, there was a mysterious strength about him that was worthy of respect.

Moreover, of late, Jerry had proved to be far from a bad investment. Jack and Harry had grown into fine, young range riders no better and no worse than a thousand others. But Jerry was different. He was a man in ten thousand.

Ever since that day of the fight, the character of Jerry had changed. He had become more sober, more quiet. Even at the age of eight he had seemed to understand that the mystery of his parentage would prove a weight hereafter. The world at large saw in him, at the age of twenty-three, a mighty-limbed young Samson with a clear blue eye and hair like blowing flame. It saw in him a bulwark of the community, a strength and support for Custis. No longer would they be unrepresented at steer-roping and mustang-riding exhibitions. In fact, they were turning to Jerry in the confident expectation that he would put them on the map.

Yet this universal esteem and all the prowess of his six-feet-two of strong muscle and bone had not served to turn the head of the young giant. Mere flattery could not affect him since that day when his foster father had told him that his real father and mother were unknown. Since that time an undercurrent of melancholy had been established in his nature. It had made him more quiet. It had tamed him, so to speak, and it had given him an air of command that was felt and admitted among young fellows of his own age.

He had developed habits of thrift from which the Peters family profited hugely. A venture at prospecting in his eighteenth year had given him a partnership in a mine that he turned over to Jeff Peters, and that partnership had become a handsome business. In reality, it was the source of Jeff's prosperity in his later life, although he carefully concealed from Jerry all knowledge of the handsome dimensions of the gift. For he and Mrs. Peters had decided at once that it would not do to allow Jerry to conceive that he had repaid all the years of care that had been given to him by a single stroke. And, by concealing the size of the donation from him, they continued to incur benefits. They became a prominent family in the town of Custis simply for the reason that Jerry brought home with him a good portion of their distinguished visitors.

What ambitious legislator could pass through the town of Custis without looking up that brilliant youngster who had won a second at the national horse-breaking contest in his twentieth year, and who had won a first on two successive years thereafter? What sheriff or federal marshal could come nearby without dropping in on so deft a marksman? Those who Jerry met, the rest of the Peters family met likewise, with the result that they were in what Mrs. Peters, more than the rest, felt to be true social clover.

As for the immediate future of Jerry, he had only to choose one of a dozen openings. He could go into lumber or cows or mining, or he could play politics or start any one of a number of careers. For men of established position had their eyes upon him. To enlist the youth would, they felt, be guaranteeing their own futures. Honesty, strength, patience—what more could be asked?

When they put these questions to Jeff Peters, the worthy storekeeper would nod and keep his own council. But all those years he had been waiting—for fifteen mortal years he had been unable to forget the picture of William, flat on his back, and the small fists of Jerry in the very act of throttling the other. That had been an indubitable outbreak of the bad blood of a black Muldoon, he had felt. And he had been waiting for another outburst, only wondering how the lightning would strike. If a child of eight, in a passion, had come so close to murder, what would this hard-handed giant do? And should he, in the meantime, risk the wrath of a black Muldoon in order to warn the boy of the bad blood that was in him?

He put off what might have seemed to others a duty, and the result was that he was out of town when the first great blow fell. A man on an outworn mustang, with a crimson-stained rag tied around his head and a shirt encrusted with red, spurred into town with tidings that a black Muldoon had just swept down with his gang upon New Custis, higher in the mountains, and blown up the safe in the store. It was the first time in twenty-three years that the famous outlaw had come near Custis, and while other districts in the mountains had suffered, the little town had come to feel that it lived a charmed life. But now that the blow had fallen on their neighbors, the men of Custis rallied gallantly for a counter attack.

The news reached Jerry in the house of Lou Donnell. As a matter of fact, most of his spare moments were spent in the house of Donnell. The Donnells were newcomers. They had not been in Custis more than half a dozen years and, although they were of rather better social position than anyone else in Custis, Jerry was the first to secure an intimate relationship with them. He secured it by dragging young Mark Donnell out of the lake when the youngster was sinking with a cramp in the bitter chill of the snow water. After that, as a matter of course, the doors to the big Donnell house were open to Jerry night and day. The reason that he darkened them so often had little to do with Mark. Mark was a fine fellow, but his chief virtue was that he had a sister. There was a singular mystery attached to Louise Donnell, and that was that any girl with so much poise and inherent dignity as she, should have had her musical name shortened to Lou. But it had happened early in her life, and she would carry the nickname to the grave.

She was an Irish beauty, was Lou. That is to say, she had blue-black, lustrous hair that swept low over a broad forehead. And under the black brows, there were deep-blue eyes. But the naming of color contrasts never paints the whole picture, and only an artist familiar with paints and their making can even faintly conceive the effect of black and blue and white and delicate pink in the face of Lou Donnell.

What is so hard to describe with words was easy to grasp at one effort of the eyes. At least Jerry had found it easy. Even six years before, when he carried Mark Donnell home on that fateful day, the sight of Lou as she ran with a cry to her brother had been a sweet and soul-thrilling shock. For six years he had been unable to disentangle from his memory the fair, young face and the grief-stricken voice. A hundred times he had wakened from his sleep in the middle of the night, so keen had been the joy and sorrow of his dream of her. What wonder that he haunted the Donnell house.

And what did the Donnells think of him? Plainly they considered him merely a boyish friend. They did not take him seriously for the simple reason that the pretty face of Lou had made them visualize a throne for her—millions or a title or some such roseate future was planned for the treading of her feet, and that the penniless young Jerry could ever draw her from the great road to fortune never came into their minds.

The swirl of horsemen stormed to a stop at the veranda of the Donnell house. And from the shade beside Lou arose Jerry.

"Jerry!" they cried. "A black Muldoon . . . Bill Muldoon . . . he's raided New Custis!"

Jerry turned pale with joy. "That's a yarn somebody's been spinning," he said. "They're always talking about a Muldoon every time there's anything goes wrong."

"I tell you," shouted one of the dusty riders, "that Oscar Little seen him with his own eyes! He's in Custis now, Oscar is. And he's got two bullets out of Muldoon's gun inside of him. And the sheriff sent us extra special to get you. He said you'd want to come, Jerry. And . . . don't turn us down, Jerry! We sure need you."

"Muldoon himself," said Jerry, and he tingled to the tips of his long fingers with an exquisite foretaste of pleasure.

The girl was turned in her chair. Leaning sidewise, she read his face with a swift and faultless accuracy, as women can. She saw him white with pleasure. She saw him literally trembling with delight. She came out of her chair and caught his hands.

"Jerry," she whispered. "Jerry." She was oblivious of all the others, yet a country girl is the most self-conscious creature under the arch of heaven.

"I'll be back tomorrow," he said to her.

But she clung to him, and the clinging was wonderfully strange and sweet to Jerry. It had always seemed to him, before, that she spoke to him from a great height, a great distance. Now she had stepped from an eternity of distance and was close to him in flesh and spirit. He looked at her in amazement. Her eyes were filled with moisture. Her face was turned up to him in human entreaty. For the first time he noticed that she was really quite small. At least she was not above an average height, and she seemed small beside his bulk.

"Jerry, if you go, there's bad luck in it. Believe me!"

"It's the hot weather, Lou," he answered. "You're nervous, that's all. But it's pretty fine of you to be nervous on my account. I sure appreciate it."

"But I mean it, Jerry. It's more than nervousness . . . it's a premonition. Besides, Jerry, I think this manhunting fever you have is horrible."

"You've never said so before."

"I've never dared to think that you'd take my thoughts seriously. But today I'm going to chance it. Today, Jerry, you've got to listen and believe me."

"Lou, it draws me wonderfully hard. But they're all waiting." His voice became a whisper. "They're all waiting and watching us, Lou."

"Do you think that I care what they see? Oh, Jerry, if you would only see half of what they can see, how happy I should be."

"What do you mean, Lou?"

"I mean that if anything should happen to you, I'd never be happy again."

"Lou!"

"Hush, Jerry . . . but . . . I mean it. Oh, how ashamed I am to tell you. But I've got to keep you from going."

"Lou, after this one time . . ."

"That's a promise you'd be sure to break. Don't make it."

"It's a promise I'd be sure to keep. Lou, on my word of honor, after this one chase I'll never ride again with the rest of 'em when they take a man trail. But this is *the* Black Muldoon . . . this is Bill Muldoon himself. Don't you see that I'd be shamed if I didn't go, just when I may be of use . . . ?"

Suddenly she turned and fled into the house. Just inside the screen door she paused, but she did not turn again, and he knew it was because she would not show her weeping face.

He turned to the waiting group of riders. Every man had a faint smile of concern and envy at the corners of his lips. It is the concern of all men, whether young or old, when a beautiful girl gives her heart away. Those smiles of understanding went out as Jerry sprang down from the porch and leaped into the saddle of his horse. In a close cluster, shouting with triumph now that they had Achilles in their midst, they raced off down the road.

IV

It was the old trail after the Muldoons. As always, they had taken to the ways leading to the rocky crests of the mountains. Above timberline the Muldoons seemed at home.

Also, they were always sure to be equipped with exactly the right sort of horses for traveling across the dangerous land where no trees grow. What their ponies lacked in speed over the level, they more than made up in ability to get about among the slippery rocks and crags of the summits. The men out of old Custis gained rapidly enough, so long as they had tolerably even ground for the running of their horses, but, when they got off the easy trails of the lower hills and entered into the precarious ways of the loftier mountains, they began to lose again. And when they came to the timberline, Sheriff Tom Smythe, old and reliable trailer that he was, gave up the battle.

"There they go yonder," he said, after he had gathered his men into a knot. "I know where they go almost as well as if I seen 'em with the eye. They're cutting around the side of the mountain, in between Custis Mountain and Mount Black. They know doggone well that before night there'll be a storm busting across the pass, and if we foller them, they get through dead easy, and we'll get caught right in the pass. And that wind would blow the life right out of us, eh?"

The others agreed. It seemed to Jerry that for sometime past they had been willing and even eager to quit the trail. Far to the north and west, a thin rift of storm clouds had been growing steadily. The prospect of being caught for a night above timberline in a wild storm was not alluring to the sheriff and his men.

"The way I figure it," suggested Jerry mildly, "is that what a Muldoon can stand the rest of us can stand, whether it's above timberline or by the seashore."

"That's the way you figure it, son," said the sheriff, and he adjusted his bandanna around his bronzed and sharply wrinkled neck. "That's the way you figure, but when you're a mite older, maybe you'll figure different again. I been following the Muldoons, off and on, about thirty years. And I ought to know their ways, pretty near, by this time."

It occurred to Jerry to suggest that thirty years of failure were fairly conclusive proof that the worthy sheriff did not know the ways of the Muldoons, but Jerry was enough of a diplomat to understand that such a challenge would destroy the favorable attitude of the sheriff and gain no desirable end.

But when the sheriff continued to say that he intended to make a detour, cross the mountains at Ball Pass, and then skirt up and down at timberline, or just below, on the chance of meeting the Black Muldoon and his gang as the latter went through to the farther side, the patience of Jerry gave out. He gritted his teeth in silence. When the sheriff actually turned to the side to start the detour, Jerry announced that, since the outright pursuit of the desperadoes had stopped, he intended to leave the party. It was in vain that the sheriff stormed and threatened that he would never again include Jerry in a posse. It was in vain that all of his fellows in the party of horsemen pleaded with him to stay. He was adamant, and at length they wound down the mountainside, growling and scowling at one another. Jerry remained behind.

He knew that he had dealt his prestige a heavy blow by this desertion, but the stupidity of the sheriff's conduct had angered him, and he decided that he would make the most of a lone hand. Had he not promised beautiful Lou Donnell that he would never again ride into the perils of a manhunt? What he could do single-handed against five desperate fighters and known villains such as Muldoon and his four companions did not enter into the calculations of Jerry. He only knew that he must get within striking range of the five, and after that he would let circumstances direct his own course of action.

But as to crossing with the sheriff to the far side of the mountains, that, of course, was absurd. There was just as great a chance that Muldoon would not cross the mountains at all, but, having ridden to an upper height, he would watch through powerful binoculars while the sheriff and his followers rode down the wrong way, and then he would double out like a fox from his lair and return by the same way he had come, to carry ruin into some mountain village. But if he did double back in that manner, he would stumble against one obstacle—Jerry, with ready guns in his hands.

He got off his mustang and led the animal to the shade of a tree. There he threw the reins and rolled a cigarette, knowing, like every good range rider, that there is nothing like tobacco to clear the head and make the brain function smoothly. While he inhaled the first draft of the smoke deeply, he looked down toward the lower hills out of which they had labored this day. They were masked in a gathering haze of heat waves. He seemed to be looking into a vast well, in the bottom of which appeared dim forms of smaller mountains. Above him rose the barren sweep of the region over the timberline, with the timberline itself swerving in and out among the hillsides like the edge of dark water. An unseen bird swooped above him, singing out of the wind as it passed. Jerry raised his head to try and mark the minstrel, and he saw, with that upward glance, a file of horsemen twisting around a boulder on the side of Custis Mountain high above him.

He clamped his binoculars to his eyes. First rode a big man who had sweeping, gray mustaches. That must be the Black Muldoon, just as he had been described when he plunged on his horse through the streets of New Custis with a revolver poised in either hand, guiding his horse with the pressure of his knees. Behind him was a flicker of red. That was Lefty, no doubt, who had been sighted in a red shirt. And behind came three more, winding into view, one by one, as they rounded the boulder, then dropping out of sight again at once.

The heart of Jerry bounded. There they came—there came five men, the capture of any one of whom meant fame to the captor. Evidently they had watched from the security of the mountainside, and hardly had they seen the sheriff lead his men to the side than they started their descent. It was plain that they were familiar from of old with the workings of the mind of the worthy sheriff.

It was hardly too late to summon back the sheriff and his men. Indeed, they could not be more than two or three miles away. But the noise that would summon them would also warn Muldoon and his followers back to safety. Jerry gripped his rifle at the balance and set his teeth.

High rocks near the tree sheltered both him and his horse from any but the most particular observation. The minutes spun out. The sun came hot and steady upon him. It seemed to press down on him with an actual and burning weight, as mountain suns will do. Perspiration streamed down his face. What if some of it ran into his eyes at the last instant? How many cool fighters had been ruined by such accidents as these? Perhaps all killers of men, in the end, were beaten by such chances as these. But his own coolness was gone. The thought of the Black Muldoon shook him as the wind shakes a dead leaf.

Another idea came to him. Would he possess the cruelty, even if he had the nerve, to shoot upon the five men from ambush? That would be murder that the law sanctioned, but it was murder no less.

The long interval drew toward an end. He heard the clink of a rock under the iron-shod hoof of a horse, and then the leader of the procession drew into sight, the Black Muldoon, to be sure, exactly as he had been described, a great body of a man, seen near at hand, active and powerful in spite of his middle age. He came with his hat pushed back on his head. His rifle was carried at a balance across the pommel of his saddle, and all his manner was one of easy command and self-assurance. And, to be sure, had he ever once been cornered? Had he ever once been beaten?

Jerry tossed the butt of his own gun into the hollow of his shoulder and drew a bead. Instantly, as the sights lined up with the head of the outlaw, his hand steadied to a rock-like firmness. Bill Muldoon was no better than a dead man. Moreover, Jerry had now a practical assurance that his nerve would by no means fail him in a pinch. All that he needed to do was to press with his trigger finger, and the notorious long rider would have been no more.

But the instant he was sure of one, he desired a greater prey. There were five men there. If he started shooting from covert, the swift action of the repeater would probably account for them all while the marksman remained uninjured. But could he shoot from covert? It was the sense that such a thing would be no better than murder that had kept him from shooting the Black Muldoon. Now all five horses were in plain view, with their heads nodding in a ragged rhythm.

Jerry leaped sidewise from his shelter among the rocks, and he fired an opening shot above the head of the last rider of the five. That was his last concession to sportsmanship. Even as he fired into the air, he was dropping prone along the ground so that he would offer a smaller target to his enemies. They had seized their guns, one and all, and reined their horses wildly back. But before they had located him, his rifle spoke again, and the last man of the five slumped in the saddle. It exploded again and knocked the fourth rider, a tall, lean man, cleanly out of his saddle.

At the same time, the three leaders found the marksman and sent a volley crashing at him, but surprise had affected their control, and every shot flew high while Jerry, in quick succession, cool as ice and wondering at his coolness, sent two more bullets home and saw the third rider and the second, he of the red shirt, struck headlong from their saddles. All the time used in the firing of those four shots had been hardly a breathing space.

There was a new explanation of why Jerry had lived to complete that string of four, however. He saw the first man, the great Muldoon himself, swing the rifle around his head with a tremendous curse and hurl it at the head of Jerry, then whip out a revolver and leap from his saddle at the same instant. The larger weapon had clogged in some manner, so that it was no longer useful. He should have opened fire with the smaller from the saddle, but a blind rage seemed to have overcome him, and he plunged in the end to combat, hand to hand.

Jerry had risen to meet him. In the flurry of that wild rush, they both fired and missed, and then they fell into each other's straining arms, dropped the revolvers, and strove for wrestling grips.

Well was it for Jerry, then, that he had youth on his side. The Black Muldoon was within a year or two of fifty, but he carried his sinewy bulk with the agility of a boy. Moreover, all the Herculean power of that great frame was used according to the methods of a trained wrestler. Opposed to that skill, Jerry had only a novice's conception of the grips. But he had tireless strength, the grip of a coiling boa constrictor, and enough lifting force to have riven up a young oak by the roots.

Even so, he found himself caught, twisted, and flung headlong onto the rocks. Only a cat-like agility in whirling over and over and throwing himself to his feet in a single effort saved him.

He dodged the next rush of the big man and, avoiding the deadly pressure of those thick arms, crashed both fists against the head of the Black Muldoon. This brought forth a terrifying roar from the giant. In he came again. Half a dozen pile-driver blows glanced uselessly from his lowered head. Again he caught Jerry, and again Jerry went down, and this time in such a manner that he could not work loose.

He labored in the moments that followed as he had never labored before and would never labor again. Had the big man followed any single plan of attack, he would have crushed Jerry infallibly in that assault, but he clung to no one plan. There was only a half-blind and consuming fury to dictate his courses. He no sooner did one thing than he saw another tempting opportunity. He quitted a grip that threatened to crack the ribs of Jerry in order to tear at his throat, and he left the throat hold for one by which he strove to crack the bone of Jerry's right arm.

But his hurrying ferocity defeated its own end. Grip after grip was changed, purposely, or else Jerry managed to writhe away from it, although the fingers of Muldoon tore his flesh like hot irons. Those terrible efforts, however, had taken the first flush of the older man's strength. Incomparably powerful though he was, his apogee of might endured only through one ecstasy of action. A hoarse and gasping breath warned Jerry that he had less to fear. With a great effort he managed to break loose, and when the Black Muldoon charged again, a well-directed blow, whipped in with all of the younger man's strength, stopped Bill Muldoon in full career and sent him staggering back. That was the turning point.

The moment big Muldoon's fighting impetus was gone, Jerry showed him the same mercy that a tiger shows to a wounded bull buffalo after a fierce battle in which both have bled. He would not at once close, for he still dreaded the bone-breaking power in the arms of the older man. But gliding around Muldoon, he slashed at him with terrible blows. Solid as was the bulk of Muldoon, it needed only that one of these blows lodge squarely on his chin to down him. And he, realizing this, held his head down, and, glaring up from under bushy, black eyebrows, he waited with a species of savage patience for a time when he might get his opponent at a new advantage.

But that time never came. A bone-crushing left hand drove against his ribs. He gasped, and instinctively his head came up as he struck hard and short in return. The raising of that head was what Jerry had been waiting for. At the same instant, his big right fist, brown as a berry and hard as a rock, slugged the Black Muldoon across the jaw and dropped him with a grunt. Yet such was the marvelous vitality of the man that, before he had well struck the ground, he was writhing to regain his feet once more.

But Jerry had had enough. He had met the huge outlaw with the latter's own weapons. He had beaten him hand-to-hand. Now that this was accomplished, he could not find it in his heart to beat the older man further with his fists. And it would have been brutally ludicrous to ask that heart of oak to surrender.

So, as the Black Muldoon came staggering and half blind to his feet, Jerry scooped up his own fallen revolver and thrust it into the giant's stomach.

"Stick up your hands," panted Jerry.

"Shoot and be damned to you," gasped Bill Muldoon, and as he spoke, a crimson stream trickled across his lips and stained his gray mustaches. "Shoot, you prancing hound . . . you skunk . . . you yaller dancer! If you'd've stopped still for five seconds, I'd've smashed you like a bad egg!"

Jerry waited patiently. Words could not harm him. Even the working hands of the outlaw, hovering perilously near his throat, could really do him no injury while the cold nose of his Colt was shoved against the stomach of his foeman. Moreover, he knew that it was the first time in Muldoon's life that the latter had surrendered to any foe.

"Now that you've finished talking," said Jerry, "get them hands up."

"I'll see you to the devil sideways, endways, or anyways you please," said the outlaw. "I've told you to shoot!"

"That was just your way of letting off steam," said Jerry. "Why, you murdering dog, d'you think I'll think twice before I blow you in two? You're worth as much to me, or any man, dead as you are alive. Get up them hands!"

The outward thrust of his jaw, and the admonitory jab of the Colt, caused the other to sag, as though his spirit were broken.

His hands came halfway to his shoulders. Then his eyes rolled to the side.

"Lemme have a look at the boys," he said. "And then I'll get up my hands as high as ever you please. Will you lemme have a look at them?"

It was, in a way, a giving or parole, and although Jerry accepted it as such, he nonetheless kept his revolver in his hand all during the time when the leader was bending over his followers.

"I'll give you my word, if you want," said the Black Muldoon.

"I want no promise from you," said the youth. "If you can get away from me, why, then you're well and welcome to get away."

V

Muldoon went at a run first to the red-shirted man, scooped him up in his arms, and then lowered him with a breathless oath.

"Lefty's done!" he gasped out. "Lord a'mighty, after all of these days, Lefty's luck run out on him, and here's the end of him, and the end of the trails that him and me rode together."

That epitaph must suffice, perforce, for poor Lefty. The giant leader had hurried on to the next man, and there he shouted with triumph as the latter opened his eyes and feebly asked for water. The third man lived also, but the fourth, who Jerry had first aimed at, was shot cleanly through the head and had never known the end that struck him down. Big Bill Muldoon, nervous with haste, panting with the labors of his battle and with his wounds dripping unheeded where the hard fists of Jerry had slashed the skin, picked up the third man, who he called Bud, and placed him beside the second, who had been previously addressed as Hank. There, where he could listen to both and work over both to the best advantage, he labored first to quench their thirst from their own canteens and the canteens of those who would never again need water. Next he examined their wounds and jerked his terrible face around to speak to Jerry.

"They're about ready to pass out. Four shots to end four men the like of them. By heaven, I wouldn't believe it even if I had seen it. No smooth-faced kid like you done that work." He dropped upon his knees in the rocks before them. "Boys," he said, "buck up. Get your chins offen your chests. You're about to die."

The man named Hank lifted his lolling head, raised a tremulous hand, and smoothed back his long, tow-colored hair. His languid eyes turned from his leader to Jerry and back again. And then a faint light of satisfaction settled upon his face.

"It sort of appears to me, old-timer . . ." he said to the Black Muldoon, "it sort of appears to me that you ain't going to be terrible backward about following us down to the devil, after leading us most of the ways to him."

Bill Muldoon shrugged his shoulders at the thrust. But through the dirt and the red stains, Jerry saw that the face of the leader was flaming with shame.

"I done my best," said Muldoon. "But . . . but . . . I was beat by a gent, here, that took me at a disadvantage."

"You lie," said Bud, gasping forth the words. "You lie, Bill. I was enough alive to see that fight . . . and I seen my money's worth. The kid beat you fair and square."

The Black Muldoon ground his teeth, and all of his great bulk of a body shook with his passion.

"No matter about me," he said, "it's you boys that I'm thinking about now."

"And I'm thinking about you, chief," said Bud, "and how you used to say that nobody but a Muldoon could ever beat a Muldoon. Was that a lie?"

"If it'll make you happier, Bud, I'll call it a lie. But now, old son, you just start in thinking about what's lying ahead for you."

Bud sneered, but the muscles of his face had grown flaccid, and the expression of defiant contempt changed to one of dismay on the instant. He reached out a fumbling hand that big Bill Muldoon received in his own.

"Steady, Bud," he said with amazing heartiness. "Steady, old-timer. It ain't more'n one twist, and then you go to sleep."

"I don't mind the pain," said Bud, a very feeble voice through his panting. "I don't mind the pain, but the kink in the mule's tail for me is that, after I'm dead, somebody else is going to ride the pinto. Come here, you fool hoss."

It was a sturdy, little, brown mare with a great white patch on her side. She came to the voice of her master and shoved her nose under his chin, with ears that quivered back and forth.

"You old fool!" gasped out Bud, passing an arm around her neck. "You old good-for-nothing, you. Lord, Bill, it sure is hard to leave a hoss like this in the middle of a trail."

"Bud," began the Black Muldoon, and then stopped short, his voice choking. And Jerry looked upon them in utter amazement. "Bud," said the Black Muldoon when he could at last speak, "I'll tell you what I'll do when you've gone along. I'll take the pinto and take the saddle offen her and turn her loose to run wild. I'll send her back to the kind that she came from."

"Good old Bill," said Bud, his voice now weakened to a horrible whisper. "Good old Bill. I sure always knew that you'd be my friend in the last pinch. You won't sell her? You won't let no other gent take the saddle on her?"

"Nary a one, Bud."

Here Bud started up, raising himself by a terrible effort upon his elbow. "But you ain't got the say no more. What about him?"

He pointed a shaking finger at Jerry, and the Black Muldoon turned with a gesture to his captor, a gesture imploring him to tell a pleasant lie.

"I'll see that the horse is turned out wild," said Jerry.

With a glance, the Black Muldoon thanked him.

And Bud stretched out his hand. Jerry took it. It was limp. There was barely enough strength in the dying man to give one pressure to that handshake, and then he dropped back, dead.

Muldoon closed his eyes, and no sooner was that duty done than he turned to the other victim of Jerry's rifle. With trembling hands, Hank had managed to roll a ragged cigarette and had lighted it, although he had barely power to lift his hand to his lips. Not a murmur escaped him, although his pallor was more from the mortal anguish he endured than from the loss of blood.

"I took a look to Bud first," explained Muldoon as he went to Hank. "I done that, because he was the weakest . . . he was the kid. I knew that he couldn't hold out so long as an ornery old critter like you, Hank."

A faint smile of gratified vanity stirred the lips of Hank, although he banished it at once.

"Yep," he said, "you can't expect much out of a kid like Bud was. Still, take him by and large, he done noble, that kid done."

Jerry looked again at the face of dead Bud, and by that second examination he saw, to his vast surprise, that Bud had really been only a youth in his twenties, a slender fellow no older than himself, although he was wrinkled and scarred by too much experience too soon acquired. And now he looked more closely at

Hank himself, and he began to see that the latter, veteran though he considered himself, could not have been more than a year or two older than poor Bud. Yet, with a half smile and a half sneer, he regarded the body of his dead companion, raised a shaking hand to his lips, and blew forth another cloud of cigarette smoke. But now death was coming upon him fast. His face was gray. His lips were a light purple. The smile was a stiff caricature of mirth upon his lips.

"Sure he done noble," said Bill Muldoon heartily. "He done his best. He wasn't quite the man that you are, Hank, but, for a kid, he done pretty well. But if all the gents that rode with me had been as hard as you, Hank, we never would've run into a mess like this one. I ain't forgetting that you was for going straight on to the far side of the mountain, or else turning back and laying an ambush for the whole posse. I ain't forgetting what you advised, Hank."

The dying face of the boy brightened.

"Well," he said, "if we'd've done that we'd've blowed about twenty fools clean to inferno instead of getting stopped, all of us, by one blamed tenderfoot . . . one . . ." He rolled his eyes up to Jerry. Inexpressible disdain curled his lip.

"That's done and over with," said Muldoon hastily. "And you can take this for a comfort for you, son . . . that the fight that finished you is the fight that finished the last of the Muldoons. Don't that please you, Hank?"

"Well, Bill, could a Muldoon have fought for you any better than I fought?"

"No, sir, they couldn't," said the Black Muldoon heartily. "You've come second to none."

"Though Lefty wouldn't've heard to that."

"Lefty was a fathead. He didn't know nothing that was really worth knowing, I guess."

"I'd like to've had him hear you say that," said Hank.

"He was about to hear it, too," said Muldoon. "I was going to let you handle the Murphysville job all by yourself and have Lefty working under you."

"The devil you were, Bill," whispered the dying marauder.

"I sure mean it."

"Well . . . I wished I might've lived to do that job."

"You can do a better job than that, partner. You can make your mind easy. You can give me any messages that you want to send down to the folks in your old hometown."

"The devil with the old hometown," said Hank. "I got no use for it or the folks that're in it."

"What about your old dad? He'd like it if he thought you remembered him when you come along toward the end."

"Would he? Well, it was little that he ever done for me, and why should I want to be thinking about him now? Let him go."

"And there's your girl, Flossie. What about her?"

The face of Hank contorted with savage pain and anger. "She'll marry that Perkins gent, and to the devil with her and him both. I hope that ranch raises more salt than cows for 'em. Yep, she'll marry him and forget about me, quick enough."

A touch of hardness came into the eyes of Bill Muldoon, but he only said: "That's a way folks have. They forget us plumb easy. But now we've got our medicine, and I guess we ain't the ones to whine about it. We'll take what's coming to us, Hank, eh?"

"Sure. You ain't heard me whining."

"Tell me what I can do to make you easy, Hank? Want me to roll you another cigarette?"

"No. Can't I roll my own? But . . . Bill . . . let's talk about the day we rode down and cleaned up Jerneytown."

"Aye, that was a day, Hank."

"D'you recollect the big, fat barber coming to the door and throwing up his hands with a yell when he seen us?"

"I recollect him like I was seeing him now."

"I shot him plumb in the belly. My Lord, how it tickled me to see him flop. What come of him, Bill?"

"He got well, by-and-by."

"The devil he did. But I remember that I was using some old shells that day. They didn't do much good. And d'you remember how the cashier . . . ?"

"Steady, Hank."

The robber's head had fallen suddenly back with a strangling sound. But now he dragged his head up again and stared at Bill Muldoon with tortured eyes.

"I'm steady enough. And . . . I got my boots on, Bill, eh?"

"You sure have, Hank. And you're the last man of the gang, too."

"Well," Hank said, breathing hard, "when you come to think of it, I am the last. And . . . and . . . Bill . . . ?"

The leader leaned low over the other.

"Bill," came the raucous whisper.

"Well, Hank? I'm right here listening."

"I guess I ain't showed any white feather, eh?"

"Nary a bit. You show the white feather? I should say not."

"Well, then, I guess there ain't nothing more for me to wish for. Bill, s'long . . ."

All his limbs contorted wildly. He started up to his knees. But to the very last he kept the cry of agony between his locked teeth. And when he slumped sidewise into the arms of Bill Muldoon, he was dead.

VI

Bill Muldoon closed the eyes of Hank as he had done those of Bud and then arose, stretched himself, and rolled a cigarette. "Well," he said, "so that's done." His forehead gleamed with perspiration, and when he had lighted the cigarette, he drew great breaths of smoke down to the bottom of his lungs. He had the appearance of one who had just completed some strenuous physical labor. "Hank was a fool," commented Muldoon to Jerry. "But he was a brave fool, right?"

"He was," said Jerry.

"About the pinto . . . I guess you ain't aiming to really turn the mare loose?"

"You heard me tell him that I would."

"That was to make him pass out plumb peaceable, I supposed."

"He was dying," said Jerry, "and I promised. There ain't no good comes out of a broken promise that's been given to a dying man."

"Suppose I was to take that saddle off of the pinto now?"

"Go ahead."

Haltingly, as though he expected a counter command at any moment, the outlaw stripped the saddle from it and sent it flying away with a stroke of the bridle reins. That done, the big man turned with a grin of satisfaction to Jerry. "I guess you didn't know what hoss that was?" he said.

"I know all about that horse," said Jerry, smiling. "That's the horse that Sheriff Galbraith and his posse followed for a whole week down south and couldn't catch up to."

"And you turned her loose?" said Bill Muldoon in great wonder. Suddenly he shrugged his shoulders, as though determined to pay no further attention to that which mystified him. "Now, partner, suppose that we get down to business."

"It's about time," said Jerry. "We got a long ride ahead of us."

"A long ride?"

Jerry smiled at the apparent misunderstanding. "We're going to get back to Custis as fast as we can move," he said.

Bill Muldoon shook his head. "I been thinking from the first that you didn't know me."

"I know you well enough, Muldoon."

"Aye, but I'm Bill Muldoon."

"What of that?"

"Why, look here, friend, I could see how a whole gang might want to take in Bill Muldoon, if they ever caught up with him, but I'm dead sure that no one man, not one as intelligent as you, partner, would ever do it."

"No?" said Jerry noncommittally.

"I say no, and the reason why is that there's too much money tied up in the taking of me."

"Money?"

"Such a pile of it, partner, that it'll make your mouth water when I tell you how much you'll get on the split."

"Half to each of us?"

"That's right. Now, what would you think I had laid up, stranger?"

"Not much, I should think," said Jerry.

"No? You ain't followed my doings, then?"

"I have."

"And you figure I ain't made enough to do any saving?"

"I figure that a gent that would rob and murder when he ain't starving for the lack of money is a hound too bad to live," Jerry said fiercely.

The big man winced suddenly, as though he had been shaken by a blow. And, staring fixedly at Jerry, he passed the tip of his tongue over his bruised lips. "It's the second time," he said slowly, "that you've laid murder at my door, friend."

"Look here, Muldoon," said Jerry, "if I stay here and listen to you, it don't mean that I'm believing what you say. Not a bit of it. I'm simply listening to a pile of interesting lies. But the facts about you, Muldoon . . . why, you're a fool if you suppose that every man jack in the mountains don't know 'em."

"I'm talking about murder," said Bill Muldoon. "First I ask you . . . write down the name of one man I've murdered?"

"Well, there's the Gaffney boys."

"They came manhunting on my trail down in the Pecos country. I met 'em both at the same time. They got the drop on me. They had me helpless. I surrendered and put my hands over my head, but them dirty yaller hounds shot me down, and while I was lying on the ground, I got out my Colt and finished the two of 'em . . . but I was laid up three months getting over the wounds that they give me."

Jerry gaped. It was impossible to doubt the veracity of this tale. How many almost-mortal wounds had cut and broken the body of this giant during his life of pillage?

"And Jud Harlan?" he asked. "I suppose that he got the drop on you?"

"He didn't," said Muldoon calmly. "There was a gentleman, was Jud Harlan. When they made him sheriff, he just sat down and wrote out a nice, polite letter that he sent to some friends of mine, and he tells them to let me know that he's about to start out on my trail, and that, when him and me sights each other, we'd better start clawing for guns. And that's exactly what he done. We met up, head on, coming around a mountain. I beat Jud by the least mite of a second and filled him full of lead, and he dropped down the mountainside, and I even rode into the next town and told them where they'd find their sheriff. And when it come to building a monument for old Jud Harlan, didn't I send in one thousand dollars in cold cash?"

Again Jerry was stunned. But how much of all this was the truth? Or had the Black Muldoon been fiercely maligned all of his life?

"You mean to stand up there and be telling me," he said at last, "that you never killed a man just for the sake of killing him?"

"So help me, partner," said the Black Muldoon, "that's just what I do mean to tell you. And if I could get them that started the lying, I'd break their backs. Why, friend, yarns like that are the things that a lot of yaller-livered cowards make up about a man they're plumb afraid to face. They ain't the stories that an honest-to-God man like you should be believing."

The flattery warmed the very soul of Jerry.

"Matter of fact," said Bill Muldoon, "what you and me are going to do is to be partners. I been waiting all my life to find just one good man, instead of a gang of bums. And you're the man for me, I can see that."

"Am I?" Jerry said, reserving his judgment.

"Sure. You had the nerve to jump out from behind the rocks and take a sporting chance when you could have killed us all dead easy from there. And then when I rushed you, instead of drilling me easy with your rifle, like you sure could've done, you met me at my own game and . . . and . . ."—he spoke through his teeth—"and you had the luck of it." He could not speak again for an instant, but then he continued more cheerfully: "The trouble with a gang is that so many men can always be followed and always be found. But a gent like you and a gent like me . . . why, we'd be as good as twenty such as them that lie back yonder."

What a consummate hypocrite the man, thought Jerry, but he said not a word. Silence more than once had undone a clever man, and it seemed about to undo the Black Muldoon, likewise. He was led on.

"To begin with," he said, "we'd split up fifty thousand dollars that I've got laid away, and you could take your share and go have a party."

"And what sort of a story should I be telling folks about how you got away?"

"They'd never know that you ever took me. But you'd be down yonder with twenty-five thousand dollars to spend, and more coming to follow it up with. And with you working free at that end of the line, we could pull off some jobs that would make the sheriffs of six states go plumb raving crazy."

"Bill," said Jerry, "it's no good. If you had two hundred and fifty thousand dollars to offer, it wouldn't be near enough. If you had two million and a half, it still wouldn't be half enough. What I say is, to the devil with you and your lies. You go to town with me and hang for what you've done. Money can't buy back them that you've killed, and money can't save you."

The outlaw answered nothing. Instead, he spent a moment looking fixedly at Jerry and then asked abruptly: "What's your name?"

"Jerry."

"Jerry is your name? You maybe ain't out of Custis?"

"I am."

The Black Muldoon, to the utter astonishment of Jerry, turned white. Then he stepped closer.

"Keep away," said Jerry, "or I'll knock you down with a gun barrel."

Bill Muldoon, upon whose lips eloquent words had been trembling, halted and closed his mouth. After a moment he said: "Well, let's be starting on."

But there was something new in his manner. There was something repressed and hidden that alarmed Jerry. It was as though the great outlaw had suddenly discovered that his captor was helplessly in the hollow of his hand.

They mounted, took the other three horses in lead, and started on down the mountain trail with big Bill Muldoon riding in the lead, his feet and hands free, although his weapons had been taken from him.

Behind rode Jerry, his revolver in its holster. And behind him came the horses of the dead men.

VII

It so happened that the worthy sheriff, having changed his mind about continuing to the far side of the range and there awaiting the possible coming of the brigand and his followers, had decided that the best possible move would be to ride straight back to Custis and there organize a larger and more efficiently mounted band, at the same time getting in touch, through telegraph, with other communities in the mountains so that they could move in harmony and throw a cordon around the probable location of the outlaws. He had ridden into Custis, therefore, with his hot and dusty followers behind him, and the townsfolk had merely sighed in their disappointment. Because, of course, there had been no real expectation that this expedition would end in the destruction of the outlaws. That would have been too much distinction to fall to the posse of any one small mountain town. No, the sheriff was not considered any the less worthy because of this failure, and indeed, when the townspeople looked up to the lofty tops of Custis Mountain and Mount Black and saw that the summits were wrapped above timberline in black storm clouds, the sheriff was simply praised for a discretion that had kept him from exposing his posse to such hard weather.

It was in the midst of such feeling that a strange murmur ran down the single street of Custis, a dumb rumor that began because a half-naked urchin had galloped bareback into town with a report that he had seen, coming down the road—but no matter what he had seen. It was disbelieved, contorted. And the rumor suddenly took form that the terrible Muldoon, the Black Muldoon himself, was about to rush upon the village with his desperate retainers and distribute death as he whirled through their midst. That rumor, in an instant, searched out every man in the village. It roused them. It put loaded guns in their hands. It made them mutter to one another: "By heaven, that Muldoon is going too far. This time we'll finish him, unless he has a charmed life."

The sheriff himself heard the story. He had just enough imagination to believe that it might be possibly true. And, gray with the shame that such an attack would bring to him, whether Muldoon fell in the attack or survived it, he got out his best rifle, looked to his revolver, and came out armed and stood at the door of his house, a conspicuous and rather absurd figure, if anyone had had an eye for humor at that moment.

Into this picture, then, came a procession, and what a procession it was. First of all came the terrible figure of the Black Muldoon, looking no less mighty in reality than he had been painted in a thousand stories about him. For thirty years he had carried terror through the mountains. Two generations had told their stories of him. And it was wonderful that he should seem as heroic in fact as in fancy.

Behind him came the conqueror, the late, treasonable defector from the sheriff's posse. Behind him came flame-haired, blue-eyed Jerry, sitting erect and jaunty on his horse, keeping his joy under restraint as befits men in great hours. And behind him came three horses. Did that mean that, besides the great leader, three of his followers had been struck down, and by the hand of that one youth? What triumph had David compared with this?

People started out into the street. Women who had been whispering together ran forth, clutching one another, and they, in turn, saw the miracle. They saw young Jerry spring down from his horse and walk up to the sheriff. They saw him point to the prisoner. They saw the sheriff wring Jerry's hand—and then all was a joyous tumult that swerved and swirled around Jerry, the foundling. Mrs. Jefferson Peters came and paraded where all the village could see her. And Elsie Dennis, who had been held to the teaching of that same school all of the last dusty, hopeless fifteen years, confined to it because her spirit was not hard enough or her face pretty enough to make her a way to greater places—poor Elsie Dennis came running out with her prematurely white head bare and found Jerry, and cast her arms around the neck of her favorite and wept on his neck.

But that was only one of many wild actions in Custis that day. For the town had awakened to the fact that it had a celebrity in its environs. No more talk of riding championships—here was a man made of that heroic clay out of which other noble forms had been molded in the history of the frontier. Here was material for the making of the youngest sheriff in the history of the West. Here was the man whose terrible name would keep all outlaws at a safe distance from Custis.

At the end of that day, Jerry sat at the table with his foster brothers and his foster mother. He said nothing at all about his exploit except to belittle it to cheer up Jack and Harry, who were terribly downhearted at this latest feat. But all during the meal, no matter what words were spoken, they all had had but one thought in their minds until Jeff Peters came home late, hungry, and tired from a day of riding.

He had not heard. Oh, the joy of telling such news to one who had not heard even an inkling of it. With compressed lips and shining eyes, they endured during the dinner he ate until he was midway in his second piece of pie, his third cup of coffee. And then they exploded.

"Dad, have you heard?"

"Heard what?" he said petulantly. "What the devil is eating you folks? You sit there and stare at me like I could be eaten."

"It's Jerry!" chanted three voices. Even Harry and Jack had lost their jealousy in a wave of family pride.

"What have you been doing, Jerry? You been out buying another hoss, maybe?"

"No, he got three hosses for nothing!"

"What the devil are you talking about?"

"Jeff, how can you use such language?"

"I can't help it, dear. It sure riles me to hear such talk. Three hosses for nothing! What d'you mean by it, Jerry?"

But Jerry, pink with happiness and dumb with modesty, was rolling a cigarette and waiting until the ordeal should be completed. He could not answer.

Mrs. Peters rose from her chair. She stood like one presiding at a meeting held to defend the rights of downtrodden American womanhood.

"It just means, Jeff, that we got a hero with us."

"Mother!" exclaimed Jerry in faint protestation.

"I mean it. That word ain't none too good for you, Jerry boy. Jefferson, today this Jerry of ours went on the trail of the Muldoon gang that raided New Custis."

Jeff Peters arose from his chair likewise. He rose as one being dragged up by the hair by an invisible hand. He said nothing. His joyous anticipation had very much the look of speechless horror.

"Go on," he urged. "Hurry."

"The sheriff missed Muldoon and Muldoon's four desperadoes," went on Mrs. Jefferson Peters, "but our boy would not follow him when he turned back. Instead, he stayed behind by himself. By himself. I'm covered with gooseflesh at the thought of it. One boy against five terrible men! But there he stayed. And the first thing you know, down they come, and out stands Jerry, and down they go, one and all."

"No!" shouted Jeff Peters.

That cry might have been taken for incredulous joy. At least, Mrs. Peters so took it.

"He killed four men and captured the Black Muldoon in a hand-to-hand fight and didn't get a scratch himself, and now Bill Muldoon is down in the jail in this very town. And six men are guarding him day and night."

She crowded the cream of all her tidings into that one great sentence. The effect upon her spouse was strange indeed. He rushed around the table to her with both hands raised high in the air as though to beat back the words he had heard and destroy the truth that they represented.

"Don't say it," he said. "For God's sake, don't say it."

"Don't say what?" shrilled his wife. "Are you gone crazy, Jefferson Peters? Ain't you got any realization of what our Jerry has done for us, and Custis, and the whole of the mountains? Why, there ain't a paper in the country that won't have a long story of this."

"You fool!" gasped out Jefferson Peters. "Heaven help us . . . poor Jerry."

Jerry came suddenly before him. "Tell me what's up," he said. "Have I done something that's wrong?"

"Done something that's wrong?" echoed the storekeeper. "Why, ain't it liable that they'll hang him?"

"Hang the Black Muldoon? Of course they will, unless he's lynched first."

"They'll hang him," wailed Peters, "and the hand that puts the rope around his neck will be yours!"

"Doesn't he deserve hanging?" asked Jerry sternly. "Is he a friend of yours? Was it by his help that you managed to buy the store when . . . ?"

"No, no . . ." stammered Peters.

"Then what do you mean by such talk?" asked his wife, advancing into the fray.

"Nothing."

"Don't talk like a fool, Jefferson. You sure got some meaning in what you've been saying."

"I don't mean nothing. I don't want to talk to you. I got to be alone . . . and heaven guide me to what's right."

The great body of Jerry blocked his path. The great hand of Jerry held his shoulder. "I've got to know," he said simply.

A sudden fury came over Jeff Peters, one of those passions with which weak men, relying on their known weakness, bully men far stronger. He tore himself away from the detaining hand. He shook his fist in the face of big Jerry.

"You blockhead!" he shouted. "You big blockhead! When they hang Bill Muldoon, they're hanging your father, and you're his murderer!"

Jerry staggered back to the door and leaned against it, weak, still blocking the escape of Peters from the room. "Say it over again," he gasped out. "Say it slow . . . so's I can understand. You ain't meaning that the Black Muldoon . . . but I knew it when I faced him. I knew it when I couldn't send the slug home into him. Oh, heaven help the two of us now."

VIII

He left those four tortured and shocked faces and stumbled out into the night. The air struck suddenly cool and sweet against his eyes. He realized that they had been on fire—that his whole body was on fire. He was in a fever of anxiety, grief, terror.

He was a Muldoon then. He was one of those terrible man destroyers, the Muldoons! He looked back over the years of his young life. When we are young, we are not fitted to criticize ourselves. And it seemed to Jerry that there were scores of facts that fitted in with what had now been told him. There were those fierce and sudden passions of his childhood, for instance. There was that murderous attack on William in the schoolyard on the never-to-be-forgotten day when he had been first told that he was really not the son of Jeff Peters. And there were other occasions when his temper had risen to a white heat. It had been bitterly hard to control himself on those occasions. The explanation was simple in the light of what he had learned on this day. It was simply the instinct of the Muldoons urging him to strike.

A black Muldoon! They would call him the *Red* Muldoon, after this. Jerry Muldoon. The very ring of the name dwelt in his mind with sinister implications. It would be a good name to give a murderer.

Jerry Muldoon, stand up! Those were the words the judge would speak. The last scene flittered before his eyes. He blotted it out with a savage oath, and, running to the barn, he saddled his strongest horse and led it out. There, the sound of softly rustling skirts met him in the darkness.

"Jerry . . . Jerry . . . Jerry!" he heard the voice of Mrs. Peters calling to him.

And to think that he had once thought of this woman as his mother.

She found him. She threw her arms around him. "Jerry, where are you going?"

"I'm going to see the girl I love."

"Ah, that'll be Louise Donnell."

"Yes."

"Jerry, don't go to see her tonight. Wait until word has been sent to her. Wait until she's been prepared."

"I'm not ashamed of being a Muldoon," he said bitterly. "I ain't a bit ashamed of it. Maybe they've been bad men, mostly, but that don't keep them from once in a while turning out an honest man, too. Am I right?"

"Of course you're right. But people won't stop to think . . . at first. There's been a horror around that name . . . Muldoon. Maybe there's a lot that's untrue blamed onto them. I don't doubt that there is. But they've got the bad name for them things, just the same. D'you see how it is, Jerry?"

"Oh, I see, right enough, but listen to me. Bill Muldoon . . . my father . . . he's a real man. When I captured him today, he found out my name and that I come from Custis, and he knew right then that I was his son. And right then he could've got clean off by telling me. But he wouldn't tell. He decided that he'd take his medicine."

"Aye, that was a terrible thing to do . . . and it was a fine thing to do, Jerry dear."

"Only a big man could've done it. He gave me to you and Jeff in the hopes that I would be raised honest. And he wouldn't spoil my life to save his own, if the name of Muldoon might spoil a man's life."

"But you ain't going to take that name, Jerry? You're still going to call yourself Jerry Peters, ain't you?"

"Lord a'mighty, d'you think that I'm ashamed of my father's name? I'm not. I'm wild proud of it."

"Jerry!" Her voice was a wail of sorrow. "Jerry, oh, Jerry boy, you're going to leave us!"

"You'll not be sorrowing very long for that," said Jerry bitterly. "I guess I've been a weight on you all these years. Keeping back Harry and Jack."

She clung to him. "Don't be saying that, Jerry." She began to weep. "Oh, Jerry, I ain't been as good to you as maybe I might have been. I've been real hard and mean to you more'n once. But when I seen you leaning against the door after Jefferson told you . . . when I seen you so sick and weak from what the words had done to you, but what the fear of bullets couldn't do . . . when I seen you standing there, Jerry dear, all at once I loved you as though you were my own child, like Harry and Jack. Can you understand, dear boy? No, no man would understand . . . but, oh, Jerry, if you're leaving us now, it's my flesh and blood that I'm losing. Stay with us, and let me show you that I love you, Jerry."

"I'm coming back, I guess," he said. "Only I'm going to see Lou Donnell first . . ."

"Won't you listen to me, Jerry?"

"Of course. But that can't change me. Besides, it's a good test. If she cares a single flip for me, this won't make any difference."

"Now you speak only because you're bitter, dear."

"No, it's the straight truth. If she was to marry me, would she be marrying my father? What difference does it make, what my father may have done?"

"The Donnells are terrible proud folks, Jerry."

"And so are the Muldoons," said Jerry.

"Are you going to talk to her like that?"

"Why not? I'm not ashamed of my blood."

"But the shock of what she hears . . . remember how the shock of it hurt you, Jerry."

"It didn't hurt me. It only staggered me sort of, for a minute. But after that . . ."

"If you go tonight, you'll lose her. Trust a woman's judgment that far, Jerry."

"If I lose her, I'll never come back to win her again."

She only sighed.

"Good-bye, and God bless you for coming out to talk," he said. "I'll never forget it, not in a hundred years."

He took her in his arms, kissed her, and then took the saddle and drove away at a smashing gallop over the gravel road. And on through the night, he never let the horse slacken until he had passed Custis, and the big, blunt outlines of the house of the Donnells rose before him. Then he stopped, threw the reins, and approached the veranda more slowly.

Luck favored him here, at least. He came through the darkness just in time to see Lou's father disappear into the house, leaving Lou herself alone on the veranda. When he walked up the steps, she rose with a cry of surprise.

"Jerry, Jerry! You've remembered us even on your great day." Then, as he came closer and into a keener light, she cried: "Jerry, there's something wrong! What is it?"

Clothes, says the resolute Westerner in his overalls and flannel shirt, clothes make no difference in man or woman. But the feeling of Jerry, at that moment, belied that maxim. For Lou Donnell was dressed all in white. Neither was it the sort of white that Jerry was used to. It was not crisp and flouncy, and apt to blow askew in the wind. Instead, it was of shimmering silk, and when Lou moved, she was accompanied by a hushing whisper of the fabric. And this dress was made, also, in a manner that suggested money—much money. Jerry knew that although he saw no details. But the clothes of Lou Donnell removed her to a strange distance. He could not talk to her with assurance. He became stiff and wretchedly self-conscious.

"I've come over to tell you some queer news," he said.

"But I know all about the fight," said the girl. "Dad was in Custis today, and he heard everything, and he's come home chanting your praises. He says that you're a hero, Jerry, and everyone else in the house agrees. Dad went to the jail with the sheriff and heard that terrible Black Muldoon tell everything. And even Muldoon didn't take away any of your credit."

The head of Jerry fell. But how could she know how cruel a cut she was giving him?

"D'you know why he wouldn't take any credit away from me?" said Jerry.

"You mustn't be mysterious about it."

"I'm going to be as plain as day. Lou, he's my father."

He had expected a cry of fear and sorrow. Instead, she merely folded her hands and blinked at him.

"You know," he explained, "that I'm not really the son of Jeff Peters. And tonight, when he heard what I'd done today, Jeff broke out and told the whole story . . . how my father had come to the store at midnight, twenty-three years ago, and made Jeff swear never to tell whose son I was, and how Jeff took the oath and promised to raise me up to be an honest man . . . and . . . Lou, are you going to take it like that?"

For she was backing toward the door. As she stepped back, the light struck across her face, and he saw that she was deathly white. He followed her a pace, but she threw up her hand.

"Don't," she whispered.

"You're afraid," said Jerry. "I might've known it. You're afraid."

"Dad!" screamed the girl.

Footfalls rushed toward them from the interior of the house. Mr. Donnell and Mark Donnell plunged out through the front door. And there they confronted Jerry and Lou with wonder.

"What on earth, Lou?" began her father.

She clung to him. "Send him away!" she cried. "Send him away!"

"What the devil have you been doing?" asked Donnell.

"He . . . he's the son of the Black Muldoon!"

"Good Lord, Jerry, what nonsense have you been telling her?"

"The truth. The flat truth," said Jerry Muldoon.

"Good Lord!" Donnell gasped.

And Mark Donnell's hand instinctively sought his gun.

Jerry waited to see no more. He turned, walked slowly down the steps, and threw himself again into the saddle.

Behind him, as the roar of the hoofs began, came the voice of Donnell calling his name, but Jerry paid no heed and spurred harder on the road back to Custis.

IX

There was no one at the sheriff's home. He was a minor figure on this great day. And when Jerry came in, the man of the law rose and greeted him with a restrained enthusiasm. In fact, he was sick of the name of Jerry, and the sight of him was very far from welcome.

"Sheriff," said Jerry seriously, as he shook hands, "I've come around to have a little private talk with you."

"Step in here, then."

They went into the sheriff's little office.

"Sheriff," said Jerry, "I thought that I'd drop around and tell you that I don't see this business the way the rest of 'em do. Not by a long shot. I know that I had no right to leave the posse . . ."

"It wasn't a particular good example for discipline, I guess," said the sheriff mildly. "Not even if it turned out good."

"Sure," said Jerry, "the luck just broke on my side. And I'm here to tell you that I know, if you'd been there, you would've done the job just as well as I did it."

"I dunno about that, but . . ."

"Matter of fact," said Jerry, "it's too easy for folks to forget how much you've done."

"Well, I can't say but that there's some truth in that, Jerry. And I'm sure glad to see that your head ain't turned by what the boys been saying to you all today."

"Well," said Jerry, "I just wanted you to know what I felt, and that, the next time you picked a posse, I'd be plumb glad to ride with you, Sheriff, and I wouldn't be breaking any orders the way I did today."

The sheriff's heart was touched. He wrung the hand of Jerry. "You're a good lad, Jerry," he said. "I always known it, but now I'm dead certain."

By tomorrow, thought Jerry bitterly, *he'll know . . . and the whole town will know. Then what will they be saying about the son of the Black Muldoon?* But he controlled his emotions so that he could continue to smile. Indeed, that he was able to act his part so easily in this interview was proof to him that the blood of Muldoon was clearly showing in him.

"But there was another thing," he went on, wondering how it was that the Peters family had kept from spreading the news during the evening, "and the other thing was that when Muldoon tried to buy me off . . ."

"He tried to do that? The hound!"

"D'you blame him?" said Jerry. "But anyway, he offered me big money. He said that twenty-five thousand . . ."

"Twenty-five thousand!" exclaimed the sheriff.

"Apiece," said Jerry. "That much for him and that much for me. That was what he offered."

"Good Lord," murmured the sheriff. "But then, there's no reason why he shouldn't have that much cached away. He's stole that much ten times over."

"But it sure seems too bad to me," went on Jerry, "that all that money should go to waste."

"It sure is a shame," said the sheriff, "but there ain't nothing that can be done, I guess."

"I'm not so sure."

"What's in your mind, Jerry?"

"Suppose I go talk to him in the jail? Suppose I talk to him all alone. Suppose that while I'm there I make a bargain with him . . . if he'll tell me where the money is cached, I'll guarantee to get him loose?"

The sheriff bowed his head to conceal a sneer that twisted his lips. Such miserable bargaining was not at all to his taste, but if Jerry was willing to do the dirty work, he felt that he had no right to refuse.

"You go do the talking, son," he suggested.

"But how'll I be able to talk to him alone?"

"You and me'll go down to the jail together. How does that suit you, old son? I'll send the others home and let you take over the guarding of the jail. After what you done today, I guess that there won't be none that kick at that idea."

So they started at once and went down the street to the little square, stone-walled building that served in Custis as a jail. It was simple, and it was unpretentious, but from those massive walls no criminal had ever escaped. Such was the formidable record of the sheriff.

It was not difficult to dismiss the volunteer guards. Jerry was this day the most popular man in the town, and he could do very much as he pleased in all matters. He would have been allowed to guard a dozen Black Muldoons, single-handed, had he so desired.

So they cleared out, and the sheriff waved good-bye. Jerry was left alone with Bill Muldoon. The latter was lying on a cot in one of the two cells that filled most of the interior of the little building. He had put his hat over his face to shut out the light, and so soundly was he sleeping that, even through all the loud talk that had greeted the arrival of Jerry, he still kept on snoring. Jerry walked to the bars and looked him over.

Lying prone, the outlaw seemed more huge than ever. In spite of Jerry's own size, he wondered how he could have stood for a moment before the assault of such a warrior.

"Muldoon!" he called.

The sleeper, who had remained impervious to all other sounds, responded instantly to the calling of his own name. He sat up, put the hat on his head, stood up, brushed back his mustaches, blinked his eyes, and on the instant was ready for whatever might come. Jerry could not but wonder at such prodigious self-control.

"So it's you, eh?" said Muldoon, advancing toward the bars and looking Jerry up and down. "You've dropped in to let me see what a great man you are, eh? Well, kid, you lay to this. It ain't you that beat me. It's the law. The law always wins. It's got loaded dice. And you . . . well, you just happened along at the right time, and the law used you for its tool. That's all that you figure in on."

Jerry smiled. "That's all, eh?" he said.

"What else?" demanded the Black Muldoon. "If I had a chance at you again, I'd smash you to bits, you young hound."

"Dad," said Jerry, very pale, "you could have that chance, I suppose."

"What?" said Muldoon, but his voice lowered quickly. "What did you call me?"

"Jeff Peters has told me everything," said Jerry quietly. "And I've come to set you free."

"Jeff Peters? Jeff Peters?" echoed the bandit, as though he had never heard the name before.

"Yep, he's the man," said Jerry.

"And he told you . . . what?"

"How you came twenty-three years ago, about midnight, and made him take me in and promise to raise me like I was one of his sons."

The Black Muldoon spread out his legs and hooked his thumbs into his belt. "So you're the brat, eh? You're the kid that I took to him that night?"

"I am," said Jerry.

"Well," said Muldoon, "Peters sure done a fine job in the raising of you. Might I be asking, did he teach you how to shoot, besides?"

Jerry watched him, amazed. There was no fatherly pride, no gleam of joyous recognition in the face of Muldoon.

"And you called me Dad on account of me bringing you to Peters?" said Muldoon.

"Didn't you tell Peters that you were my father?" gasped out Jerry, as a flash of hope sprang into his breast.

"Tell Peters? Did I tell him that?" Suddenly the giant broke into tremendous laughter and smote his thighs with his hand. "By God," he said, "I begin to remember chunks out of that night. And . . . it seems to me that I did tell the little storekeeper something like that."

"And it wasn't true?"

"No, you fool! Do you look like me? Nope, I picked you up out of a sheepherder's cabin. He was dead, and his wife was dying. I watched her pass out, and then I picked you up and brought you along for luck. That's all there was to it. I gave the storekeeper a yarn so's he would be kept amused. And there you are."

X

But Jerry, startled though he was, kept a steady eye fixed upon the outlaw, and it seemed to him, as he did so, that the fellow could hardly meet his gaze but, turning away, stalked up and down the cell and now and again indulged in fits of heavy laughter.

"Listen to me," said Jerry suddenly, "if you can prove that you're my father, Bill Muldoon, you go free out of this jail. I've come here for that reason. I've got the keys turned over to me. I've got guns for two. I've got a horse outside, and I can get another horse while we travel. Say the word, Bill, and you and me go on together and do what you was trying to buy and bribe me into doing this morning."

Bill Muldoon halted in his pacing, strode to the bars with a muttered word of triumph, and then stepped back once more with an oath.

"I'll see you to the devil, first," he said. "I'll see you to the devil before I call you any son of mine."

But Jerry, watching very closely, saw that the face of the older man was shining with perspiration, and all of his great body was quivering and trembling as though with exhaustion. Suddenly Jerry unlocked the door to the cell and stepped in. Onto the bed of Muldoon he tossed a bunch of keys.

"There's what'll get you safely out of the jail," he said. "And here's a gun for you to start working with." As he spoke, he passed a Colt into the hand of the Black Muldoon. "Muldoon," he said, "if you're not my father . . . if I'm only a stranger to you . . . the son of a sheepherder that you never knew . . . why, Muldoon, what's to keep you from shooting your way out of this jail? Start going, for when you make a pass with your gun, I'll know certain sure that you aren't any father of mine. Start up some action."

Bill Muldoon, facing him in anguish, suddenly tossed the gun from him with a shudder. "Jerry," he said, his voice changing to a peculiar moan, "the Lord is witness that I didn't ever want you to find out. And your mother that's watching somewheres . . . she'll sure put a curse on me for what I've done today."

Jerry Muldoon thrust his own weapon back into the holster. He leaned by the iron bars only the fraction of a second. Then he stepped forward and held out his hand. At his touch the anguish melted wonderfully out of the eyes of the Black Muldoon, to be replaced by a sort of childish marvel.

"Dad," said Jerry, "when I saw you up there on the roof of Custis Mountain, I must've known you. Something kept me from shooting when I had the bead drawn on you. It was something working in both of us, Dad, that kept us from doing a killing up yonder."

"Jerry," whispered the other.

"Aye, Dad?"

"D'ye mean it, Jerry? D'ye mean that you ain't hating me and despising me and wishing me dead?"

"Me? Why in heaven's name should I wish you dead?"

"Lad, I've busted my word to your mother. When she was a-dying with her heart plumb broken, I swore to her that I'd never let you know that a black Muldoon was your father. Because she knowed well enough that it might lead on to all kinds of bad luck in your life."

The arm of Jerry Muldoon passed around the wide shoulders of his father.

"There's only one thing worth thinking about," he said, "and that is that you and I have found each other. And after that, the next thing in order is for us to get you out of this jail."

"So that the blame of it can come on you, Jerry?"

"D'you think I could ever hold up my head among folks if they didn't know that I'd done my best for my own father?"

"Jerry, I'm fighting hard to be honest and to do what's right by you, but how can I talk against you?"

"You can't, because it isn't natural or right. Dad, we're going to do what's right for both of us. D'you think that I'm ashamed of being a Muldoon? I'm not. I'm glad to find out that I am one. It makes me a pile stronger. It makes me a pile surer of myself. It's . . . it's the biggest day in my life!"

He thought back to the girl he loved and the terror in her face as she had heard his true name and denied him. And in a fury he repeated: "To the devil with them that hate the Muldoons! There've been black Muldoons before . . . but now I'll show them what a red Muldoon can do."

"Jerry . . ."

"Only say you'll do what I want for tonight."

"I'll do that, Jerry . . . and God bless you, lad. When I heard your name up yonder on the mountain, and when you told me that you came out of Custis, right off I knew you, and right off I begun to think what we two could do if we was to start teaming it together . . . y'understand, Jerry?"

"There's nothing to keep me back," declared Jerry. "I've busted loose from everything that might hold, Dad."

"How come that? Jerry, is there a girl in it?"

"She got the horrors when she heard what my full name was," said Jerry. "She got the horrors and called for help. Well . . . she'll need no help to keep me away from her. Why should a Muldoon be ashamed? We've never backed down to no man that ever stepped, and why don't we figure as well with a girl? But I'm through, Dad . . . I'm plumb through with the whole job."

"Wait a minute," said the father, his fleshy brow corrugated with thought. "Just wait a minute, Jerry boy. How long have you been fond of her?"

"That doesn't count . . . about six years, maybe."

"Six years . . . and that doesn't count? Listen to me, Jerry. There was a time when I started to break loose from the old life. There was a time when I figured that one woman was worth more'n the whole rest of the world, Jerry. And so her and me got married and . . . so help me God . . . I fought to lead a clean and honest life. But it wasn't no use. I'd done too much before. Folks found me out and hunted me down. They drove me away from her. They broke up our home. But right up to the very end, Jerry, I've always figured that one happy year with her to be worth more'n all the rest of my life rolled into a lump. D'you hear? And you, lad, haven't made the break yet. You've been honest, so far. Maybe it'll be a hard thing for you to live down . . . but, after a time, folks'll see that you ain't following in my footsteps. They'll see that you're trying to be square all around . . . and then you've got a happy chance for a real life opening up to you. You understand, Jerry?"

"Dad," said the boy solemnly, "you're trying to hang yourself."

"I'm an old man," said the Black Muldoon. "I ain't fifty, but I've lived enough to fill five hundred years. And I'm ready to die . . . I deserve to die."

"It's no good," said Jerry. "Why . . . Dad . . . every word you speak simply makes me love you. Give you up? I'd go through anything for you."

The father was silent for a long moment. At length he made a gesture of surrender.

"Go get the hosses, lad," he said. "Before morning we'll show them what two Muldoons can do. But first . . . before you go, Jerry, give me the picture of the girl."

"What girl?"

"Give me her picture, I say!" roared the Black Muldoon suddenly, and Jerry, in humble obedience, took out his wallet and gave him the treasured picture.

"Now get out and rustle the hosses," said Bill Muldoon. "There's got to be a head in this family, and I reckon that I'm it."

XI

That last sentence seemed to Jerry to reveal more of the true nature of his father than everything that had been said before. And, passing slowly up the street, he sketched to himself the life that was before him, the constant alarm, the many dangers, the brutal companions, the more brutal adventures. There would be the first robbery, the first holdup, the first safecracking, the first murder!

Yes, call it what they would, a battle of guns between one possessing his skill and an ordinary man was nothing better than a murder. Many a brave man in the West, Jerry knew, had accepted a challenge and fought a fight of which he knew, before the start, the inevitable outcome. But in such battles as these, he loathed the thought of himself as the aggressor.

There would be ruthless raiding of houses in search of provisions. There would be the stealing of horses in the midst of pursuits. There would be stealthy night approaches and sudden flights. There would be the price laid upon his head, as it was laid upon the head of his father. These were the thoughts that thronged in the unhappy brain of Jerry Muldoon as he went up the street of Custis, wondering why God permitted such unhappiness in any man.

At the hitching rack in the front of the Peters house, he saw a horse that he did not recognize as any of theirs. He paused to look more closely. There was something very familiar about the neat-limbed creature—he looked more closely still, and his heart leaped, for it was the mare that Lou Donnell rode.

He circled hastily to the side of the house and then slipped up onto the side veranda, his blood turning cold as he realized that this was only the first of a thousand similar maneuvers that he must execute in his life as it now promised to stretch before him. The sound of voices came out to him through the opened window. Lou had just arrived. Mrs. Peters was busy making her welcome and at the same time herding the Peters men out of the room. The door closed behind the last of them as Jerry reached the window, and looking in, he saw Lou drawing off her riding gloves and wringing them nervously.

"Missus Peters," she said, "I have to see Jerry."

"You haven't seen him already?" asked Mrs. Peters.

"I . . . yes, but I must see him again . . . at once. Where can he be if he isn't here?"

"I can't say. He'll come back, I suppose, in a short time."

"Then . . . ?"

"Shall I give him a message?"

"Yes . . . no . . . but tell him that I came and that I'm very eager to see him at once and . . . but, oh, if he doesn't understand!"

"Lou, I think I know what he went to talk to you about this evening."

"He came to tell me that his father is the Black Muldoon."

"Yes."

"And at first it was a horror to me. I turned away from him . . . I . . . I . . ."

"You either fainted or you called for help."

"I called for help. Dad came out. And then Jerry swore he was proud of being a Muldoon, and he turned away with a face as black as thunder and went off into the night. The moment he was gone, we all tried to call him back, but it was too late . . . and here I am, Missus Peters. And I must see him!"

"Does Mister Donnell know that you've come?"

"Yes. He sent me. He was the one who vowed that it made no difference. He said, too, that any man was a cur who was not proud of his father's blood, no matter what that father might have done, and the rest of us agreed with him. I agreed, at least. What difference is it to me if Jerry's father is the Black Muldoon? The Black Muldoon is simply a man who was stronger than other men and has not been careful enough of his strength. Suppose my father grew up wild? Might he not have been just like the Black Muldoon? At least, that's what I feel and why I have to find Jerry, so that I can tell him."

Jerry stepped back from the window. He was almost too stunned with surprise and with anguish to keep from following the first wild impulse to rush into the room. But he ruled himself. His decision was not to be made here. It was made long before, when he promised his father liberty. And what was a woman, no matter how he loved her, compared with the tie of blood between him and his father?

He staggered across the veranda, dropped to the ground beyond, and then made for the corral. Even in that anguished moment, he made sure that the horse his father was to bestride was the best on the place. What matter whether or not that horse belonged to him? They could pay for that horse later out of Jerry's own money.

He chose a mighty, gray gelding strong enough to drag a plow but surprisingly fast, likewise. That gelding he roped and saddled at the barn, and then he made a long detour back to the jail, cutting around behind the houses so that there should be a smaller chance of detecting him. He tethered the gelding beside his own horse, and then, with a last, agonized look down the street, where the twinkling lights of Peters home told that Lou Donnell was waiting for him, he entered the jail.

There was no Black Muldoon waiting for him. The great outlaw had ridden his last ride, fought his last fight, cursed his last oath. He lay prone on his back in the middle of the floor, with the Colt clasped in one hand and the other relaxing from a bit of paper. And when Jerry examined the fingers of the left hand, he discovered that they had been gripped around the picture of Lou Donnell.

* * * * *

They buried the Black Muldoon on the highest hill overlooking Custis, and they heaped for him a great monument of rough stones. Sometimes, in the days that came, Jerry would say to his wife: "But, Lou, how can we tell the children everything that my father did?"

"Are you yourself ashamed of him?" she would say.

"No," he would always answer.

"Then," said Lou, "tell them everything from the first. Half-truths don't help. Because, you see, no matter how many crimes he committed during his life, he knew how to die like a brave man for the sake of others, and I think that death makes his whole life beautiful."

There were others, and they were numerous, who did not agree with Lou. They held that the Black Muldoon had been terrible and graceless to the very end, and they explained his death as an accident. But as for Jerry—as for the Red Muldoon—if any had their doubts of his virtue, if any waited for the bad strain to show, at least they were afraid to speak up where other men could hear them talk.

THE END

About the Author

Max Brand is the best-known pen name of Frederick Faust, creator of Dr. Kildare, Destry, and many other fictional characters popular with readers and viewers worldwide. Faust wrote for a variety of audiences in many genres. His enormous output, totaling approximately 30,000,000 words, or the equivalent of 530 ordinary books, covered nearly every field: crime, fantasy, historical romance, espionage, Westerns, science fiction, adventure, animal stories, love, war, and fashionable society, big business and big medicine. Eighty motion pictures have been based on his work, along with many radio and television programs. For good measure he also published four volumes of poetry. Perhaps no other author has reached more people in more different ways.

Born in Seattle in 1892, orphaned early, Faust grew up in the rural San Joaquin Valley of California. At Berkeley he became a student rebel and one-man literary movement, contributing prodigiously to all campus publications. Denied a degree because of unconventional conduct, he embarked on a series of adventures, culminating in New York City where, after a period of near starvation, he received simultaneous recognition as a serious poet and successful popular-prose writer. Later, he traveled widely, making his home in New York, then in Florence, and finally in Los Angeles.

Once the United States entered the Second World War, Faust abandoned his lucrative writing career and his work as a screenwriter to serve as a war correspondent with the infantry in Italy, despite his fifty-one years and a bad heart. He was killed during a night attack on a hilltop village held by the German army. New books based on magazine serials, unpublished manuscripts, or restored versions continue to appear so that, alive or dead, he has averaged a new book every four months for seventy-five years. Beyond this, some work by him is newly reprinted every week of every year in one or another format somewhere in the world. A great deal more about this author and his work can be found in *The Max Brand Companion* (Greenwood Press, 1997) edited by Jon Tuska and Vicki Piekarski. His website is www.MaxBrandOnline.com.